Fire in the Rain

Paul Cox

Llumina Press

ISBN: 978-1-62550-469-2

Chapter One

Western Slope of the Rocky Mountains

Sixty Miles South of the Canadian Border
Sandpoint, Idaho

The Beginning
June 15th
8:16 PM (PST)

Sitting in the shade of a young maple tree, Justin Mabry watched his son Billy through the chain-link backstop. Billy was small for his age but a whirlwind of enthusiasm when it came to playing baseball. Even in the ninety-degree heat, with dirt and sweat pasting his face with mud, his bright grin came through the catchers mask. Billy loved the game.

Billy glanced back at his dad and saw him smile and nod his head. Mabry's simple expressions communicated all that was necessary. Unlike the other fathers, he did not coach from behind the fence. There would be plenty of time later to talk about practice. Then they would share stories of the day's events and plan the next. They were together now and, for Justin Mabry, that was all that mattered.

His divorce was less than a year old and, except for Billy, Mabry lost everything. His wife wanted it all and to get what she wanted, she gave up her custody rights. According to her, father and son were just alike anyway; what did she care if they moved to Idaho. She was moving back to Los Angeles where she belonged, with her friends, the shopping, and her new boyfriend. She said she was finally happy but that may have been the cocaine talking. Who knew anymore?

This was the first Little League All-Star practice Mabry had been able to attend and it was the last one before the playoffs. With the coach doing the pitching, the day had been devoted entirely to batting. For the last two weeks, Billy had been the only catcher. Though battered and bruised, he sweated behind the plate in full gear for hours each day. He never got a break and never complained.

At the beginning of the All-Star season, Billy had shared the catching position with a boy named Johnny and the days were far less grueling. But Johnny mysteriously disappeared from practice. The All-Star coach had Johnny on his team throughout the regular season and didn't hide the fact that the twelve-year-old was his favorite player. Other than that, Mabry knew nothing about the boy, or Coach Burns, for that matter.

It was nearing time to end practice but Billy hadn't yet had his chance to bat. One more boy, then Billy would hit last. He would be exhausted by then but would not mention it. Even during the divorce, Billy had said little. His heart was broken, he was confused, but his concern was mostly for his mom and dad. He was a good boy, tender hearted and innocent.

Other parents began arriving to pick up their players and, as usual, gathered into a tight cluster talking amongst themselves. Occasionally, some would glance Mabry's way, but none of them had ever met Billy's father. Most agreed he was unsociable anyway. Billy had been selected from the Clark Fork team and was clearly good enough to be on the All Stars but he was new to North Idaho. He wasn't a local and most of the boys didn't like him much either. And the Mabrys were from California.

Mabry had seen their kind before and gave them little thought. He was comfortable being left alone. It was simpler that way, and peaceful. This was all for Billy.

Finally, the last batter was finished, and it was Billy's turn to hit. As he eagerly started unbuckling his shin guards, Coach Burns called everyone in from the field. Knowing practice was about to end and he had been overlooked, Billy squatted in the dirt looking expectantly towards his coach.

Mabry had been in athletics most of his life and knew coaches. He didn't care for Kal Burns, but it was only his instinctive reaction to the man. As yet, he had done nothing specific. But no matter what the sport, the time always came when a defining moment, an action or even a single word revealed the essence of a man's character. It provided a glimpse into the soul, into the bedrock foundation of beliefs on which all decisions were ultimately made. And this looked like it was that time for Kal Burns.

Mabry came to his feet and felt his face flush. Saying anything to a coach, no matter how diplomatic, was usually considered the unforgivable sin. Nothing good ever came from it. But to say nothing when it was warranted was an act of submission and by the end of his athletic career, Mabry discovered that coaches no longer intimidated him.

The look on Billy's face was all it took. Just as Mabry started to speak up, a defiant young voice rang out,

"Billy didn't bat, yet."

It was Matt Jordan, the only other boy from Clark Fork and the only child Billy called a friend, at school or on the baseball diamond.

Matt was the biggest boy on the team and forever in need of a haircut. His parents never attended his games and if it weren't for the ride he got from the Mabrys, he wouldn't have been able to play at all. Each day, he rode his bicycle to the bottom of a narrow dirt road where he was picked up. Even when they got back from practice after dark, he adamantly refused a ride the rest of the way up to his house. His family was reclusive and, like several others in the area, lived "off the grid." They had no electricity except that supplied by a generator. He was the same age as Billy yet tough and street-wise. But there wasn't a street within ten miles of the Jordans' cabin.

Burns, acting surprised, turned to Billy, who still sat behind him in the dirt.

"Oh, Billy, I guess I forgot," he said clearly but with an intentional hint of insincerity. Looking back at Matt, his eyes held on him for a moment. "Thank you, Matt," he said, then flashed a humorless smile. "O.K., everybody back out on the field."

Most of the players, and some of the parents, moaned and rolled their eyes as the boys reluctantly returned to their positions. Burns folded his arms. After watching Billy hurriedly remove his shin guards then fumble with the straps of his chest protector, Burns picked up a bucket of baseballs and slowly walked back to the mound.

Mabry stared at Burns through the fence and studied his every move. A gold chain hung loosely around Burns' neck, the only bright feature surrounding a dark, oily face. His chin was framed by a black Manchu mustache and, under it, his thick lips were curled into a smirk of arrogant confidence. But the eyes were shaded by the cap on his head, and Mabry found him hard to read.

Burns stood on the pitcher's mound and glanced around the field. He seemed pleased with himself and with his team. They had a chance to win it all for the first time in years so a certain amount of pride was understandable. But it was no secret Burns wanted the championship trophy in the window of his front office for everyone to admire. Kal Burns owned one of the biggest car dealerships in Sandpoint.

In such a small town it was easy to see that Burns was an influential man, and Mabry knew that being the Little League coach only added to his status. He alone had the power to decide who played and who was benched in the All-Star games, and every parent wanted to see their child get on the field. Some, if not all, would do almost anything to gain the coach's approval. And some coaches would do anything to win.

Clenching his teeth, Mabry took a step closer to the fence then stopped. For the first time since the post-season practices started, he knew something was not right. He had felt uneasy about the coach before, yet it had only been a vague sensation. Now it was right in front of him. But what exactly was he seeing? Was this part of a coaching strategy to benefit the entire team…or was it something else?

Billy adjusted his batting helmet to block the glare of the setting sun. It didn't help, so he merely squinted and stepped into the box. Before he could take a practice swing, a pitch was on its way. Caught unprepared, Billy swung clumsily and missed.

Mabry saw the quick-pitch and his jaws tightened even more. But there would be more pitches and Billy was a good hitter.

A second pitch came over the plate and again Billy missed. Then a third came with the same result as scattered moans filtered in from the outfielders.

On the fourth pitch, Mabry switched his attention from his son to Burns and watched the ball leave his hand. The velocity was the same as he had thrown all day, but even in the fading light, Mabry could see there was no rotation on the ball. He was throwing knuckleballs, something no twelve-year-old could be expected to hit!

Suppressing his anger, Mabry casually started for the grass behind the chain-link backstop, but his move was noticed by everyone. The players and the parents froze. This was not expected, certainly not from the father of Billy Mabry. Only Burns was at ease.

Mabry positioned himself directly behind home plate and with no one catching the pitches and no umpire, he would see perfectly what type of pitch Burns was throwing. Mabry forced the suspicion from his eyes and casually looked directly at the man who now was smirking back at him.

Noticing the change in his coach, Billy glanced over his shoulder to see his father behind the screen. But this time his father did not smile.

"Just relax," said Mabry calmly. He raised his right index finger almost imperceptibly. "You can hit the next one."

Billy caught the movement of the finger and understood the baseball signal. He was to look for a fastball.

Burns was intentionally making Billy look bad by throwing knuckleballs that, from a distance, appeared to be normal pitches. Now with someone watching and knowing Billy could hit a curve, the only pitch Burns could hope to get past him was a fastball. And for whatever reason, he would throw it just slow enough to go unnoticed by the other players and dads, but fast enough to make a Little Leaguer miss.

The fifth pitch came speeding out of the sun but heading for the center of the plate. As he had done before, Burns wanted the pitch to look perfect to everyone. Hopefully, Billy would be able to adjust his swing and catch up to the ball.

Having choked up slightly on his bat, Billy was ready and swung hard. With a loud metallic ping, the ball exploded off the barrel of the bat. As everyone watched, the white speck sailed toward the right field line, landing just short of the home-run fence but a few inches foul. He was a little late with his swing, but it was an impressive hit.

When Mabry looked back at Burns, the greasy arrogance had been wiped from his face but what replaced it was unreadable. Before Burns could say anything or start another pitch, Mabry looked at his son. This would be hard on him, but it had to be done. Whatever was going on, his son would not be a part of it.

"Put your bat up, Billy," he said. "You're too tired to hit right now. It's time for everyone to go home."

Billy looked quizzically at his father and hesitated for a moment. There was a firmness to his father's tone. His eyes were hard, but they were not focused on him. They were locked on his coach.

"We've got time for a few more," said Burns amiably, as he took another ball from the bucket.

Mabry smiled politely but knowingly. The man's authority had been challenged. If Burns was like most coaches he'd known, he would do his best to get even. "Thanks. But Billy's spent."

Burns paused for several seconds, then his smile returned. But behind the straight row of porcelain capped teeth, his tongue was silently swearing.

"Okay," he said, raising his voice. "Practice is over. Everybody in."

As the players once again ran off the field, Billy walked back to the rear of the backstop, puzzled that he was allowed only one hit. He knew his father had a reason and would explain. He always did.

"That last pitch was the only good pitch you got out of the five. So you went one for one. That's batting a thousand. It's best to end practice on a good hit and you are worn out. Tomorrow you can bat for real."

Grinning and nodding, Billy turned and trotted away to help put away the gear. He was an amazingly resilient child and could endure enormous hardship with only the slightest amount of encouragement. But certainly there were limits. And how long would such innocence last? As Billy rejoined the other players, one of the parents called out to him.

"Lucky hit."

If Billy heard the comment he didn't act like it and that, at least, was good. But like so many other things, there seemed to be less and less about sports that was respectable and few who cared about its degradation. There had been a time when it was said that sports and sportsmanship were inseparable but that was long ago. Mabry shook his head. How long would his son, how long *could* his son last in such an environment?

After all the equipment had been shoved into olive-green duffle bags, they were laid at the feet of Coach Burns who waited with his arms folded, poised to speak. The young boys crowded around him in a half circle and gazed upwards expectantly. Directly behind them, the parents stood elbow to elbow. Mabry was off to the side, an arm's length from everyone, clearly sensing their disdain. He had interfered. And he was an outsider.

Mabry was now able to see Burns' face and could detect nothing unusual. He appeared to have been unaffected by the subtle confrontation. There was no trace of anger or even irritation and for a man like Kal Burns, that could mean but one thing.

Coaches only came in a handful of varieties and Mabry had seen them all. From Pop Warner football to Division II college baseball, he had witnessed some of the best and endured some of the worst in sports. Too many coaches were dictators with a myopic view of life, incapable of wielding their power without becoming tyrants. Sooner or later their egos overcame what little common sense they had and most would eventually self-destruct. But in the wake of their reign of terror, the damage inflicted on young athletes was immeasurable.

"Good practice today," began Burns. "We're looking good and we're ready for tomorrow. You've all done your jobs well and you all deserve to play. But this is a double elimination playoff and we can't afford a loss. Tonight, I'll have to come up with our starting lineup. It won't be easy, but I have to put the best players on the field to keep us in contention. Those of you that will be on the bench are just as much a part of the team as those on the field and I expect you to support them. If I get a chance, you'll all get in the game.

"We have a game at ten in the morning and another at four. I'll have the starting lineup ready before our pre-game warm up at nine o'clock."

Pausing to inhale and smile, Burns glanced over the small gathering.

"Any questions?" he asked pleasantly, then his eyes met and held on Mabry. "Mr. Mabry, do *you* have any questions...or maybe some pointers for the team?"

So there it was--a couple of simple questions but ones that would force him to respond. It was an old technique employed by slick trial lawyers and used-car salesmen. It was a method of manipulation, a chance to gain control. In this case, the technique was designed to embarrass Mabry and show everyone who was in charge. This was likely just the first step in his reprisal, but Burns was behaving like a small-time crook. Justin Mabry wasn't impressed.

Instead of answering the questions dictated to him, Mabry countered with one of his own.

"Should we bring lunch or will it be provided?"

The smile on the coach's face vanished as he looked more closely at Mabry. For a moment Burns seemed confused.

"Uh, bring your own lunch," replied Burns, attempting to maintain his poise. "The mothers will have an ice chest with things to drink."

Burns had been caught off guard and obviously didn't like it. Despite his efforts to hide his irritation, Mabry detected a twitch in the man's eyes but the movement was almost imperceptible. The car dealer was smooth.

"That's it then," said Burns cheerfully. "See you all in the morning."

Glad that practice was over, Matt and Billy ran to the parking lot and tossed their gloves in the back of Mabry's battered Ford pickup truck then hopped inside the cab. Mabry followed behind, then after getting in and starting the engine, took a moment to watch Burns load the team's gear in the back of a silver Cadillac with dealer plates.

"It'll be close to dark when we let you off, Matt."

"Almost," answered Matt, also observing the coach. "My dad doesn't like Coach Burns, either."

From what Mabry could gather, the Jordans were very private people and Matt seldom spoke of anything related to his home life. It was an unusual comment and one best left alone. Asking questions about his family at this stage in their relationship might seem like prying.

"Well, it's good to have the practices over with, anyway," offered Mabry. "The games are when the fun starts."

On the long drive back to Clark Fork, the cab of the truck was unusually quiet. No one spoke until they had passed through the small town and turned onto Lightning Creek Road. As they left the pavement and rumbled onto the gravel road, Matt finally spoke again.

"He's done that to Billy before."

"Done what?" asked Mabry. "Who has?"

"The coach. He's been throwing to Billy like that. Like he did today. Junk stuff."

Keeping his eyes straight ahead, Mabry unconsciously let off the gas. He had been trying to make sense of what happened for the last twenty minutes.

"Are you sure, Matt?"

"Yeah."

Mabry thought for a moment. "Did you know that, Billy?"

"No."

"Matt, are you sure he only threw that way to Billy? Are you certain there was no one else?"

"I could see it all from right field. I know what I saw. Dad always tells me to mind my own business and not to …well, I just thought you should know. After today and all. I could see you knew he was throwing junk anyway."

They drove in silence the rest of the way to Matt's drop-off point. As he got out of the truck, Matt turned.

"And I think I know why he's doing it, why he wants to make Billy look like he can't hit the ball. It's on account of Johnny, the other catcher. I heard from some of the other players that he's coming back. He didn't quit like most of us thought. While we've been practicing for the last two weeks, he's been on vacation in Hawaii."

Mabry was stunned.

"Coming back for what?"

Matt shrugged.

"Johnny's father and the coach are drinking buddies. Everybody knows it. Dad says a bunch of people go to Johnny's father to get money to buy cars from the coach. Dad and I think Johnny's going to play."

Billy cocked his head to one side.

"But the coach told us at the start of All Stars that if we didn't come to practice we couldn't play. Remember, Dad, when he sent that letter home and you had to sign it? It had all the rules on it. And that was on it, too."

Mabry's head started to swim as a flood of emotions engulfed him. He tried to shake them off but could not. All the pieces were suddenly crashing into place. Burns was going to play Johnny instead of Billy. And his innocent twelve-year-old child, his son that had been working so hard, would be humiliated in front of everyone.

"I remember, Billy," he said as evenly as he could. "We'll just wait and see what happens. Maybe if you guys win a few games and you're ahead, the coach may let Johnny in for a few innings. He shouldn't, but he may. That must be what the boys meant. That's the only way he could hope to get in the games now."

Matt shut the door and grabbed the handlebars of his bicycle.

"See you tomorrow, Billy," he said, then looked at Billy's father. "Mr. Mabry, you stood up to Kal Burns. I never knew anyone but my dad to have done that. Thanks for the ride."

As Matt watched the truck pull away, a bearded man dressed in full camouflage and carrying a rifle, stepped from the deep shadows.

"Did you tell him, son?"

"Yeah, Dad. But he almost had it figured out hisself."

"Seems like a decent man. He should know who he's dealing with."

"I think you'd like him, Dad. He's a lot like you."

Placing a big hand on the shoulder of his son, Luke Jordan looked down the gravel road as the dust began to settle and the distant sound of the Ford's engine faded away.

"Maybe. What he does tomorrow will tell his story."

Washington D.C.
White House Lawn
June 16th
8:00 AM (EST)

A woman in her fifties, wearing a dark blue suit with white blouse and matching brooch, approached the podium. Her hair, cut short, was light brown with wisps of gray. She was average height and slightly overweight. Her smile was soft but the eyes that surveyed the news reporters were hard as granite.

"This morning at seven o'clock, I signed into law the Federal Child Protection Act. Congress and I worked together on this historic legislation, which is designed to protect our nation's children from those who would do them harm. As you know, this has long been a goal of my administration and today, I can say it does indeed 'take a village to raise a child,' but it takes a nation to protect them."

Without taking questions, Madeline Stark, President of the United States, turned and walked back inside the White House.

Washington D.C.
Democratic National Headquarters
June 16th
8:12 AM (EST)

"I'm only her campaign manager, Harry. You're the damn DNC chairman. You tell her!"

The man speaking was short, fat and bald. His white shirt was stained with arm-pit sweat and his face was an angry shade of red.

Harry glanced across the table at a man in a neat gray suit and power tie.

"What do you think, Senator Warren? Will she listen to the Majority Leader?"

Senator Warren swore, then took a puff on his cigar. "I've tried. You've tried. Even Stan here, her personal advisor, can't get through. She's more interested in her legacy now than helping Congressmen get reelected. And she thinks she can win again by just sweeping the states on both the East and West Coasts. To her, the 'fly-over' states are just full of hicks."

"Those states could be full of crap-covered rednecks, but they still vote," growled Harry. "And what if she loses Washington or even Oregon? The eastern parts of those states are already sympathizing with that 'sagebrush rebellion' movement. And now she's rammed that Child Protection Act through. If that thing goes sour, we'll lose everything but the Northeast. As it's written now, that legislation is a damned time bomb and we all better be prepared to distance ourselves from it if it gets out of hand."

"Why'd you vote for it, Senator?" Stan demanded. "You're on record. You even lobbied for it."

Senator Warren smiled.

"Let me worry about that, Stanley. If you want to get her re-elected president, you make sure that Protection Act doesn't blow up in her face before election day. And you better convince her to move back towards the center and pick up some of those 'hick' states or she won't get a second term. We need Ohio, Iowa and Illinois at least. She can forget the inland western states all together. They hate her out there."

Washington D.C.
FBI Building
Third-floor conference room
Domestic Terrorism Unit
June 16th
8:47 AM (EST)

Five men and one woman sat facing each other across a polished walnut table. In front of each was a seventy-two-page summary report. At the head of the table, a sixth agent sporting a crew cut and thick bull neck thoughtfully tapped his fingers. His eyes glanced appraisingly at each field agent.

"Okay, what do you make of it? Increased membership, the meetings, the rhetoric? Is this just another up-cycle because of the recession? What have we got in this report, people?"

After a long silence, a middle-aged man to the left of the crew cut spoke up.

"It's just the usual pattern in my area, Agent Berger. We see the same scattered groups with lots of complaints. No new faces in the leadership. Our informants are still well embedded and we're getting good intelligence. Nothing unusual seems to be going on."

Three others at the table agreed, offering similar reports to Agent Berger but the two remaining agents hesitated.

D.J. Francis was a six-foot redhead with green eyes. She always wore a pinstripe suit and a chip on her shoulder. She was a model of efficiency and, at twenty-nine years old, the youngest FBI agent at the conference on paramilitary organizations.

"I disagree," she said flatly. There was seldom any emotion in her tone, yet she routinely telegraphed her impatience for those around her with lesser intellects. Within the Bureau, her ambition and arrogance was a constant source of friction but her skills as an FBI agent were unquestionable.

"Seattle is stable," she continued, "and so is Portland. But get out to Ellensburg or to Bend, Oregon and the situation changes distinctly. The unrest is more palpable and the rhetoric is intensifying. Land-use issues, water rights, environmental restrictions. They are taking a toll. I believe we're approaching a level where civil demonstrations may grow in size and might intensify."

A sandy-haired man of medium height and build waited for Francis to finish. He was a few years older than she but hadn't been considered an expert in domestic terrorism quite as long. Having grown up on an Idaho cattle ranch, he had dealt with stubborn cows, rank horses and a tough-as-nails mother. He was the only field agent who could get along with Agent Francis and the only man who liked her as a woman. He was also the only agent she couldn't intimidate.

Berger turned to him next.

"Agent Anderson, what's your take on all this?"

John Anderson straightened in his chair.

"I agree with Agent Francis. My feel for it is that we need to defuse things a bit. Emotions are running high, especially in North Idaho and Montana. I think this is much different than the usual cycle."

"What the hell does it mean when you say a 'feel for it'?" demanded Berger.

A round of laughter broke the tension in the room. They all were aware that Anderson was a farm boy. They made fun of that fact, but they knew his background afforded him a unique understanding of the region's character and temperament. And anyone who could work with D.J. Francis had their respect.

"Well, sir, in my estimation, the communication in the Inland Northwest has actually decreased. There's a normal amount of chatter, but the content isn't there. It's as if they have changed the manner in which they're communicating somehow. Even the open meetings are noticeably subdued. On paper, you might say things look normal, but these people are not the type to soften their rhetoric or shut up all together unless there is a good reason. It's a feeling, sir. It's a gut feeling."

"It's just a feeling, then?"

"No, sir," replied Anderson. "It's a bad feeling."

Chapter Two

June 16th
Cody Gazette (Cody, Wyoming)
Morning edition
Dead Wolf Dumped at Federal Building

June 16th
Daily Bee (Sandpoint, Idaho)
Morning edition
Dead Grizzly Found at Federal Building

June 16th
Mountain Tribune (Billings, Montana)
Morning edition
Federal Vehicles Torched, Arsonist Sought

June 16th
Sandpoint, Idaho

By the time the Mabrys arrived at the baseball fields, the parking lot was nearly full. Six teams, from as many surrounding towns, were to play throughout the day. Adults and children of all ages filled the park. The concession stands were open, and the smell of coffee and shouts of excited young ball players permeated the cool morning air.

Ordinarily, it would have been an exciting time, but Mabry had not slept all night. Matt called early that morning from a payphone and explained that his father was able to make the game and would drive him in. Billy had been unusually quiet all the way from Clark Fork.

Starting for the field, Mabry put his hand on Billy's shoulder. As they walked, he kept it there. He could think of nothing to say, nothing that could prepare his son for what might happen next. Or *was* there anything to worry about? Maybe he was wrong. Maybe he had misread all the signs. Perhaps Coach Burns would surprise him and stand by the rules. Billy had worked hard. He had done everything asked of him without complaint, and he was a good player. Mabry felt sick to his stomach.

The team was taking a seat in one of the bleachers next to a baseball diamond. Near it, Kal Burns stood alone concentrating on a clipboard he was holding. The fathers were clustered a few feet from Burns. Johnny, the boy that had been missing for the last two weeks, was nowhere in sight.

Mabry stopped twenty paces from the other men, took a deep breath and exhaled slowly. Taking his hand from his son's shoulder, he forced a smile and looked into his eyes. "You will do just fine, Billy. Have a good game."

Billy's face was a mixture of trust and uncertainty, of bravery and fear. He nodded, then without speaking, turned and went to join his team. Mabry watched his son walk away from him towards Burns. He was only twelve but Mabry had to let him go.

Taking a seat on a picnic table, Mabry was out of hearing distance when Burns walked to the front of the bleachers and started speaking to the team. There seemed to be some activity in the group as players' heads suddenly turned from side to side, but the commotion quickly subsided. Burns was announcing the starting lineup and, of course, there would be excitement. There was nothing to worry about.

Johnny had not shown up after all. With the first game only minutes away, Mabry finally started to relax, but when he noticed a white BMW speeding up the street, he caught his breath. When the car turned sharply into the crowded parking lot, there was no doubt who was in it. The sedan drove up onto the grass and all the way to the bleachers before stopping.

Still wearing a flowered shirt and lei, Johnny stepped out to greet the cheering players. A moment later, Johnny's father appeared with a cell phone to his ear. He wore a matching Hawaiian shirt but had two leis around his neck.

Burns quickly crossed the short distance between them and vigorously shook hands with Johnny's father. Staring in disbelief, Mabry failed to notice that one of the other fathers had come up beside him.

"Looks like Johnny made it back in time after all," the man said.

Mabry looked at the man. His face was familiar but he didn't know his name. "You mean, Johnny made it in time to watch the game?"

The man pointed to Johnny's father, who was now opening the trunk of his car. "No. To play."

"He hasn't practiced in two weeks," retorted Mabry, barely suppressing his irritation. "It looks to me like he's been on a vacation."

The man glared at Mabry.

"Oh, he told the coach he was going ahead of time, so it's all right that he gets to play."

Mabry's eyes blazed but his voice was even as he looked directly into the man's eyes. "It's not all right with me."

The man blinked twice then turned and walked back towards the other fathers without responding. Mabry watched him for a moment, swore, then looked back at the BMW as Johnny took his uniform and shoes from the trunk and headed for the restroom to change. He was certainly going to suit up, but would he be allowed to play? And if he did get in the game, how much would he play? And how would that affect Billy? Just how much emotional damage would there be?

A half-dozen players followed Johnny to the restroom while the team meeting appeared to have come to a sudden halt. Most of the players stayed in the bleachers but Billy and Matt climbed down and started walking slowly towards him. Mabry's eyes were fixed on his son, but his mind was a complete blank. For the next few seconds, as his heart began to pound, every thought, every impulse, was put on hold.

Billy did not speak until he stopped in front of his father. He was only inches away but instead of looking up, he hung his head.

"Johnny is going to start."

His voice was that of a child attempting to be an adult. Matt was next to him. Matt was tough and Billy was trying to be.

"He's letting Johnny bat in my cleanup spot and put me ninth," added Matt. "I said it wasn't right benching Billy, and the coach threatened to kick me off the team if I didn't shut up."

Mabry nodded. Struggling to recover from the shock of what he had just heard, he glanced at Matt.

"Thank you," he managed, as his throat tightened and his eyes began to smolder with anger. "Thanks for speaking up."

All night long, he had vainly tried to rein in his imagination, to convince himself his worst prediction of what this day might bring was nonsense. He could not fall asleep for thinking of what might happen and of what he would have to do in response. He told himself repeatedly the whole idea was an absurdity. Johnny would not show up, he wouldn't be allowed to play even if he did, forget about it, get some sleep, it was ridiculous. And yet, here it was. The impossible was now reality.

Billy had suffered tremendously during the divorce and was just beginning to recover. Baseball was his life and all he wanted to do was play the game. He followed all the rules. He did everything Coach Burns asked of him but instead of being rewarded for his enthusiasm, the coach had betrayed him. He was too young to comprehend the reasons his mother had changed and gone away. And now, after all his hard work, Billy would be unable to understand why his chance to play in the game had been stolen from him and blatantly given to another.

For the sake of his son, Mabry managed to endure the countless lies and insults of divorce court and learned to suppress his anger when, one by one, the judge and the lawyers took everything he owned. But watching his innocent boy being subjected to the same outrageous brand of injustice was pushing him over the edge.

Feeling the stinging heat in his face and the blood rushing through his body, Mabry struggled to restrain the savage impulse boiling up inside him. He wanted to beat Kal Burns with his bare fists, to physically destroy the man. The one responsible for brutally humiliating his child in front of everyone deserved nothing less than to be beaten to the ground and left in a bloody heap. Burns was good at bullying children, but he was about to meet a man.

Mabry's hands clenched into fists as his eyes bored into Burns. Nothing was more important than protecting Billy and no one would ever be allowed to get away with hurting him like this. But before going after Burns, Mabry glanced down at his son.

Billy now gazed up at him, and his face was a tragic portrait of pain and confusion. Mabry had seen that look once before when Billy first learned of the pending divorce. On that day, Mabry swore to do everything in his power never to see it again. It was the return of that vivid and awful memory that broke through the blinding rage. The instant Mabry looked into his son's tear-filled eyes, the flames of hatred that had so quickly consumed him were smothered by an even greater passion.

There was one thing more important than avenging his son. For Billy, he had sacrificed everything. And for him, for him alone, he would allow Burns to go unpunished. Justin Mabry would not further disgrace his son brawling over what others would flippantly refer to as "just a game."

With his blood beginning to cool, Mabry recalled the decision he had made the previous night. If Johnny was allowed to play and Billy was benched, there was only one path to follow. It was a matter of principle, but more importantly, it was about taking a stand for what was right even when the cost was high. Billy may not understand for years and most likely would be even more devastated but it had to be done. No one would be allowed to embarrass his son and treat him with such disregard, not without consequence. And under no circumstances would Burns retain the authority to control any aspect of Billy's life.

Looking down at Billy, Mabry paused. He knew his son could not grasp what was about to happen. How could he?

"Go get your gear," he said firmly. "You won't play for a man like that. Not now. Not ever."

Billy had already been humiliated by being benched and now was going to be hit with a barrage of conflicting emotions. Mabry knew his son trusted him without reservation but he would naturally feel a loyalty to his teammates. He would want to be a part of the team, to belong, even if it meant sitting on the sidelines. Anything was better than quitting. But he would do as he was told. He was only twelve.

Mabry looked at the expression on his son's face and his heart sank. As Billy obediently dropped his head and slowly turned towards the bleachers, Mabry's stomach twisted into knots.

Before Billy took a step, Matt spoke up.

"I'll quit, too," he said defiantly.

Mabry shook his head.

"You're a good boy to offer, Matt, but this shouldn't be your battle. You go on and play. We'll be all right."

"No," replied Matt. "We talked it over last night."

"Who did?" asked Mabry.

Before the boy could answer, a deep baritone voice rolled over Mabry's shoulder. "We did."

Mabry turned and looked up several inches into the gruff, bearded face of a mountain man. He wore heavy black logging boots and canvas pants. Over a plaid flannel shirt, a pair of red suspenders stretched across powerful shoulders. The man extended a massive hand.

"I'm Matt's father. Luke Jordan. You'd be Justin Mabry?"

Shaking hands firmly, Mabry nodded.

"Yes."

Billy gazed in awe at the size of Luke Jordan and for a moment was distracted from his predicament. As Matt went to his father's side, Billy went to his.

"Matt and me, more or less, knew what was going on a week ago. I'm sorry for Billy, but Burns is a...well, I've had dealings with him before, and this was no surprise. Matt was only playing because he got along with Billy so well, and that made it fun for a while. But Burns is as crooked as a snake. If Billy don't play, then Matt don't, either."

"Thanks," said Mabry. "But this will lead to bad feelings and in a small town, that's not good. I don't want you to have problems because of us."

Jordan laughed.

"That won't be nothing new, nothing at all. We're hill-people! We don't care what they think in town."

"Well, Billy's through with this team. He was just going to get his gear and then we're leaving."

"Then let's all go over," said Jordan, as a smile showed through the black hairs on his face. "I want to see the look on Burns' face when he finds out what's going on. But I guarantee you he isn't going to say a word. The man's a born coward. I've known him all my life."

No one seemed to notice as Matt and Billy entered the dugout. But when they gathered their bats and gloves and walked back out, the players and parents watched in stunned silence. Burns, who had been standing on the third-base pad and joking with Johnny's father, now stood with his mouth half open. He wore a stupefied expression on his face but, true to Jordan's prediction, said absolutely nothing.

All eyes were on the two fathers and their sons as they walked away from the field, but none of the observers moved a muscle or uttered a single sound. What was happening in full view of everyone was inconceivable.

In the parking lot, Billy quietly crawled into the cab of the truck and rolled down the window. His sad bloodshot eyes glanced at Matt.

"See ya."

Matt only nodded as his father again extended his hand. As Mabry took it, Jordan's brow wrinkled with concern.

"Your boy won't know why you did this for some years yet. But this country needs men that will stand their ground, even when it costs them. You got my respect."

Mabry sighed.

"Thank you," he said. "I was beginning to think I was alone in that regard."

"Oh, you're not alone. No sir. You're not alone at all. Not around here." Jordan smiled, his eyes lighting with admiration. "I knew Burns wouldn't say nothing, but I was surprised at the other parents. You must have either intimidated or shamed them all into silence. And that was quite a sight to see."

Mabry stepped into his pickup and watched the Jordans walk away. They were obviously close, just as a father and son should be. And at least they understood. It felt good to know there were still some people that shared the same values.

"Billy," said Mabry softly, "I can't begin to tell you how sorry I am this happened. I know how bad you wanted to play. But I won't allow you to be treated that way. What the coach did was wrong, but doing nothing about it would have been even more wrong."

Only a faint nod came from Billy. His eyes were downcast, his shoulders slumped, but he held back the tears.

"I think we'll stop by Bobbin's Donuts in Clark Fork before we go home. We can get some of those jelly-filled donuts you like. Maybe we'll get some extra to take with us."

Billy still made no reply. He tried to smile but failed miserably. It was the best he could do.

Kelly Anson flicked a donut crumb from her Bonner County Sheriff uniform and took a sip of steaming coffee. She had been on duty since 2:00 AM and it was time for her second break. Not being accustomed to the graveyard shift, she needed the caffeine.

Another deputy sat across a small table that was covered with a white cloth. He was stocky, bald and wore a sarcastic smile.

"You've been on the force for less than a year, Kelly, and you're already eating at the donut shop! You're the one that's always getting on me about stereotypes. And here you are turning into one."

"Funny, Gill. Very funny."

Kelly Anson wasn't in the mood to take the ribbing. Like all rookie cops, she had to work the late shifts and she was tired. Gill Jacobson was a likeable guy, but sometimes he didn't know when to stop.

"You going out with anyone this weekend?" asked Jacobson. "Oh, I forgot. You got the graveyard shift again. You won't have time for any sweet-talking man. You'll have to settle for donuts."

Anson's lips curled into a humorless smile.

"One donut, Gill. I only had one."

Patting his round belly, Jacobson leaned back in his chair.

"Yep. That's just how I started out. When I was a rookie, I was a wiry one hundred and sixty pounds. It all started with that one donut.

"Sure, you've got that sexy little figure now, Kelly, but you just wait a few years. Now, how in hell will you ever get married if you look like me?"

"Knock it off or I'll tell your wife you were flirting with me."

At the thought of his wife, Jacobson's mood sobered and his grin bent downward into a frown. He hunched forward, leaning his thick forearms on the table.

"Where are you patrolling next?"

"I'm going up Lightning Creek."

"What for?" asked Jacobson with a hint of fatherly concern.

"Another property line dispute. More and more people moving in up there."

"You be real careful," advised the older officer. "That's drug country up there and, rumor is, there's a bunch of those militia types out in the woods, too."

Anson sighed patiently.

"Gill, I was raised here, too. Remember?"

"I know and I don't give a tinker's damn about political correctness. You're a young woman and you're pretty. You barely made the height requirement and I bet you don't weigh as much as my right leg. You know how I feel about women cops, especially the young pretty ones."

"You're stereotyping again, Gill. And flirting."

"Bull! Bull on both counts! I'm just stating the facts. You listen to what I said. When you get in that country, or any of the mountains around here, you be careful. If something doesn't feel right, make up an excuse and get out. Then you can go back in with some backup if you want."

"Nobody's going to bother a cop," said Anson. "They know better."

Jacobson shook his head.

"I told you, you should have taken that new federal job they offered you. It would have been perfect. You'd be looking out for kids, making sure they're not abused. As softhearted as you are, that would have been right up your alley. Now they gave that job to that idiot, Jeff Brown. He was a bad deputy and they promoted him to a federal officer. It should have been you, Kelly."

"I didn't want to be a babysitter. Besides, it gets Brown out of the department and moves him up the ladder and away from us. That's what he wants, so let him have it. I mean, really. Federal Child Protection--how lame."

Jacobson shrugged.

"Your loss," he said then leaned closer to Anson. He lowered his voice, but his tone was suddenly commanding.

"You do what I say when you get out there. You only have two eyes and the woods are thick. Someone could get behind you in a second and you'd never know it. You know these people, but not like I do. I've seen the ugly side of some of them. And to some others, you aren't a sheriff. You represent the government and that's a whole different ball game."

"Those kind have been in North Idaho since before I was born," Anson replied. "They've never done much to anyone. They're mostly just a lot of talk. I know plenty of them and have known them since I was in grade school."

Jacobson stood up.

"I promised your father I'd look after you. Now, you be careful like I said and watch your back."

Anson rolled her eyes then smiled flatly.

"I will, Gill. I'll see you back at the station."

As Jacobson left the donut shop, Kelly Anson stared for a moment at her half-eaten donut, then glanced down at her stomach. It was flat and her waistline was small, but she was less active now that she spent so much time in a patrol car. She would take Gill's advice about the hill-people and about the donuts. Gill was old-school and sometimes hard to take, but he was one of the best cops in the state and it paid to listen when he gave advice.

Suddenly, her thoughts were interrupted by a young boy's voice. It was soft, almost mournful, yet carried with it a tone of respect. Looking up, she saw what obviously was a father and son standing at the counter with their back to her. The small boy wore a baseball uniform, and the father had dark hair and broad shoulders.

It was her job to be observant, especially when she met people she did not know or weren't part of the community. The man, whom she estimated to be in his mid-thirties, spoke softly to the boy then gently put his hand on his shoulder. The boy stood close to his father, leaning slightly against him. There was no dirt or grass stain on the uniform. It was clean.

When the pair turned towards the tables, Anson met the man's eyes. His were gray-blue and very troubled. The boy was as cute as she had ever seen and a duplicate of his father. But the look in the boy's eyes broke her heart.

Kelly Anson smiled and the father attempted to smile back, but whatever was on his mind smothered the effort. She then glanced back at the son and immediately understood that something terrible had happened. She was suddenly concerned, but it had nothing to do with her training as a police officer. This was more personal.

Before she could give it more thought, the father and son sat down a few feet from her at one of the tables in the small shop.

Impulsively, she said, "You two have a game today?"

The man again tried to be courteous and smiled faintly.

"Yes and no," he offered dejectedly. "It's been a very tough morning for Billy."

Anson leaned over and extended her hand to the young boy.

"You must be Billy," she said cheerfully. "I'm Officer Anson. But you can call me Kelly."

Billy's face brightened as he took the officer's hand.

"Hi."

Glancing at the patch on the shoulder of Billy's uniform, Anson was surprised to see that the boy and father were local.

"You play for Clark Fork. You must be new to the area."

"We've been here three months," said Billy.

Noticing the sadness in the boys voice Anson wanted to hug him, but instead she asked another question. "Then you must be on Kal Burns' team, the All Stars? What time is your game today?"

Billy's face darkened and he dropped his head. Anson looked to the father for an explanation, but he too stared down at the table. Suddenly she knew, at least in part, what had occurred.

"Well, it is just a game."

The man slowly raised his head and looked into Kelly Anson's eyes.

"Baseball *is* just a game. But games are governed by rules designed to make the competition fair for both sides. Like all games throughout history, they're a contest to determine which team has the best athletes. And no matter how corrupt a given society might become, the people still despise cheaters in sports. If nothing else, we want purity in competition so that a winner is truly a champion. We insist the rules are followed. But there are no rules that govern ethics and morals in sports. A lot of people think anything goes, just so you win. But I don't. When morality and ethics are ignored, especially when it affects my son, it's *not* just a game anymore."

The statement was simple, profound and unarguably true, but it was also on the verge of being a lecture. As Anson wondered what recent event had triggered such a response, she studied the man sitting across from her. He was handsome, apparently a man of principle and a father that obviously loved his son. But there was something else about him. Was it in his eyes or his voice? Or was it neither? It was almost like a vibration, a vague sort of magnetism she could sense, yet not define. When he took a sip of coffee, she checked for a wedding ring and felt an unexpected sense of relief when she saw none.

"I'm sorry. I was in sports myself. I should know better," she said. Then, offering her hand, she added, "You are right, of course. I'm Officer Kelly Anson, Bonner County Sheriff's Department."

The man took her hand.

"Justin Mabry," he said. "And thank you for caring."

Anson leaned back in her chair with a question forming on her lips. Before she could ask it, Mabry nodded towards Billy, who still hung his head.

Silently, Anson acknowledged the signal and immediately understood her role.

"I played fast-pitch softball in high school. Some of those girls threw a pitch that equaled a ninety-mile-per-hour baseball pitch."

Billy lifted his head and his eyes widened.

"Ninety?"

"Yep. Baseball just keeps getting better the older you get. You wait. Next year will be much more fun, and you'll be bigger and better than ever. As long as you and your father keep practicing."

"Could you hit the ball?" asked Billy with genuine interest. "At ninety, I mean?"

Smiling as she remembered, Anson said, "Not at first. I couldn't do anything but strike out. There were times I went home and just cried, but I practiced hard and I learned. By my junior year, I was on the varsity team and the lead-off hitter. I hit over three hundred for the next two seasons."

"Really? Wow! You were good when you were a girl."

Checking her watch, Anson moved her chair back and stood up.

"Time for me to get back to work but, Billy, you keep your chin up. Every athlete has a disaster from time to time. And if there were more people like your dad around, police officers would have a much easier job."

Both father and son watched the officer as she walked out the door. They continued watching through the window, as she passed their truck and got inside her patrol car. After she drove away Billy looked at his father. "She was nice," he said. Then after a thoughtful pause, he asked, "Was she pretty?"

Justin Mabry glanced at his son and felt a twinge of sadness. His little boy was growing up. "Yes, Billy. She is very pretty".

"I thought so," replied Billy as if one of life's mysteries had just been solved. "So, she was pretty."

"More than that, Billy. She's smart and she cares about people."

Billy nodded approvingly. "And she knows baseball!"

Mabry leaned across the table and whispered, "After we finish eating, let's speed through town and see if she'll give us a ticket."

Grinning, the twinkle in Billy's eyes returned. "Can we?"

Chapter Three

Washington D.C.
FBI Building
Third-floor conference room
June 16th
8:14 PM (EST)

Agent Berger paced the floor. His bull neck was red.

"So there it is--a dead bear, a dead wolf and torched cars and trucks. All on the same night and all in the inland northwest region. Is it coincidence?"

Agent Anderson paused, knowing Agent Francis was usually the first to respond. Unlike other agents that worked with her, he didn't care that she always wanted to be first at everything. Like anyone else, D.J. Francis wasn't perfect. Her ambition was a minor flaw, nothing more. He understood her completely and accepted her for who and what she was. He hoped that someday she would feel the same way about him.

"Definitely not, sir," answered Francis. "I would say that, at the minimum, the bear and wolf drops were coordinated."

Berger glanced at Anderson, who casually sat back in his chair with his arms folded.

"I agree," said Anderson. "But I have no doubts all three events are linked."

Rubbing the back of his neck, Berger swore.

"All right. I want the two of you on this now. Get out there and find out what's going on. Get those field agents moving! I want this defused as quickly and quietly as possible. This is another damn election cycle and the administration doesn't want any more trouble in the western states."

"We'll be on a flight for Boise this evening," said Francis.

Anderson smiled.

"Sure thing, sir."

As the two agents stood to leave, Berger looked squarely at Francis.

"And I want Anderson in charge. It's more his turf and they're his kind of people you'll be investigating. Am I clear on that?"

The redhead stood to her full six feet. She straightened her vest with a snap of her wrists .

"Perfectly, sir."

June 17th
Spokesman Review (Spokane, Washington)
Morning Edition
Firefighters Die; Endangered Species Act Blamed

June 17th
Desert Review (Winnemucca, Nevada)
Forest Service Bans Land Use for Ranchers

June 17th
San Francisco Chronicle (San Francisco, California)
Ninth Circuit Court Rules Anti-Gay Churches Illegal

Taking a red-eye flight out of Washington D.C., it was just past sun-up when Agents Francis and Anderson landed in Denver. The flight transfer there was delayed an hour and Francis found the airport food nauseating. She was now on board a half empty connecting flight preparing to take off for Idaho. Boise was bad for the complexion. It would be hot and dry this time of year, and it was a hick town in a hick state.

As the jet roared down the runway, Francis ignored the seat-belt light above her and unbuckled the strap around her waist. With her lap-top resting on her thighs, she waited impatiently to open it and catch up on her work.

Hearing the metallic click of the safety belt next to him, Anderson glanced at Francis and smiled.

"Well," he said, continuing their previous conversation. "I think Berger was right to send us. We need to be there on the scene. Sure, we have our implants and our snitches, but you know as well as I do, they're not that reliable. You don't get the feel of things unless you meet the people, hear the tone of their voices. Sometimes what we need to know is in their eyes or their subtle mannerisms. It's especially in the eyes. You won't get that by fax or e-mail."

"More hayseed logic," replied Francis, but there was no sarcasm in her tone. She had known Anderson to be right too many times.

Anderson laughed.

"They're my people, D.J. I grew up out there, remember? When we work the big cities, you can tell me how it's done. When we travel to the Inland Northwest, I think I have the advantage."

"I hope this isn't another false alarm, John. These *people* of yours are usually just a bunch of blowhards with beer bellies. Most likely, we're wasting our time."

As the passenger jet leveled off, the seat-belt light chimed and disappeared, but Anderson only loosened his belt and left the buckle locked.

"Probability says you're right, D.J. The whole key to this, though, is the climate. For forty years or so, there has been unrest of one kind or another but, like little grass fires, we've quietly snuffed them out. And except for the Waco disaster, the general public hasn't cared how we've done it.

"But given the right conditions, fires spread fast. They can get so hot nothing can put them out. It's not uncommon at all to see fires burning in the rain."

Francis opened her computer and thought for a moment. The recession was in its third year, energy prices were soaring and unemployment was rising. Congress was talking about a tax hike along with an increase in welfare spending. The West was in its fifth year of drought and several states were fighting with the federal authorities over water rights. Discounting the East and West Coasts, the country as a whole was angry. But this was nothing new. It was a typical cycle and would run its course. Everything would then turn around and the past would soon be forgotten.

"I don't see the present situation being any different than others we've experienced," said Francis. "At times like this, these right-wing groups always become more active. It will pass."

"Again, you have mathematical probability on your side. But in the last four decades there has always been one missing factor. It's because of that missing ingredient that we've had no major problems with domestic unrest."

Francis looked at Anderson with a humorless smile on her lips.

"Let me guess. The missing ingredient is a spark."

Anderson nodded.

"Sort of. It needs something, or someone, to unite them. If that happens under the right conditions, the escalation of civil disobedience may be too rapid for our usual 'low intensity warfare' strategies to stop it. There won't be enough time for our provocateurs to generate internal conflicts, and there won't be time enough to harass them legally or even illegally. None of the tactics we've used for the last seventy years will be effective.

"The covert operations we traditionally use take time and planning and they only work when we know who we're after and why. So far, the Bureau has been successful because all the groups we've identified and successfully infiltrated are fragmented and unorganized. And what leadership they've had has been systematically neutralized by our techniques. But what will happen if one single event or person brings all the domestic unrest, all the little organizations together? What will we do then?"

Francis looked at Anderson.

"What is it with you? You never worry about anything, and now you come up with this 'fire in the rain' theory? It's not going to happen, John. Not in our lifetime, anyway. You're talking about civil war, or close to it. Americans have no stomach for anything even remotely resembling such a thing. We're a society that likes to fight, but only as long as someone else, or some machine, does it for us. No, John. The days you're thinking about are long gone. We don't grow messiahs anymore. And if we did, there would be a file on them in West Virginia and they would already be under surveillance."

Anderson was silent for a moment.

"You may be right, D.J. But I hope you're wrong about the people. It would be sad to believe that Americans no longer possess what it took to build this country in the first place, that there will be no more great leaders. No more Patrick Henrys, no more Sam Houstons. It would be tragic. It would mean we no longer exist as Americans. And I don't believe that, for a minute."

Naples, Idaho
Forty miles south of the Canadian border
June 17th
7:24 AM (PST)

Inside an aspen thicket, six men in full camouflage strapped on their bulletproof vests. On a rock ledge above them, a seventh man scanned the forest and valley below for any signs of movement. All seven participants wore military-style helmets and carried VHF radios. After fastening their vests, each man slung an assault shotgun over his shoulder, then grabbed an AK-47 rifle and started for the edge of the trees.

Forming a single file, they broke into an easy dog-trot and headed into the dense forest. Eight minutes later, despite the rough terrain, they were a mile away from their starting point. In a small clearing, the men spread out and dropped to the ground. Unfolding the bipods fastened to their rifles, each man took careful aim at a life-size target stationed four-hundred yards across a canyon. Shots blasted rapid-fire from the muzzle of each weapon and echoed off the distant mountain, and a fraction of a second later, thirty white-hot bullets tore through a black paper silhouette.

Without a word, the small platoon folded the bipods, reformed their line and trotted to the next training stage. "Leaderless Resistance" was stitched in blue thread on the left shoulder of each jacket. Over the left pocket, in red thread, was "Phantom Cell" and sewn over the right, in white thread, was "Idaho Militia."

From the rocky ledge, should anyone be monitoring the airwaves, only one word was sent.

"Clear."

Then, over hundreds of square miles of national forest, there was nothing but silence.

It was almost noon when Kal Burns opened his bloodshot eyes and tried to focus on the clock next to his bed. He was hung over in his own bedroom and for a moment could not remember why. But then he began to swear through gritted teeth.

Yesterday, his All-Star baseball team had barely lost their first game, but in their second attempt to advance in the playoffs, they had been eliminated from the tournament by Post Falls, ten runs to nothing. And, naturally excluding himself, the only one to blame for their defeat was Justin Mabry!

Taking his son off the team had an unexpected negative effect on the other players, and without Matt Jordan's hitting ability, they never had a chance. Burns had been humiliated in front of everyone at the ballpark, and today's newspaper would make it even worse.

Going out the front door in his underwear, Burns bent over and snatched the paper from the steps. A passing car honked its horn, and he came up with a jerk. Not recognizing the driver, he flipped him off and swore some more.

Tossing the Daily Bee on the dinning room table, he went to his cupboards for coffee. As he loaded the grounds into the pot, he scanned the front page. There it was in bold print.

Sandpoint All-Stars Gone in Two. Story on B3.

While the coffee perked, Burns simmered as he read the report on the team's poor performance. It pointed out in graphic detail how they were expected to be state champions, how much of an upset it was to lose to lowly Post Falls, and how if it weren't for the ten-run mercy rule, the players would have suffered an even greater defeat and further embarrassment.

Hunched over the paper and resting his hairy elbows on the table, Burns gritted his teeth and clenched his fists. Mabry had done this! That nothing-of-a-man had ruined everything. Who would have guessed a total failure like him would take his precious little Billy off the team? The kid was a naïve sap, and so was his father. He was a loser that lived in a run-down rental on the edge of town. And yet, that loser had beaten him at his own game!

Winning was everything to Burns and he had grown accustomed to it. But on rare occasions such as this one, revenge was the next best thing. Before he had gotten drunk the night before, he decided the first thing to do was explain to everyone what Mabry had done, how he had forced his kid to quit, then talked Matt Jordan into quitting as well. It would then take little time to turn the small town of Clark Fork against the newcomer. There would be satisfaction in that, but Burns was an impatient man. And after reading the newspaper article, he wanted something more palatable than social rejection for Justin Mabry. He wanted something he could savor immediately.

Burns went to the counter and poured himself a cup of coffee. Scratching at the black stubble on his face, he racked his aching brain for a plan of attack. As he stood finishing his second cup, he thought of his past accomplishments and smiled. No one ever got the best of Kal Burns. What would it be this time? He had to think of something big, something deserving, something to fit the crime. Crime?

Burns swore, but this time his profanity rang with excitement. He slammed his coffee cup down on the kitchen counter and went to his trash can. Rummaging past the damp garbage and coffee grounds, he retrieved two newspapers. What he wanted, he had read in one of them a few days earlier. After a quick search he found what he was looking for.

"Gotcha!"

He spread the paper on the counter top. He refilled his cup with fresh coffee, then sat down. This was going to be good!

On the front page of the June 16th *Daily Bee* was a photograph of a police officer. The caption below the photo said that Jeff Brown had recently been appointed Bonner County's first Federal Child Protection officer. Burns took a sip of steaming coffee and eagerly scanned the story.

No proof necessary, the article said. A person need only have a strong suspicion to make a report, and the concerned citizen would be assured complete anonymity. The perpetrator could be charged with a federal offense and, if convicted of severe abuse, jail time would be mandatory.

Burns thought of the many baseballs that had slammed into Billy Mabry's arms and the bruises they had left. Some were new, some were old; they were made to order. This was going to be sweet, possibly his most cunning payback ever.

Of course, Mabry would never be found guilty, but the interrogation, the threat of being jailed and taken away from his precious Billy, would cause him an enormous amount of anxiety and grief. It was perfect and Mabry had asked for it.

Picking up the phone, Burns excitedly paced the floor as he punched the number. He began to laugh.

"And the best part is," he said to himself, "the son-of-a-bitch is going to know it was me that turned him in!"

Officer Jeff Brown sat at his new desk inside the Federal Building in Sandpoint. He was moving up. No longer was he a mere cop with a minimal salary and bad hours. He was a federal agent and didn't have to take orders anymore, at least not from people he had grown up with. Now they would work for him. When he needed an escort, they would have to give it to him. When he demanded extra support, they would send more police officers to assist him. He would call the shots now, and there was nothing they could do about it.

Brown looked in the small mirror he had just hung on his wall. He liked wearing a suit now and had chosen to buy a dark gray one like those the FBI wore. Under his coat, he also wore a new shoulder holster with a quick release scabbard for his pistol. He had spent most of the morning practicing his quick draw.

As Brown smoothed some hair that was out of place, his phone rang for the first time. With his heart instantly pounding, he deepened his voice and answered his first call.

"Child Protection," he said gruffly. "Agent Brown speaking."

He listened for a moment.

"Yes, that is correct."

Brown's eyes narrowed as he picked up a pen.

"I see. And your name is...? Oh, hello, Mr. Burns. Completely anonymous, yes. And why do you believe that has happened, sir? I see. I see. How long do you think this abuse has been going on? Bruises on both arms. Any other marks? Contusions? And the name? Can you spell the last name? And you say he lives in Clark Fork. And you have the address? No, that should do it. No, not at all. Rest assured that you have done the right thing, Mr. Burns. The children are our first concern. It's everyone's duty, sir. You have done the entire community a service."

There was nothing moving on the blacktop but rippling heat waves and an occasional jackrabbit. The Wyoming interstate was wide open and a Peterbilt diesel engine, deep inside an eighteen-wheeler, barely strained at ninety miles per hour. The windows of the cab were down. An arm, tattooed with a black snake head, rested on the door and glistened with sweat in the blazing sun. A red and white Dixie flag waved from the grill of the truck. A voice blasted from the radio.

"I tell you, folks, they're not happy out there in the West. Well, let's make it clear--the Inland West, not those wackos out on the coast. These westerners are *not* happy. The environmentalists have gotten control of every branch of the government that affects their lives. These federal officials are after their water rights, their grazing rights, the timber, the mining, you name it. It's another Sagebrush Rebellion, like the ones they had back in the seventies and eighties.

"That's why they're meeting right now at the Conference of Western Governors. It hasn't gotten much press, but they're gathering up in

Coeur d'Alene, Idaho, both Democrats *and* Republicans, folks. They don't like the president's policies and, mark my words, folks, these governors are going to make their feelings known when that meeting is over.

"Okay, it's almost noon. We have time for one more caller. We have Dillon from Ellensburg, Washington. What's on your mind, sir?"

"Ah, yeah, Hank. Great show. What I was wondering about was this new Child Protection law, the one that just became federal law. I haven't heard much talk about it out here. What do you think about this thing? It seems kind of scary to me."

"You get the prize, Dillon! I've been waiting for this to come up all morning! We only have a few seconds before we have to go but let me just say, this is *big*. Maybe the biggest intrusion into family rights since teens were allowed to have abortions without parental consent. No, it's bigger than that even.

"You just wait, folks. This thing is going to backfire big time. This is going to cause nothing but more trouble for Madam President. Personally, I think this is a bombshell. Well, got to go, folks. Great callers today. More tomorrow on the Hank Sprey Show. Until then, 'Sprey 'em down' with the unvarnished truth!"

Officer Anson was finally off duty. Her shift had started at 2 AM and it was noon when she walked through the rear entrance of the Bonner County Sheriff's office. She was headed for the lockers when Sally from dispatch yelled to her from down the hall.

"Sorry, Kelly. We're short-handed again. You're going to get some more overtime."

Anson frowned and sighed.

"What is it?"

"You're to pick up Jeff Brown at the Federal Building and take him out to Clark Fork. He's got his first case."

Shaking her head, Anson rolled her eyes.

"So when does he get a car to go along with his fancy new job? How long can we expect this nonsense to go on?"

"Got me," answered the dispatcher. "He just called a minute ago or I would have radioed you. He sounds...motivated."

"You mean impatient, pushy and rude, don't you?"

The dispatcher smiled knowingly.

"Your lucky day."

Sliding into the patrol car, Anson adjusted her pistol to a more comfortable position and shoved the keys into the ignition. She was tired and in no mood to deal with Jeff Brown. It was a twenty-minute drive to Clark Fork and she already had a headache.

Starting the engine, Anson leaned back for a moment. She removed her sunglasses and massaged her forehead for a few seconds, then stopped suddenly. The thought of the donut shop drifted into her mind and of the father and son she had met there. The man was certainly handsome enough, but she had seen plenty of that sort before. There was something different about him though, something…attractive. She had felt it yesterday when she met him, but had been too busy to think about anything but work since then. The encounter was so brief but still, she was curious. As she drove out of the parking lot, she found herself hoping to see him again.

When she pulled up in front of the Federal Building, Brown was waiting in his new suit and holding a leather briefcase. Recognizing Anson, he smirked as he opened the passenger side door.

"How's it going, rookie?" he asked with unveiled impudence.

Anson glared at Brown.

"How's the babysitting going?"

Brown snorted and smiled, yet there was no humor.

"You're about to find out. And you're about to make history."

Pulling out into light traffic, Anson kept her eyes straight ahead.

"History?"

"Yeah. If this isn't the first Federal Child Protection case, it's going to be one of the first. And the president herself will likely take an interest in it."

"How do you know you even have a case? You've only been doing this one day. You may not find any evidence on your first call."

Brown took a deep breath and let it out slowly.

"Oh, I have a case all right. The caller I had was very specific and very reliable. There will be bruises and there's an established history of bruises. It's a pattern of abuse, observed firsthand by the caller. It's an open-and-shut case. At the very least, there's plenty of suspicion, enough to place the child under federal protection."

"How old is the child?" asked Anson, turning eastbound on Highway 200.

"Twelve."

"Anyone we know?"

Brown shook his head, unsnapped his briefcase and opened it. He took out a single sheet of paper and glanced at it.

"The name is Mabry. Justin Mabry. His son's name is Billy. They just moved up here about three months ago."

Anson abruptly pulled off the blacktop onto the shoulder. Slowly, she turned her head and stared at Brown.

"Does this have anything to do with…baseball?"

Looking up from the report in his hand, Brown glanced at Anson then slowly returned the paper to his briefcase and snapped it shut.

"How did you know that?"

"Who called in the report?"

"You know I can't tell you that. But it is a reliable source. There's no question about that. Let's just say he's well known in this area and a long-time resident. This is legitimate."

Anson shook her head.

"If the person that called in that report is who I think it is, there's been some kind of mistake. This is too important to go rushing in without proof."

"First of all," said Brown, with a hint of irritation in his voice, "proof is *not* what this call is about. That comes from the investigation. Protection comes before proof. And second of all, what do you know about this?"

"I met the father and son yesterday. I saw how they were together. It's a feeling, but I trust my instincts. There is no way he's guilty of abuse."

Brown relaxed and smiled.

"That's one of the first things they taught us at the federal academy. Don't use your *feelings* to do this job. You can never tell what goes on inside someone's home or when no one is looking. How did you think this guy would act towards his son with you standing there in uniform? Come on, Kelly!"

Anson thought about what Brown said for a moment. There was an element of truth to it, but what she had seen was real. The father and son weren't even aware of her presence when she first observed them.

"Jeff, I'm just saying to go slow. Accusing a parent who's devoted to his child, of abuse. Who knows what could happen?"

Opening his suit-coat, Brown exposed his shoulder holster and pistol.

"That was part of our training, too. Even you local cops know that domestic disputes are some of the most dangerous calls you'll ever make. And, of course, I have you along to protect me."

"I don't like this. I don't like it at all. This whole Federal Protection law is unnecessary. It should have stayed in the hands of local law enforcement."

"It's a new day, Kelly. Laws are always changing whether you like it or not. But it's your job to enforce the laws, not give them your personal stamp of approval. You'll get the hang of it after a few years on the force. You'll do your time and go home, just like everyone else. We're enforcers, not priests. The work is hard enough without worrying about morality. They don't pay us enough to do that."

Kelly Anson took her foot off the brake and reluctantly pulled back onto the highway.

"I didn't become a cop for the money, Jeff. How we do our jobs shouldn't be influenced by how much we're paid."

Wondering about his son's state of mind had kept Mabry awake for a second night, and at 4:00 AM, he decided to get up and make coffee. As it perked, he kept asking himself the same questions. Could Billy possibly grasp what had happened? Would he remember yesterday as the time his father had done something for him, or the day he had done something *to* him? Certainly, it was confusing to Billy and such a traumatic experience could easily strain their relationship, if not permanently damage it. And it was that relationship, that bond that Mabry treasured. And yet, what he had done as a father was equally important. It was a lesson in right and wrong, and in the price of justice. If Billy did not understand these principles today, he would tomorrow. Hopefully.

Some roads in life were rough no matter which way they turn, and that, too, Billy must learn. But why did it have to start so soon? Mabry wanted to protect his son's childhood as long as possible. The divorce was devastating, and there was so little time left for him to be a child. Why did the coach have to be someone like Kal Burns? Why couldn't Burns have at least made a pretense of being fair? How could a grown man treat a child that way? And for what?

The questions came and went without resolution and after a second pot of coffee, Mabry felt no better than he had when he left the baseball field the previous morning. All he knew for sure was that he and Billy needed time away, time together.

It was close to ten o'clock when Billy woke up and staggered into the kitchen.

After a bowl of cereal, Mabry suggested an overnight fishing trip to Roman Nose Lake. Billy seemed genuinely excited to go, and for two hours they packed all the camping gear they owned into their backpacks. They had the packs just inside the front door and were getting their fishing gear together when a white sheriff's car pulled up in their driveway.

Billy saw the car first.

"Dad, that pretty lady is here," he said, looking out the front window.

Mabry was tying a final knot around his sleeping bag.

"What? What pretty lady?"

"The police lady. The one from the donut store."

Mabry stood slowly, feeling his heart rate increase. The divorce had taught him never to expect anything good from such a visit. There had been too many papers to sign and too many legal battles lost. His ex-wife had everything she wanted. What more could she want?

"And there's a man with her."

Mabry glanced out the window and felt his stomach turn. The man looked like one of the many attorneys he had grown to despise. They always seemed to need a briefcase.

Not waiting for the knock, Mabry opened the door. He looked only at the woman that had been so nice to them the day before. Whatever this was about, it had nothing to do with her. And no matter what message the lawyer brought, she, at least, was beautiful.

"Justin Mabry?" the man said.

Mabry didn't care for the tone of the man's voice and reluctantly shifted his attention to him. He saw a pair of arrogant eyes, eyes that reflected a desire to exert power.

"That's right. What can I do for you?"

"I'm Agent Brown, from the Federal Child Protection Service. I have some questions for you."

Only half listening to the introduction, Mabry sighed as Billy came and stood beside him. Placing a hand on his son's shoulder, he spoke in a monotone voice.

"If you're representing my ex-wife, I would prefer you go through my attorney."

"This has nothing to do with your wife," Brown replied. "We're here to see you."

Mabry thought for a moment, still uncomprehending.

"Well, we haven't lived here very long. I don't think we can be of much help."

"What?" Brown said.

"We don't know any kids well enough to help you. I assume you want to know about someone around here, but we just haven't had a chance to get to know anyone. The only real contact we've had with anyone is through baseball and that's not been very much."

"Mr. Mabry, you don't understand. We're investigating *you*. You have been accused of domestic child abuse."

Mabry blinked his bloodshot eyes. His head began to spin as the words sank in. In a fraction of a heartbeat, his mind had been flooded with a tangled mass of conflicting thoughts and emotions. For several seconds, he was in shock. Then, as rapidly as the wave of confusion slammed into him, it subsided, leaving only one simple instinct behind. And it was primordial.

Brown bent down and looked at Billy.

"I assume that this is your son."

Mabry made no reply. His predatory eyes were locked on Brown. His pulse was pounding, his muscles pumping adrenaline.

"We have reports of bruises, especially on the arms. Billy, isn't it? You want to show me your arms, Billy?"

Billy moved closer to his father, keeping his arms close to his side.

"He has lots of bruises," said Mabry defiantly. "And he earned every one of them behind the plate as a catcher on the baseball team."

Still looking at Billy, Brown said, "I was told he had these bruises before the season started and I have that report from a reliable source. The source was very concerned, enough to go over my head, to Washington, if I didn't investigate you. The source said Billy showed signs of emotional distress as well."

The rage within Mabry was white-hot, but he struggled to keep his mind clear. "Your 'source,' as you call it, said the bruises were there before baseball?"

"That is correct."

"That means your 'source' is lying. And that 'source' has to be associated with baseball. And the most likely person to be such a damn liar is Kal Burns."

Agent Jeff Brown hid his surprise. Mabry had guessed the name of his source within seconds. But what did it matter? He was still guessing, and Brown had known Kal Burns for years. He was an important man and a good connection to have in a small town. Why would he lie?

"We never reveal our sources. It's for the protection of the children. If we did, no one would come forward. They would be afraid of retaliation."

"What about my right to face my accuser?" snapped Mabry. "What about my rights as a parent?"

"Mr. Mabry, you have no rights in this situation. The child's safety supersedes the rights of any parent."

Without warning, Brown took hold of Billy's left arm and pulled it forward. Billy jerked his arm back, but the bruises were easy to see.

"Don't you ever do that again," said Mabry. His words came slowly, deliberately. The tone of his voice carried an unmistakable threat.

"Those look like baseball injuries to me," Anson said, attempting to defuse the situation. "Agent Brown, catchers get them all the time."

Ignoring Anson's comment, Brown came to his full height, a full three inches above Mabry.

"I have the authority," he sneered, "to take this child from you by federal law. And I have the authority to examine him anytime and in any way I choose."

"No," said Mabry, his eyes flickering with a wicked light. "That may or may not be the law, but you don't have that right. Not with my son."

Brown raised an eyebrow as a smirk curved the corner of his mouth.

"I have all the evidence I need." He reached towards Billy. "This child is now under federal protection."

The federal agent grabbed Billy by the shoulder and pulled him forward. Brown started to say something more but a fist slammed into his jaw. His head jerked with such force that the two-hundred-pound body spun with the impact of the blow. Brown staggered for two steps, then fell face down in the front yard. He did not move.

Kelly Anson was stunned.

"Oh! My God! Oh, my God! What have you done?"

"What I had to," growled Mabry. "Are you part of this, too?"

Anson slowly took her eyes off the unconscious Brown. When she looked at Mabry, her eyes were filled with horror.

"That's a federal crime! I know him. He'll make you pay. Oh, my Lord. You'll go to jail. They'll take your son. You should have done what he said. Oh, Jesus. What do I do? You should have just done what he said!"

"No, ma'am," said Mabry flatly. "I should *not* have. No one should have."

Mabry knelt down in front of Billy.

"I'm sorry, Billy. I'll try to fix this. Meantime, you go to the only other place you'll be safe. Do you know where I'm talking about?"

Billy whispered in his father's ear.

"That's right. Stay until I come. I love you, Billy."

After hugging and kissing his father, Billy picked up his pack.

"I know what the right thing is," Billy said. "Now I know. I love you, Dad."

With his backpack on, Billy ran across the road and through a horse pasture then disappeared into the thick forest. When he was out of sight, Mabry grabbed his own pack then went to Brown and rolled him over. Taking the agent's pistol from its holster, he shoved it behind his belt then turned back to Anson.

"Just tell them I escaped and you'll be fine."

"I'm supposed to put you under arrest," Anson said feebly.

Mabry nodded.

"You're too good a person to do that. I'll try and straighten this out. You know the truth. The truth about the bruises, about Kal Burns. And the truth about that big idiot lying there.

"I appreciate what you were trying to do and what you are doing now, Officer, and what it may cost you. All I can offer is my gratitude...and my deepest respect. It's not worth much, but it's all I have to give."

Hoisting the backpack to his shoulders, he glanced at his small house. Then, after one long look in the direction he had last seen his son, Mabry headed in the opposite direction. He stopped in the middle of a field and tossed the pistol into some weeds and then, a moment later, he, too, was in the deep woods headed for the mountains.

Chapter Four

"Dispatch, this is Officer Anson. We have a situation."
Anson completed her call to the Sheriff's department. While making the report, her attention was divided between a slowly recovering Jeff Brown and a distant range of mountains. When she turned around, she was startled to see a man standing at arm's length behind her.

He wore a red and black plaid cap that covered a head of white hair. His thumbs were hooked into wide suspenders that held up a battered pair of heavy denim pants. On his feet were heavily scarred logger boots.

Anson's eyes opened wide.

"Mr. Hickey!" she said. "I didn't hear you come up."

The old man nodded then glared at Brown.

"Never did like him," he grunted. "That other fella, he can damn well through a punch can't he?"

"You saw that?

"I seen it all. And heard it from my front yard. I heard it all from the very get-go. If he'd have come on my property and tried to take my child, I'd have shot his sorry ass."

Anson said, "I don't know. I…I'll probably lose my job over this. I should have stopped him from leaving."

Mr. Hickey smiled.

"The way I seen it from across the street, Kelly, was like this. He punched Brown and grabbed his hide-out pistol. The child was in your way so you couldn't use your gun and they got away. You had to stay and check on Brown. It all happened too fast. Remember what he told you--he 'escaped.' He was protecting you when he gave you that idea. All hell was breaking loose and he was thinking of your welfare. That there is a *man's* man!"

The faint sound of sirens echoed off the mountains as other deputies responded to Anson's call to dispatch.

"I'll be going now," said the old man. "And I was never here, if you get my drift. You just tell it like I told you and everything will come off fine."

Walt Hickey walked away, briskly for an eighty-year-old man. He was almost to the corner gas station before he paused to watch the ambulance and two sheriff's cars speed past him. Hickey had seen the man and his son move in across the street a few months back. They kept to themselves but were good people. What just happened to them was a result of pure stupidity and as far as it went, Jeff Brown was lucky to have gotten off so easy. The old man shook his head and swore as he continued walking. The whole world was going to hell on a freight train.

Inside the small gas station, three white-haired men sat at a card table drinking coffee and swapping hunting stories. When Hickey walked in, they looked up.

"Hey, Walt," greeted the man nearest the door. "What's going on out there? We thought you'd gone and had a heart attack on us. That ambulance was headed down your way."

Hickey took a seat at the table. As he poured himself some coffee, a stranger wearing a cap full of fishhooks came in to pay for his gas. Hickey glanced at the fisherman then turned back to his friends.

"There's going to be hell to pay, the way I hear it," he said. "They say that new neighbor of mine just cold-cocked one of them new Feds. You know, one of them government child abductors."

"That would be Jim Brown's boy, Jeff," said a second old man. "And he's a big bastard."

The man paying for his gas went to a shelf and picked up a candy bar. He slowly put it down and looked at another. He seemed to be in no hurry.

"That new fella took off into the mountains," continued Hickey, "and you can bet the Feds will come hunting for him. We'll have TV cameras and newshounds all over town before sundown."

The stranger paid for his gas and walked out to his car. He started the engine then flipped open his cell phone. Driving towards where he had last seen the ambulance and police units, he dialed a number.

"John, this is Seth. Yeah, the fishing was fine, but I may have something. How's that Governor's Conference going?...When do you think they'll wind it up?...Well, this just could be bigger, much bigger. We can leave camera one there and bring camera two down here. We could be the only ones in Spokane to get this story…Well, for instance, how about the president's Child Protection Act gets its first test and fails…That's right…Hang on. I see the cops…This looks legitimate, John…Get that damn camera crew down here now!"

Just minutes after getting the call from dispatch, Deputy Jacobson slid to an abrupt halt in front of the Mabry residence. Quickly crossing the freshly mowed lawn, he helped Anson get Jeff Brown to his feet.

"Are you all right, Jeff?" Anson asked. "I called for an ambulance."

Brown wobbled clumsily and tried to focus his eyes on Anson as some garbled swear words dribbled passed his lips. He steadied himself for a moment, then jerked away from Jacobson's supporting grip.

"I don't need a damn ambulance!" he blurted. "Where is he? Where the hell is that bastard?"

"He escaped," Anson said. "With his son."

Barely suppressing his rage, Brown glared at Anson.

"Why didn't you stop him? How could he have gotten away with you standing right there?"

"The boy was too close. The father took your weapon before I could respond. I couldn't endanger the boy. It was too fast. We were both caught off guard…weren't we?"

Another deputy handed Brown an ice pack for his jaw that was now starting to bruise. He pressed it to his face.

Brown reached for his pistol which wasn't there, then inside his coat pocket for the report he had filled out for the case. They were both missing.

"Which way did he go?"

"Into the mountains," Anson said. "He threw your pistol away. It's out in that pasture somewhere."

Shaking his head, Brown muttered, "He's got the case file. He's going to know who turned him in."

Jacobson sighed.

"This is going to get messy. You're going to have to warn the informant that's in that file. I wouldn't want to be in his shoes."

Taking his cell phone from his belt, Brown walked away from the deputies and punched in a number. While he waited for a response, he held the ice to the side of his face.

"What a jerk," said Anson. She spoke softly but her voice was laced with anger. "This is all his fault. He shouldn't have reached for the boy like he did. That's when he got hit. None of this had to happen."

Jacobson shrugged indifferently.

"Yeah. Knowing Jeff, you're probably right. But the guy assaulted a law enforcement officer. We can't allow that. For any reason."

"But Jeff pushed him into a corner. You know how arrogant he can be, how obnoxious he is. Is everyone supposed to just bow down to us because we wear a badge?"

"Tough break for this Mabry character, but it's water under the bridge now," said Jacobson, feeling his stomach growl. "That's the way the mop flops. I'm getting hungry."

Anson glanced at Jacobson disapprovingly.

"I think Jeff got what he deserved. He's the one that went over the line."

Jacobson had known Anson's father and seen her grow up. She had always been a little spitfire.

"So, is that why you let Mabry get away? Just between you and me, I think that part of your report needs some work."

Her face flushing red, Anson gazed off towards the mountains and for a moment did not respond.

"No," she said finally. "That wasn't it. It was…something else."

"Like what?"

Again, Anson hesitated. "I can't explain it. He is…different from anyone I've ever met. It was like he knew what I was going to do before I did. Like he'd already known me for a long time."

A sarcastic smile spread across Jacobson's round face.

"So, you finally meet the man of your dreams and he turns out to be a felon. I always knew you had a soft heart but I never figured you'd be the type that goes for bad men."

"Shut up, Gill! I should have known you'd come up with something like that."

Anson and Jacobson had been leaning against a squad car for a half-hour before Brown received the instructions he was waiting for by phone. At first, his conversation was inaudible, but then his voice became louder as his confidence grew.

"Yes, sir," he said, his eyes widening in surprise. "Yes, sir. I understand, sir."

Snapping his phone shut with one hand, Brown shoved it onto his belt as if it were a magnum-sized pistol, then strutted towards the two deputies.

"They're calling in the U.S. Marshals to take over. Until they get here, I'm to secure the area and conduct a preliminary investigation."

Anson's eyes reflected her disgust, but Jacobson only chuckled. Glancing to his left down the empty street and then to his right, the older officer smiled.

"Looks secure enough to me. Let's go to lunch."

Snorting through a nose covered with large pores, Brown's lips tightened.

"The Attorney General of Idaho wants this site secured. He said this could be a landmark case and doesn't want any screw-ups. So, what you two are used to calling secure isn't good enough for a federal investigation."

"Attorney General!" exclaimed Anson. "What's next, the Air Force?"

"That's right. I was just on the phone with the United States Attorney General of Idaho," said Brown, pausing for effect. "And he was speaking for the president. Until the Marshals get here, I'm the Agent in Charge. So, it looks like you'll be working for me today."

Anson started to swear but faltered and was cut off by Jacobson.

"I'll call in and see what the sheriff wants us to do," he offered casually but with an unmistakable firmness in his tone. "Could be he'll want us to help out. Could be he won't."

Under a thick mat of short blond hair, Brown's skin turned red with stifled anger, but he knew better than to butt heads with Jacobson.

Jacobson's eyes grew hard, but still he wore a smile as he spoke.

"Sheriff Whitman has to worry about the budget and all. More than likely, you federal boys will be mostly on your own. You know how it is up here in the sticks."

"What if he didn't do it, Jeff?" asked Anson. "What if all this is one huge mistake? How's that going to look?"

"I was told to keep this low-profile for now. Until the Marshals get here, I'm..."

Brown stopped in mid-sentence and looked down towards the street corner. A white van with bright red-and-blue lettering was turning towards them. On the roof was a satellite feed and on its door was *Channel 6 News*.

The two deputies turned simultaneously to see the Spokane news van come to a sudden stop a few feet from where they stood. Two men stepped out. One wore a sport coat and tie above a pair of shorts, while the other, carrying a TV camera, had on a flowered shirt and baggy sweat pants.

"Good afternoon," greeted the man with the tie. "I'm Steve Spence of the Channel Six News. We got a call about an altercation involving a Federal Child Protection officer. Would any of you care to make a comment?"

Brown recognized Spence from the evening news. For a moment the idea that Spence wore shorts while broadcasting disrupted his thoughts, but then he glanced at the camera. Brown felt a wave of uncertainty.

"There's nothing to report here," he said.

Spence noticed the ice bag and then the bruise on Brown's face.

"Are you the one that was attacked?"

Seeing the camera focused in on him, Brown wondered how he would look on television. He stood a little taller.

"Yes. I'm the one."

Grabbing a microphone, Spence took a step closer to Brown then turned back towards the camera.

"I'm standing here in the small town of Clark Fork, Idaho, with one of our nation's first Federal Child Protection officers, and reporting what could be the first battle for this newly formed institution."

Spence moved the microphone closer to Brown.

"Your name?"

"Agent Jeff Brown."

"Can you tell us what happened here today?"

"The matter is under investigation. I can't make any comment at this time."

Spence lowered the microphone and held it at his side. He smiled.

"O.K., we can go with that if you want. We'll just report what we've already heard."

Brown faltered.

"You couldn't have heard anything. This just happened."

The reporter raised an eyebrow.

"It happened nearly two hours ago, and we have it from an eyewitness that you were knocked unconscious. The man escaped with his child, leaving you and the president's pet project looking inept. Is that the way you want it on the news this evening, or would you rather have a more positive slant?"

As he tried to think, beads of sweat began to form on Brown's short forehead.

"I have to make a call," he said finally. "I need to clear this with Boise."

"By all means," said Spence.

As Brown walked away for more privacy, the reporter nodded to Jacobson and Anson.

"How about you two? Anything you want to say?"

"I wasn't on scene," offered Jacobson. "And we've been advised that the situation is going to be handled by the U.S. Marshals. They'll have someone here in a couple of hours to answer all your questions."

"We can't wait around that long," said Spence. "This is going out on the six o'clock broadcast."

Anson had been trying to listen to Brown's conversation, but he was too far away and now cupped his hand over the phone.

Turning her attention to the reporter, she said, "Off the record, this is a bunch of bull. The entire incident was started by a false report of child abuse. Now it's turned into ...this."

Noticing the irritation in Anson's voice, Spence's eyes narrowed with interest. "Are you sure of that?"

Anson had been raised to tell the truth, and it was now an ingrained characteristic. She wanted to answer the question truthfully, but feeling a whisper of doubt, she hesitated. People could do terrible things in the privacy of their own homes or when they were out of public view. Was there a chance Justin Mabry was guilty?

But then she remembered their encounter in the donut shop and the expression on Mabry's face when he looked into his son's eyes and told him he loved him. Her confidence returned.

"I'm certain."

Spence's eyes flickered.

"But he did assault a federal officer, right?"

"Yes. There is no doubt about that," admitted Anson. "But we haven't heard his side of it yet. I think there are mitigating circumstances that need to be heard before everyone gets worked up into a feeding frenzy."

Dismissing her concern, Spence shook his head and glanced at Brown.

"Hitting a federal officer is a felony assault. Everybody knows that. And that's going to be the big story, especially with this being the president's pet project. I don't think his side of it is going to matter."

"You could still report it," insisted Anson, "that at least there is another side, and people should wait until they hear it before they pass judgment."

The cameraman snickered.

"You don't know our boss. He has what you might call a political persuasion. When it comes to stuff like this, he sends us out to get the facts then he spins them the way he wants. He was part of the political machine that worked on the president's campaign in the last election. I can tell you for sure. This dude is going down!"

Clipping his cell phone to his belt, Agent Brown returned to the camera crew and deputies, but this time he walked with a swagger and wore a know-it-all smirk on his face.

"I'll answer a few of your questions now," he said, then planted his feet wide apart and arched his lower lip into a tough-guy frown.

Spence hurriedly ran his fingers through his hair and straightened his tie. Taking his place beside Brown, he waited for his queue.

"Steve Spence reporting this breaking story from the small town of Clark Fork, Idaho. Here in this peaceful community, only minutes ago, one of the nation's newest federal officers was brutally assaulted by a man suspected of child abuse. This is shaping up to be the first major challenge to President Stark's Federal Child Protection Act, just signed into law two days ago.

"This legislation, as you recall, was designed to protect the nation's children from abuse by adding the enforcement capabilities of the federal government. And standing next to me now is Agent Jeff Brown of the newly formed FCPA. What can you tell us, Agent Brown?"

As the reporter tilted the microphone towards Brown, he felt his legs weaken. His knees began to quiver but then, seeing his own reflection in the lens of the camera, he began to relax.

"This morning," he said, then coughed to clear his throat. "This morning at approximately 10:00 AM, I approached a suspect, Justin

Mabry, to investigate a charge of child abuse. Based on the complaints against Mr. Mabry and upon my own observations of his behavior and of visible bruises seen on the child, I informed the father that I was taking the child into custody. At this point, without warning, I was attacked and rendered unconscious for a considerable length of time. During this interval, Mabry escaped, taking with him his twelve-year-old son. It is believed he headed into the nearby Cabinet Mountains."

"Does the father have any previous history of violent behavior?"

"A full investigation by the U.S. Marshals will begin immediately. Then we'll have a complete profile on Mr. Mabry. The State Attorney General has promised an extensive manhunt and prosecution of Mabry on the charges of assaulting a federal officer, illegal flight, obstruction of justice and kidnapping."

Looking over his shoulder at the mountains and then back at the camera, Spence feigned grave concern.

"And where, in this vast wilderness, would the Marshals begin?"

For a few seconds, Brown was speechless.

"Ah, I don't think they will search the mountains. Few people can last more than a day or two out there. We'll be looking at known associates and relatives and interviewing neighbors. He'll likely show up in a place he finds familiar and thinks is safe."

"If Mr. Mabry is convicted of the charges you mentioned, what would be the consequences?"

Already having been assured of the answer to this question, Brown regained his confidence.

"The Attorney General has informed me that he'll get twenty years in a federal prison. That is almost a certainty."

Spence glanced at Brown curiously.

"Why do you say that?"

Brown inhaled deeply, as if bored with the questioning.

"The president has been advised of this development and has taken a personal interest in its outcome. She is very committed to protecting our nation's children and wants everyone to understand that the full force of the law is behind the Child Protection Act and its officers."

Peering dramatically into the camera, Spence's voice was ominous.

"There you have it. The President of the United States committed to protecting the children of this great country and one man, Justin Mabry,

50

is standing in her way. This is Steve Spence, reporting from Clark Fork, Idaho, Channel Six News."

Anson eyed Spence with contempt as he lowered the microphone and loosened his tie.

"That was a quick trial," she snapped, then glared at Brown. "And you! Twenty years! Why should he give himself up now? You just broadcast to the whole world that he's got no chance to ever be with his son again. You may as well have declared war on him. And you know as well as I do, you never can tell what will happen in a court of law."

Brown snickered.

"You've always been such a Pollyanna. You have no idea how things work, do you?"

"Did you get all of what you just said on camera from your phone conversations?" asked Jacobson.

"Yeah. And a lot more."

"So, you're sure about everything?"

"You think I would have said it if I wasn't? And why not? We all know he's guilty of assaulting an officer. And it's like a slap in the face to the president. You think she's going to let some nobody from Jerkwater, Idaho show her up?"

Jacobson scratched his jaw and chuckled.

"Then you better catch him early. You and the president just raised the black flag. This guy won't come in now under any circumstances, and likely he'll try and get to Canada. The way the prime minister and President Stark have been going at it, the Canucks will take him just to spite her. The longer this goes on, the dumber you're all going to look to the rest of the world."

"That's right," added Anson. "And you know what happens when you spook the elk. They head into the deep woods and nobody can find them. And you sure as hell have spooked him now."

Steve Spence grinned as he slid into the news van and then stuck his head out the window.

"We'll be seeing a lot of each other before this is over. I can smell a good story, and this is going to be the one that gets me on the national links."

As the van sped away, he slapped the outside door and looked back at the officers. "Yeah, baby!" he yelled. "This is going to be it! Yeah!"

No one spoke as the van disappeared around the corner. A meadowlark called from the field behind the Mabrys' house, its call carried on a gust of wind that stirred the pine trees across the street.

"I feel...ashamed," said Anson, as the breeze brushed the back of her neck. "I want to go home and take this uniform off and never put it on again."

"You'll get used to it, Kelly," muttered Jacobson. "It's just part of the job."

"That's right," said Anson. "We're not paid to think. Just blindly enforce. No, to force the law on people. We're just black-booted enforcers."

"I'm going to lunch," said Jacobson. "Take it from me--when you're in law enforcement, it doesn't pay to think too much."

Chapter Five

June 17th
4:15 PM (PST)

June 17th
4:15 PM (PST)

Mabry gasped for air and wiped the stinging sweat out of his eyes. From his house, with a heavy pack on his back, he had gone over a barbed wire fence, jogged across a forty-acre field, and for the last hour, hiked straight up a steep mountain slope. Now he was hundreds of feet above Clark Fork, peering down at the small town.

Standing in a small clearing, he could easily make out his house and the pasture behind it. As far as he could tell, no one had followed him. The pounding in his chest finally began to ease. Mabry slid the pack off his back and after removing a pair of binoculars, dropped it onto a bed of dry pine needles. His sweat-soaked shirt clung to him, but as a gentle mountain breeze brushed by, the sticky cotton immediately began to cool his skin.

Mabry sat down in the shade of a large Ponderosa pine, his eyes locked on his house and the sheriff's cars in front of it. He took a few seconds to listen for any hint of pursuit, but except for the soft rush of the wind through the trees, there was almost perfect silence. If anyone were coming up the mountain after him, they would have to make noise. But there was no sound of rocks rolling or branches snapping. He was alone.

Mabry looked through the binoculars at his house and the field behind it. Nothing was moving, and discounting the presence of the police cars, nothing seemed different.

The running and climbing had been all consuming, however, at least for now, he was safe. It was time to gather his thoughts, but for a brief moment he tried not to think of anything at all. Closing his eyes, he listened to the wind and smelled the sweet aroma of pine trees. For half a minute, he allowed himself to do nothing, to merely exist on the side of a mountain.

Then he took a deep breath and let it out slowly.

"God, what have I done?" he asked, then once again looked down into the valley below. "What have I done?"

For the next several hours, Mabry wrestled with the nightmare that had become his life. But no matter how he arranged and rearranged the events in his mind, nothing changed the gravity of his dilemma.

An agent of the government, the same government that had been designed to be a servant of the people, had forcibly tried to take his son from him. Without a shred of proof, he was pronounced guilty on the steps of his own home and was expected to meekly submit as the agent abducted his only child. But Mabry would not, Mabry *could* not, accept such barbarism.

He had endured his divorce in virtual silence, forfeiting nearly everything he owned, in order to get custody of Billy. And now, he was the victim of an incomprehensible form of tyranny. He could not tolerate such injustice, yet it was his intolerance that caused him to commit a felony, a crime that might permanently separate him from the only thing in life he valued.

Desperate to grasp the slightest ray of hope and unable to accept the impossibility of his predicament, Mabry finally shook his head and wiped his face with both hands. It just simply could not be as bad as it seemed. Surely, he was making too much of it. The solution might be as simple as making a few phone calls. His divorce attorney could give him some advice or at least refer him to someone who could help. Then, they would explain to the authorities the tremendous stress he had been under, the recent divorce and the devastating settlement agreement. That would help explain his actions and give him time to clear himself of the false charges leveled by Kal Burns. It was just a simple misunderstanding, a heated moment, a mistake that anyone in his state of mind could have made. He was, after all, merely the innocent victim of a series of unfortunate circumstances. If not a judge, certainly a jury would understand.

The strained logic used to form his untenable conclusion brought a welcome relief, and Mabry felt as if a crushing weight had been removed from his chest. A few phone calls would set everything in motion. Soon, all would be right side up again. He would wait until dark, then go to his house or the payphone at the gas station and start the process of reconciliation. By tomorrow, or maybe the next day, he and Billy might even sleep in their own beds. In a week, surely no more than a month, what had happened would be old news and the whole thing nearly forgotten.

Mabry's pulse was beginning to drop and his breaths came more evenly, yet deep within flickered the knowledge that he could be wrong, that life was full of injustices and terrible things *did* happen to innocent people. And barely suppressed beneath that admission, lurking in the darkest recesses of his soul, was the familiar sensation that something primitive, something savage, was prowling back and forth, waiting for its chance to escape…or to climb to the surface should he choose to summon it.

Billy Mabry sat at a dining table in Luke Jordan's house. Matt, with wide expectant eyes, was seated next to his friend and looking across the table at his father and four other men.

Luke Jordan glanced at the men on his right and left, then back at Billy.

"Thanks for telling it all over again, Billy. I wanted everyone to hear it firsthand. Now, you and Matt go on outside and play awhile. And don't you worry about your father. He'll be fine."

Billy nodded, scooted his chair back and stood.

"Thanks for letting me stay here, Mr. Jordan. Dad didn't know what else to do, I think."

Jordan smiled through his beard.

"You and your dad are welcome anytime, Billy. Anytime at all."

After the boys had gone, Jordan stood up and placed his big hands on the heavy wood planks of the table.

"Like I told you, Mabry's the one. And this is going to be it. All agreed, raise a hand."

Looking at each man in the room, Jordan filled his barrel chest with air and let it out slowly.

"Then it's unanimous."

Jordan stepped away from the table, picked up a small piece of paper and wrote a few words. He rolled the message and carefully slid it into a tiny metal cylinder. From a small cage, he took a pigeon and attached the cylinder.

With one last look around the room, Jordan went to an open window and released the bird.

"It's time," he said solemnly. "It's finally time."

Fifteen minutes after landing at the Boise airport, Agents Anderson and Francis passed through the security check at the Federal Building. Waiting for them was an older agent that eyed the new arrivals through a pair of black-framed glasses. A security tag dangling from his shirt pocket had "Wilson, B." printed in bold letters across the bottom.

Agent Wilson extended his meaty hand.

"How was your flight, John?"

"Long," answered Anderson. "Bob, this is Agent D. J. Francis."

Bob nodded and half-heartedly shook hands with Francis. His eyes narrowed with disapproval.

"Welcome to Boise, Agent Francis. I'm familiar with your work."

With a flat smile, Francis answered, "Charmed."

A single eyebrow raised behind Wilson's glasses, but other than that he ignored her rudeness.

"If you two will follow me, there's a conference call waiting for you in my office. There are some reports that were faxed over, also."

"Are they calling from Coeur d'Alene?" asked Anderson.

Shaking his head, Wilson started down the hall towards his office.

"No. The call is from Assistant Director Berger in Washington. He's going to send you two up to the Panhandle."

Wilson paused in front of his office door. Before turning the knob he smiled wryly at Francis.

"If you like Boise, you're going to love Clark Fork."

Wilson opened the door and stepped aside.

"You know where everything is, John. Call me if you need anything."

Once inside the office, Francis took a seat in a cushioned leather chair. Anderson went behind the desk and stood by the phone.

Glancing around the small room, Francis' eyes focused on a set of family photos on the wall. She took a deep breath and exhaled her irritation.

"Where--or should I say *what*--is Clark Fork?"

His finger on the conference button, Anderson tried to look serious. He enjoyed ruffling the fine feathers of D.J. Francis.

"It's a small city just past Hog Wallow and just shy of Possum Jump," he said. Before she could formulate a snide response, Anderson pushed the button and spoke again.

"Agents Anderson and Francis here."

A voice on the phone answered, "Hold, please, for the assistant director."

Anderson picked up two folders that were on the desk and handed one to Francis. She took the report from his hand and mouthed a silent "asshole" to her partner as he returned a mischievous smile.

The agents scanned the four-page report while they waited. Francis, among other things, was a speed reader and closed her folder before Anderson finished his first page.

Tossing the file back onto the desk, Francis glanced at Anderson.

"Assaulting a federal officer and kidnapping. This could be handled by any of our field agents."

Anderson said nothing and slowly turned to the second page. A wrinkle formed between his eyes. A moment later, he began to shake his head and swear softly to himself.

"What?" asked Francis with her usual impatience.

Before she could get an answer, the speakerphone came alive.

"Good afternoon, agents. Have you had an opportunity to review the preliminary report?"

"In progress, sir. But I have the general idea."

"Good. This situation has come to the personal attention of the president. She wants it handled as a politically sensitive event."

"Yes, sir," replied Anderson as he continued to read.

"First, I am naming Agent Francis as Special Agent in Charge. The president prefers to have a woman heading the operation. She's convinced that it would sell better to the general public since a child's safety is involved. Election-year politics, Anderson. That sort of thing."

Anderson's face flushed with a faint shade of red. This was his territory, his specialty. D. J. knew almost nothing of the Inland Northwest or its people.

"Understood, sir," he said evenly.

"Agent Francis?"

"Yes, sir."

"We want this incident brought to a close as quickly and decisively as possible. You will have immediate command of the U.S. Marshals assigned to the case as well as other field agents. And this is to be handled high-profile."

"High profile, sir?" asked Francis.

"This involves the president's personal legislation. She wants to demonstrate her leadership and her compassion. She wants to show her commitment to certain fundamental ideals, at least for the next few months.

"That's why she wants your face on TV instead of Agent Anderson's. She's counting on the female vote to swing the election again."

"I'll handle it, sir."

"Agent Anderson, you will accompany Agent Francis as Supervisory Special Agent. Your assignment is to keep a lid on this. You know what could happen up there better than anyone."

Anderson hesitated. "Sir, may I speak freely?"

There was a brief pause from the assistant director.

"Go ahead."

"I don't like the looks of this, sir. That area of the country is not the place to put our agents on parade. I would advise all concerned to designate this a low-profile operation. In fact, I would suggest we back off entirely. With all due respect to the president, I think the risk is too high."

The speaker box on the desk was quiet for a full half-minute before it broke the silence.

"Your concern is duly noted, Agent Anderson. I voiced those same concerns to the president. It's your job to eliminate those risks . Now, if you would please step outside the room for a moment. Agent Francis, we'll not use the speakerphone."

Having been with the Bureau for ten years, Anderson knew its protocol and its tactics. Additional instructions were about to be delivered verbally and without witnesses. It was standard operational procedure whenever plausible deniability might be necessary to protect the top of the food chain. He was being eliminated from the inner circle and perhaps being set up as a scapegoat should the need to offer a sacrifice arise.

With the folder still in his hand and without looking at Francis, Anderson stepped through the door and into the halls of the Federal Building. It wouldn't be the first time he turned his back on such activities, but at least they had not required him to be a co-conspirator. He still had his integrity. More or less.

He walked to a nearby bench, sat down and finished reading the incident report which included a description of Justin Mabry. The only encouraging bit of information was that Mabry had recently moved into the Clark Fork area. In all likelihood, he would arouse little support or sympathy from the established residents. But the rest of the report left Anderson increasingly uncomfortable.

Mabry was adopted at the age of four, had been a good student and athlete through college, and now was a high-school history teacher. He had recently gone through a divorce and somehow gained custody of his twelve-year-old son. And he'd never had so much as a parking ticket.

His banking account showed no unusual activity and he regularly made out checks to a community church. He was renting a small house in Clark Fork and had been recently hired by the high school to start teaching in the fall. He was also financially broke.

Mabry needed to be caught and immediately found guilty. If not, if he put up a good defense and the case was covered by the media, it would be hard to convince the public that a law-abiding, church-going, poor schoolteacher was a child beater. And from the photo that was included in the report, Mabry would undoubtedly capture the attention of women everywhere. He was the wrong person to falsely vilify, and North Idaho was the worst possible place for the FBI to be caught doing it.

The Conference of Western Governors was running twenty minutes past its scheduled ending, and the lobby of the Coeur d'Alene Resort was full of impatient news crews. Most reporters had prepared questions they hoped to get answered and with the deadline for the evening news coming up, everyone was getting anxious. Everyone, except Steve Spence and his cameraman.

The drive back from Clark Fork had taken them almost an hour and a half, but with the governors getting out late, Spence had arrived with time to spare. Smugly, he waited for his chance to break the news to the governor of Idaho. How would Pierce Fulton respond when informed that his state was the first to test the power of President Stark's new child abuse legislation? It was common knowledge that neither Governor Fulton, nor any of the governors at the conference, cared for President Stark, but Fulton was the most outspoken.

The bustling sound of doors opening and shoes shuffling over stiff carpet finally drifted into the lobby. Six uniformed security guards blocked off the main entrance to the hotel as a small crowd of men and women rounded a corner and worked their way towards the lobby.

Two dozen camera lights lit up. Reporters scrambled out of their cushioned seats and fought their way to the politician of their choice. Voices erupted simultaneously as each governor staked out a section of the lobby floor to field the incoming barrage of questions. Spence, however, took his time and casually walked up behind the cluster of reporters surrounding Fulton.

Several predictable questions were followed by equally predictable answers. Spence was normally annoyed with political interviews, but not this time. Like a cat in a hay barn, he waited with eyes full of lethal confidence. He had the story, and he alone would break it. And it would undoubtedly go national.

The fervor of the reporters' inquiries was beginning to wane. As the governor turned to leave, Spence spoke out over the other voices.

"Governor Fulton, what do you plan to do about the assault of a Federal Child Protection officer that occurred in the city of Clark Fork this morning?"

The governor froze as a hush fell over the small gathering. Fulton shaded his eyes, trying to see past the glaring lights and identify who had asked the question.

"I'm sorry," he said. "Could you repeat the question?"

Spence wasn't buying the stall and pressed on.

"Won't this bring in the FBI and, if it does, will you be supportive of their efforts in lieu of the fact that you have been an outspoken critic of the Child Protection Act and of President Stark?"

Fulton paused. The practiced smile melted away and the political mask came off. In its place was an expression of conviction and anger.

"I'll take that up with the proper authorities. But I will say this. The FCPA was an ill-conceived and poorly written piece of legislation. And it was enacted prematurely. It was never made clear, for instance, who would finance its enforcement on a local and state level. My first inclination is to answer your question this way. Until I have more information, the state of Idaho will offer only minimal support to any investigation that involves the Child Protection Act."

Spence knew he had the attention of everyone and enjoyed his moment. "Governor Fulton, Channel Six News has just learned that the man accused of the assault, Justin Mabry, has already fled with his son into the mountains near Clark Fork. Will you offer assistance in any kind of manhunt?'"

The governor's eyes narrowed and his lips turned into a faint smile.

"We don't have the funding for something like that. If he's any kind of outdoorsman, it'll take hundreds of thousands of dollars, if not more, to get him out of those hills. And if I were the federal government, I would stay out of there."

Spence was surprised at Fulton's candid response, but he was satisfied and asked no follow-up questions. It had turned out even better than he thought. The story now had momentum and would likely continue to build and eventually spread across the country. It was his exclusive, and he planned to ride that wave of notoriety into the national spotlight.

Holding up his hand, Governor Fulton indicated the interview was over and the cameras were lowered. Keeping his eyes on Spence, he motioned for him to come closer.

Spence glanced at his cameraman, handed over the microphone and shrugged. He walked up to the governor and waited to be spoken to.

"You're Steve Spence, aren't you?" asked Fulton.

"Yes," answered Spence uneasily. "Channel Six News."

"Yes. You said that."

Spence suddenly felt small. This was the governor of Idaho. And he was no fool.

"Can you tell me what you know?"

"Ah, sure. But it's not much. A guy punched an officer and took off. The local police were there when we arrived, and the federal officer was on the phone asking someone for advice. We got a short interview with him for our coverage."

"How many local cops were there?"

"Just two. A man and a woman. I don't think the woman cop agreed with what was going on. She seemed pretty hot. I mean *upset*."

"Is that it?"

"That's all I know. But we just got a call to go back to Clark Fork for a live transmission at six o'clock."

Fulton thought for several seconds.

"This will make the local news tonight?"

"Yes, sir. At six and eleven. Our six o'clock will be picked up by our sister stations and be national, for sure, by eleven."

Nodding thoughtfully, Fulton eyed Spence with penetrating eyes.

"KSPN leans hard to the left. How do you think this story will air?"

"Same as always. To the left, I would think."

Fulton laughed softly.

"Good," he said, then started to walk away. "Make sure it does."

Kelly Anson had been in her patrol car for three hours and the U.S. Marshals still had not arrived at the Mabry residence. Jeff Brown was pacing back and forth in front of the house and growing more agitated by the minute.

Finally, Anson stepped out of the car and started for the house. As she passed Brown she said, "I'm going in to use the bathroom, crime scene or not."

Brown stopped pacing.

"To hell with them," he said. "We'll both go in. The USAG already faxed my office the Affidavit of Probable Cause Warrant. We have legal right to enter. And anyway, until the Marshals get here, I'm in charge."

The lights were off in the small living room, but the sunlight came through the windows and reflected off a bare wooden floor. A well-worn couch, framed by two cheap end tables, was against the far wall. Opposite the couch, a twelve-inch television sat on top of a stand made out of two-by-fours. The remainder of the room was empty, but the walls were decorated with photographs of father and son hung in various arrangements.

Pointing to her left, Anson said, "Well, the kitchen is over there so the bathroom has to be this way."

As Anson walked down a short hallway, Brown went into the kitchen and began opening cabinet doors. On the shelves, he found several cans of food and two boxes of cereal. The refrigerator contained a carton of milk, some bread, a few slices of sandwich meat and a jar of mayonnaise. On the kitchen cabinet was a coffee maker and a few pots and pans. A hand towel hung over the oven door. There was nothing unusual about anything other than its general neatness. It was an average kitchen.

Brown went to the refrigerator and opened the freezer compartment. He was looking into it when he heard Anson's voice behind him.

"Frozen dinners, right? And I bet you were hoping to find drug paraphernalia."

Brown let the freezer door slam shut then closed the refrigerator door. Ignoring her comment, he turned to face her.

"And what did you find it the bathroom? I know you looked."

Anson nodded.

"Yeah, I looked. I shouldn't have, but I knew you would anyway. And I saw the same thing you're seeing. Nothing. Not even any towels on the floor. No underwear on the shower door either. But there was toothpaste and toothbrushes. And get this--even dental floss.

"Do you have floss, Jeff? I bet you don't have floss in your medicine cabinet, do you? Justin Mabry has floss."

"Funny," replied Brown, then stepped past Anson. "Let's see what he has in his bedroom."

Anson hesitated for a moment then shook her head.

"You're not going to find anything in there, either," she said. Raising her voice as Brown disappeared, she added, "You're wasting your time."

"We'll see," Brown replied from around the corner. "We'll see!"

Returning to the photographs on the walls, Anson began to study each one in detail. At first, she took note of the surroundings in each picture, the background, time of year and the activities taking place. Next, she concentrated on the expressions of father and son and in a matter of seconds knew everything she needed to know. Not only did they go places and do things together, they loved each other. She had felt it when she met them in the donut shop, but now she was certain. Justin Mabry would never abuse his son. This was all a terrible mistake, a mistake that had to be corrected before it did even more damage to an innocent man and his son. Someone had to do something to help them.

Anson headed towards the bedrooms and called out, "Jeff, you need to come see these pictures."

Hearing nothing, Anson looked into the first bedroom then the second, but Brown was nowhere to be seen. A few steps in front of her, the door to the attached garage swung open.

"Out here," said Brown. "Look what I found."

Anson looked into the dimly lit garage to see the agent standing next to a full- sized punching bag that hung by a chain from the ceiling rafters. A smile on Brown's face spread his thick cheeks apart. "It appears your 'good father' likes to hit things."

"All that explains," said Anson, "is why he was able to knock you out."

Brown smirked, then gave the seventy-pound bag a shove. As he watched it sway back and forth, he said confidently, "He hits the bag for fun, he hit me…and he hits his kid. It all adds up."

With Mabry's truck parked out in the driveway, the garage was nearly empty.

A few tools, along with a broom and dust pan, hung on one wall. On the adjacent wall, a homemade shelf was stacked with cardboard boxes that had been taped shut. On each box, the words "Billy's Toys" were printed in black.

In the far corner, a dust-covered box sat alone. The tape that kept it closed was aged and cracked. Nothing on it identified its contents. Brown started for it and took out a small pocketknife.

"What are you doing, Jeff?"

"Looking for more evidence."

"Evidence of what? Evidence that helps you justify what you did this morning?"

"That's right. Not that I need any. I had enough to start with."

"I don't think you have the right to open that box."

"Probable cause," muttered Brown. He then squatted down beside the box and started cutting the tape. "The warrant says I have the right."

As Brown started cutting the tape, Anson went down the steps into the garage and peered over his shoulder.

"What do you think you're going to find in that box," she asked, "a map to his secret hideout up in the mountains?"

"Maybe," grunted Brown, then slid his fingers under the cardboard lid and gave it a jerk.

For a moment, he merely stared. When he began to swear, Anson stepped around him and took a closer look at the collection of metallic gold figures inside the box. "That's a *lot* of trophies!"

Brown came to his feet and started back inside the house as Anson picked up two of the trophies.

"Justin Mabry, Most Valuable Defensive Player. Justin Mabry, All-League Shortstop," she recited. "Is this the evidence you were looking for, Jeff? If it is, there are a dozen more of these you should take with you."

"Up yours, Anson," snapped Brown. "Up yours!"

After reading the brass engravings of several trophies, Anson closed the lid to the box and looked it over closely. At the coffee shop where she had first met the Mabrys, the boy said they had moved just three months before. Yet this box full of awards had been sealed for years, so many, in fact, that it was very likely Billy Mabry had no idea what was inside.

Wondering why the trophies had been packed away for so long, Anson went back inside the house and found Brown sitting on the couch thumbing through a large book. When he heard her steps he looked up. His face was twisted with frustration.

"You're enjoying this, aren't you?"

Anson recognized the book Brown was holding and was totally confused.

"What are you doing with a Bible?"

Brown snapped the book shut and tossed it further down the couch.

"I found it in his room. Sometimes people hide things in them."

"Why don't you just admit you made a mistake, Jeff? It happens. Just call this whole thing off before it gets out of hand."

"I didn't make any mistakes; I followed procedure. I didn't violate any law. He did."

"Jeff, the man has a Bible in his bedroom!"

"So the hell what?" retorted Brown.

Kelly Anson's eyes ignited.

"Watch your mouth, Jeff," she said, and Brown did just that.

"Well, it doesn't mean anything," said Brown. "Anybody can have one. The Aryan Nations people quote from the Bible all the time."

Throwing up her hands, Anson exclaimed, "So, now he's a White Supremacist. What next, an alien life force? Face it, Jeff, you screwed up. You've got nothing on this guy and you're going to get nothing. You tried to take a child from a good father and he busted your chops. Like any real man would have done."

Brown suddenly bristled with anger.

"He assaulted a federal officer in the line of duty. That was the only mistake made around here, and he made it. Nothing else is going to matter. I don't have to prove anything. What he did is a matter of fact and you were a witness to it. He's going to learn, everybody's going to learn what happens if you go against the federal government!"

Before Anson could respond, the slamming of a car door filtered through the thin walls of the living room and was followed by the sound of two more doors shutting. Both officers looked out the front window to see three men in dark suits approaching. The man in the rear carried a small leather suitcase. All three wore sunglasses.

Brown opened the door and waited as the men came closer. Before he could ask who they were, the first suit extended his right hand while flashing a badge with his left. "FBI," he said, as he shook Brown's hand. "I'm Agent Degan, this is Agent Jones and that's Agent Flin. And you must be Agent Brown."

"Child Protection Service," replied Brown, trying to sound official. "I was expecting U.S. Marshals."

Degan's eyes held appraisingly on Brown. A derisive smile betrayed the FBI agent's evaluation of the man.

"There was a change of operational plans," said Degan, with a faint wisp of insult in his tone. "Agent Brown, I see you've entered the premises. Have you found anything or disturbed anything?"

"No, sir. We just came in a few minutes ago. Officer Anson had to use the restroom. But we haven't done a search of any significance. Just a walk-through."

Degan looked at Anson but not as another officer of the law. Behind the dark glasses his eyes lingered on her tight-fitting shirt and how it curved across her chest.

"So, you two saw nothing out of the ordinary in the house?"

Brown answered, "Not in the house, but the garage."

Taking his eyes off Anson, Degan removed his sunglasses and put them in his inside coat pocket. Now looking with half interest at Brown, he asked, "What's in the garage?"

"A body-size punching bag, sir."

Nodding, Degan seemed genuinely impressed, if not pleased.

"Good work, Brown. The perp may be into the martial arts. We'll keep that in mind. He might be more dangerous than we thought."

There was a moment of silence, then Degan glanced at Anson.

"Officer Anson, what do you make of all this? Did you find anything we could use?"

Taking an immediate dislike to Degan, Anson deliberately hesitated before she answered and when she did, it was with an unmistakable edge to her voice.

"No."

Degan took a closer look at Anson.

"Officer Anson, we were briefed on Agent Brown's report, but I'm still unclear about one thing."

"What's that?"

"What happened to Agent Brown's weapon?"

"The suspect took the pistol from Agent Brown after he was knocked down. He threw it away as he crossed the field behind the house and ran for the mountains."

"Have you made any effort to recover the weapon?"

"No. It's a big field. Likely, it would take a metal detector due to the tall weeds."

"Approximately, how far away from you was the suspect when he threw away the weapon?"

"Maybe one hundred yards."

Degan gave Anson a calculating glance.

"One hundred yards? Are you certain it was the gun he tossed away? That's quite a distance to be so sure. Maybe it was something else."

Anson's eyes were steady. There was something about the man she didn't like.

"Search the field. You'll find it."

The federal agent hesitated, then nodded.

"We'll do just that; we'll get right on it. Now, does the Sheriff's Department have any bloodhounds or some breed of tracking dogs at its disposal?"

"They're owned by volunteers for Search and Rescue," said Anson. "They donate their time if we ask them."

Agent Degan waited for Anson to offer more, but she merely stared at him in silence. Slowly, a patronizing smile spread his thick lips. He intentionally glanced at Anson's breasts.

"How soon can we get them out here, Officer Anson?"

"I can't say. All I can do is make the request," answered Anson. Not missing the arrogant grin and the city-slick hairstyle, she added, "Could be old Smitty is out hunting 'coons or running cats. You never know about old Smitty."

Degan's smile evaporated.

"If you would, please," he said with practiced sincerity, "put in the request. We need them here ASAP."

"I'll put in the request, but all we can do is ask. It *is* on a volunteer basis."

"Agent Brown, you have been very helpful. Thank you for securing the premises. We were briefed by the Idaho Attorney General's Office. He gave us your report. If we have any need of clarification, we'll call you. Otherwise, we will take over from here. If we have any questions, we will be in contact."

Expecting another handshake, Brown hesitated for a moment but after receiving none, awkwardly joined Anson who had already started for the patrol car.

Anson glanced at Brown and said, "You know they think we're a bunch of hicks, don't you?"

Brown merely shrugged but his pride was obviously bruised.

"Will you call for the dogs?"

"Yeah. But dispatch may have a hard time locating Smitty."

Looking over his shoulder, Brown watched the three men go inside the house and shut the door.

"I have the feeling I missed something."

"I have the same feeling, Jeff. And it's not a good feeling."

The drive back to Sandpoint took a half hour, but neither Brown nor Anson were in a talkative mood. By the time Anson dropped off her passenger and went home to her apartment, it was nearing six o'clock. Not wanting to miss the Spokane News telecast, she quickly grabbed her mail, unlocked the door and let her cat inside.

Bending down, she scratched the cat on top of its head.

"I hope your day was better than mine, Weasel. You wouldn't believe what happened. But you're just a cat aren't you? And cats don't care about people stuff. Now, if you were a dog we could talk, but then I'd have to have a big yard, wouldn't I?"

After placing the mail on the kitchen counter and feeding Weasel, Anson turned on her television and tossed a frozen dinner into the microwave.

Maybe there would be nothing about Clark Fork on the news. It was such an insignificant town with a population of less than a thousand. And what had happened today was really quite trivial if viewed as a domestic disturbance. Hopefully, there were more urgent matters to report, and the story involving Justin Mabry would be left out all together. Then, after everyone cooled off, it could be resolved calmly and without political interference.

As the microwave hummed and the cat noisily crunched its dried food, Anson sat down on her couch. A commercial was on the television, but she heard none of it. Kelly Anson's mind was on Justin Mabry.

The first time they met in the donut shop, she had watched him closely as he sat with his son. Why she paid him so much attention still puzzled her, but even in that brief encounter, she knew that somehow he was different from other men. He possessed an innate quality, an almost tangible sense of integrity. When he looked at her, his eyes conveyed an inner strength but they also carried a message. It was a message that could easily be read as a warning. This was a man that had endured a great deal, but was nearing the end of his rope.

Her father and grandfather, both lawmen, had talked of such men, men that were old-school. Those they spoke of were even-tempered, always fair and impeccably honest but pure hell if someone insisted on making trouble and pushed them too far.

Mabry's home was small. By most standards, he appeared to be living at the poverty level, but the house was neat and clean. He had just moved to Clark Fork with his son but no wife. Was he a widower or divorced? Why had he moved here and why were his athletic trophies kept hidden from his son?

The promo for the evening news interrupted her thoughts.

"Tonight, an exclusive from Clark Fork, Idaho, where a manhunt promises to bring in a federal fugitive. You don't want to miss this breaking story. Stay tuned for Channel Six News at six."

As the station ran one last commercial, Anson sighed and shook her head. Suddenly she was no longer hungry. It was all so unnecessary. What would Mabry do if they came after him with dogs? Would he try to run? Would he even consider surrendering, knowing that he likely would be convicted of a felony and sent away from his son?

Anson wanted to swear but she had been taught better. As the station switched to a commercial for headache pain, she scolded the TV.

"If you chase him, he's going to run. Idiots! He doesn't deserve any of this."

Weasel jumped onto Anson's lap and started to purr just as the commercial ended.

She began to pet the cat with one hand, and with the other she took the remote and turned up the volume.

"For our top story, we go live to Steve Spence in the town of Clark Fork, Idaho. Steve."

When Spence came on the screen, Anson leaned forward and looked closely at the reporter and then the house and yard in the background. Trash was scattered across the lawn and the curtains in the living room were crooked.

"What did they do to his house?" she asked, as Spence brought up his microphone. "What a bunch of pigs. And what happened to the interview with Jeff?"

Spence began to speak.

"Who would have thought that here, in this peaceful small town, the president's newest piece of legislation would be defied before her signature was even dry? Earlier today, KSPN broke this story to the whole country. I was on the scene only minutes after Justin Mabry allegedly struck a newly appointed Child Protection officer while in the line of duty. And who is this Justin Mabry? What kind of man has dared challenge this new law, a law designed to better protect our nation's children from those that would do them harm? Who, indeed, is Justin Mabry?

"I have just concluded another exclusive interview with an FBI agent here at the scene. All we know at this juncture is that Mabry is to be considered armed and dangerous and that he has fled the scene. To the best of the FBI's knowledge this evening, he is now hiding in the rough terrain of the vast Cabinet Mountains. And with the arrival of several FBI field agents in the morning, tomorrow promises to be an eventful day for this quiet little town, nestled in the forests of the beautiful but rugged Idaho Panhandle.

"This is Steve Spence, reporting from Clark Fork, Channel Six News. Robert, back to you."

With a few rehearsed comments, the news anchor moved on to the next story but Anson was not interested. Pressing the mute button, she absentmindedly continued stroking the cat. She tried to recall how the curtains looked when she and Brown first went inside Mabry's house.

In her mind, she entered the living room. She could see the couch, the end tables and the pictures on the walls. Then she remembered the curtains. They were light green and likely made of bed sheets, but they were straight. Like everything else in the house, they were neat and orderly.

A few coffee cups, some napkins and fast-food sacks discarded by the FBI agents before the newscast might explain the cluttered appearance of the front yard. But why were the curtains so obviously misaligned? Instead of being notoriously meticulous, it was as if the Evidence Recovery Team that was sent in had trashed the scene of the crime. Or had they intentionally made it look run-down and dirty? And if they had, for what purpose?

When Steve Spence interviewed Jeff Brown earlier in the day, the camera was aimed in such a way that most of the yard and house would have been in the background. In that video, the house would have looked almost quaint, but the six o'clock live broadcast left the impression that it was the home of a low-life.

Anson's thoughts quickly switched to Agent Degan and she frowned.

"Weasel," she said to the cat, "that man gives you a bad name. Agent or not, I don't trust him."

Recalling how he had questioned her about Mabry discarding Brown's pistol, she began to wonder about Degan's motives. He immediately tried to make her second-guess what she had witnessed. Why would he want there to be doubt about the pistol? Did he actually believe that Mabry was armed, or was he merely being cautious? Yet Spence had called Mabry armed and dangerous. Spence could only have gotten that information from one of the federal agents.

There was no question Mabry had thrown the gun away. What if the FBI team had actually *found* it but claimed they hadn't? What then?

If the issue came up, they would say she simply was mistaken, that she was too far away to know what he threw away. They could then continue to claim Mabry was armed and dangerous and only the FBI would ever know what happened to the pistol.

Kelly Anson shook her head.

"Come on," she said out loud. "You're getting carried away with this stuff. Get a grip, girl. Get a grip. They probably didn't have time to look for the pistol, that's all."

But the questions kept coming. Perhaps it was being a third-generation cop, or perhaps it was something more personal, but she could not stop thinking about Mabry. She had only interacted with him for a few minutes, but she immediately felt attracted to him. And it was not a simple attraction. There were facets she could not define, sensations she could not identify, but one thing was perfectly clear. Despite her family background, despite her training, she felt an irrepressible desire to help him.

If he was still in the mountains, which was almost a certainty, he could not know of the evening news broadcast. He likely would think the incident was still a local issue, something to be handled through the county courts. He would know enough to seek legal counsel before making his next move, and there were no attorneys in Clark Fork. To contact one, he would need a phone.

From the looks of the house, the Mabrys were on a very limited income and money was probably tight. He would not be able to afford a cell phone. He would have to use a pay phone and Clark Fork only had two. Near sundown, or shortly afterwards, Mabry would come to town and try to contact some sort of legal counsel. He would show up at one of the pay phones.

Anyone that had seen the inside of Mabry's house would easily surmise his financial situation. And anyone familiar with the case would certainly come to the same conclusions as to what his next move would be. Agent Degan had been inside the house. By now he would have men posted at both phone booths and unless someone intervened, Mabry would be apprehended within hours!

Setting Weasel aside, Anson checked the time. It was six-fifteen. In the middle of June, the sun would not set in North Idaho until nine-thirty. She would have to be in Clark Fork at least by nine o'clock if she was to intercept Mabry.

Chapter Six

June 17th
6:26 PM (PST)

Agent Francis was driving when she and Anderson finally crossed over the clear, rushing waters of Lightning Creek. A narrow metal suspension bridge showing signs of corrosion marked the official entrance to Clark Fork, Idaho. They had flown out of Washington D.C. almost twelve hours earlier, and as far as Francis was concerned, had left all semblance of civilization back at the Spokane airport.

Sneering at Anderson, Francis asked, "Is this the kind of town you grew up in?"

Anderson laughed. He had been enjoying her acidic comments and sarcastic questions since they crossed the border into Idaho.

"No. I grew up in the Coeur d'Alene area. This is a little small, even for me."

Francis drove a few hundred yards, passing several two-bedroom houses and a few scattered single-wide mobile homes. There was a bar on her right and a gas station on her left.

"Oh look," she said, "we can buy gas and beer. And I was worried I would be bored."

Anderson replied, "An eighth of a mile ahead, on the *other* edge of town, is another gas station, a market and a liquor store. We'll have everything we need. Some of the towns in North Idaho aren't as sophisticated as this one."

Looking out the window as she drove through town, Francis swore under her breath.

"Where did they hide our motel?"

"Oh, it's next to the Ranch and Feed store. It looks out onto majestic Mosquito Creek."

"Do they have indoor plumbing?" snipped Francis. "I think I hear banjo music, Anderson. You better watch your back."

As Francis turned into the motel parking lot, Anderson smiled.

"I'm the local boy, Francis. You're the out-of-towner. You're the one that should worry. With all the Viking genes floating around, they grow some mighty big women up here."

Francis spotted a car with government plates and changed the subject.

"The field agents are already here. They rented a room for us that connects with theirs. Agent Phil Degan is in charge of evidence recovery. Do you know him?"

"We've met a few times," answered Anderson, but did not mention that neither liked the other. "But I didn't know he had changed to the evidence team. He was more into domestic terrorism the last I heard. I think he's based in Spokane."

Francis turned into a parking space but left the engine running.

"It's about six-thirty. Do you want to meet with Degan, or go interview…what was the man's name?"

Pulling a small spiral notebook from his coat pocket, Anderson scanned it for a moment.

"The name is Kal Burns. He made the report of child abuse and was the boy's baseball coach. He's the one most likely to give us Mabry's known associates. The information we have from the field agents is that Mabry is new to Clark Fork, and that Burns is our best bet to get a line on Mabry."

"Does Burns live in town, or is he one of those hillbillies that you're always talking about?"

"Hillbillies, as you call them, don't coach baseball. Hopefully, you won't…hopefully, *we* won't have occasion to meet any. Burns works in Sandpoint but lives near here. We could go see him."

"So, what do you say?"

"Let's go," said Anderson. "We still have a lot of daylight and the sooner this case is taken care of the better. I still believe this entire region is one big powder keg."

Francis shifted into reverse and backed out of the parking lot.

"From the looks of the people I've seen, beer keg would be more accurate. Where do we go?"

Anderson again glanced at the paper in his hand.

"Go right. At the liquor store, turn left. He lives along the river."

"What's the name of the river?" asked Francis.

Anderson grinned.

"Clark Fork."

Francis sighed, "I should have known."

Just south of town, Francis drove across a narrow bridge, then turned west and followed the Clark Fork River for half a mile before turning into a gravel driveway. Even she was impressed with the appearance of the two-story house and expansive green lawn in front of it.

"Apparently Mr. Burns has some money," said Anderson. He stepped out of the car admiring the view of the river and the Cabinet Mountains beyond. "Let's see what he knows."

Francis pushed the doorbell and stood back. Anderson stood to her side but slightly to the rear.

Kal Burns opened the heavy oak door with a what-do-you-want look on his face. The top of his white shirt was unbuttoned, displaying the heavy gold chain around his neck. In one hand he clutched a can of beer and in the other a smoldering cigar was wedged between his thick fingers. Before he could speak, Francis flashed her badge.

"I'm Agent Francis of the FBI and this is Agent Anderson. Are you Kal Burns?"

Burn's expression became defensive.

"Yeah. What of it?"

Francis was blunt.

"We have some questions concerning Justin Mabry and your association with him. May we come inside, Mr. Burns?"

Hearing he was not the subject of an investigation, Burns replied more civilly, "Sure. Come on in. I was just listening to the news on TV about that. I never figured he would assault an officer of the law. Whack his kid maybe, but not an adult."

As the two agents walked inside and sat down on a plush leather couch, Anderson asked, "Why did you think he would not hit an adult?"

Burns took a seat across from the agents.

"I don't know," he said, shrugging. "He never said much to anybody. Kept to himself. He never showed much emotion at the games, you know, never yelled at the umpire if his kid got a bad call, things like that. He just didn't strike me as much of a man, if you know what I mean."

Anderson smiled and glanced up at the elk antler chandelier that hung from a vaulted ceiling of knotty pine.

"Yeah, I know what you mean. But you never can tell about those quiet ones. Did you shoot all those elk?"

Burns snickered.

"No! I'm no hunter. Those antlers are all fake. They look real, don't they? They're a hell of a lot cheaper than the real ones."

"Mr. Burns," said Francis, "if you saw the news, I assume you are aware that Mabry has fled. He is now a fugitive. We need to know who his friends are, who he may turn to for help. Our report says he's new in this area but that you might be able to give us some names. We need to know of any known associates."

Burns sat back in his padded chair and shrugged.

"That's simple. He doesn't have any friends from what I could see. But his boy had one. And they gave him a ride to practice every day. I'm pretty sure that's the only friend in town he might have."

Taking out a small note pad, Francis said, "And what would the name be?"

Leaning forward as if he wanted no mistakes, Burns spoke clearly.

"Matt Jordan. That's the boy's name. His father is Luke Jordan. They live somewhere up in the hills. I don't know where, though."

Francis methodically wrote down the information, but Anderson's eyes narrowed. He knew the name of Luke Jordan and had known it for years. Hopefully, the connection between him and Mabry was purely coincidental. But even if the two men had no previous interaction, the fact that Justin Mabry and Luke Jordan were now being mentioned in the same sentence could mean more trouble than anyone imagined.

"Is there anything else you know about Justin Mabry?" asked Anderson. "Anything about his social life?"

Burns took a puff on his cigar and thought for a moment.

"I heard he was going to be a teacher at the high school. And that he just got a divorce."

"We've done some preliminary investigations," continued Anderson, "and his bank records show church contributions here in town. Did you know he went to church?"

"Yeah. I do recall them missing practice for that reason. Or at least that's what the kid *said*."

Francis looked up from her writing and glanced curiously at Anderson but said nothing as he continued.

"You said this Mabry was not very emotional at the games, you were aware he was a teacher and went to church, yet you accused him of child abuse. I'm curious, Mr. Burns. What made you believe he abused his son?"

Burns was silent for several seconds. His face showed a tinge of red and a hint of guilt.

"Well, it was all those bruises," he said finally. "He always had bruises."

"Where did you see the bruises?"

"Oh, they were all over his arms. If you find him you'll see them. They're all over. Some of them are old and some are new ones."

"Did you see any on his face, or anywhere else?"

"No. Just his arms. But that was enough to make me wonder. I thought, you know, for the safety of the kid, to be on the safe side and make the report. I would hate to think he was being abused and I just let it go unreported."

Anderson came to his feet. Francis stood also, and sensing Anderson was on to something, allowed her partner to continue the questioning.

"That answers all our questions for now. Thank you for your cooperation." Anderson started to turn and leave but hesitated.

"By the way, Mr. Burns, what position did Billy Mabry play on your baseball team?"

Burns rose out of his chair.

"He was a catcher."

As Francis and Anderson neared the door, Anderson stopped and looked casually at Burns.

"I played a little baseball myself when I was young. It's a good game."

Burns smiled.

"What position did you play?"

Anderson opened the door. Just before he stepped outside he said, "I played catcher, Mr. Burns. I played catcher all through high school."

Anderson studied Burns' face.

"I think it would be in your best interest, Mr. Burns, if you kept your doors locked until this is over."

Francis did not say anything until they had driven back across the Clark Fork River, and Anderson had offered nothing to explain his line of questioning. Pulling off to the side of the road, Francis put the car in park and turned off the engine.

"Okay, John. I let you go on in there with your questioning because I could see you were on to something. Now, tell me what you know."

Anderson was grim.

"First of all, Kal Burns is lying about the child abuse. He knows Mabry didn't hurt his child. Mabry is innocent, at least of that charge."

A wrinkle of interest showed on Francis' forehead.

"Explain."

"Any baseball coach knows that a catcher gets bruises on his arms. It comes from blocking pitches that hit the dirt and bounce. The catcher uses his body and arms to stop the ball. Their arms are always bruised. And Burns knows, too, that this Mabry is not a hot head. He has something against Mabry. He turned him in to get back at him for something, and now we're caught in the middle."

"What else?" asked Francis. Her lips tightened as she waited for an answer.

Anderson sighed and shook his head.

"Luke Jordan is a major leader of the Patriots and is associated with several other right-wing groups that cover all of Idaho, Montana, Nevada and Eastern Washington. That's just the organizations we know about. Given today's political unrest, his influence may have spread even further.

"The way I see it, either this Mabry knew Jordan before he moved here or he never met him before and their connection is pure chance. If it's just a coincidence, there may be nothing to worry about. I say maybe. But if they knew each other through some of these political groups, we'll definitely have more trouble than we bargained for…if we don't back off."

"We won't be backing off," said Francis.

Anderson glanced at his partner from the corners of his eyes.

"You sound certain. Is there something I should know?"

Ignoring Anderson's question, Francis started the car.

"Let's get back to the motel. They'll have an updated report on Mabry by now. We'll check his association with Jordan and get some more background. I'll contact headquarters about the possible connection between the two men and have the office advise us how to proceed. As I see it, nothing has changed."

Mulling over the last comment, Anderson thought of the closed-door phone conversation between D.J. and Assistant Director Berger before they left Boise. Francis was cold and calculating, but this time she had let something slip. A person with her intellect would recall the name of Luke Jordan from her own records. The name would be a familiar one, even in her district. Yet, she was acting as if she had never heard it and confidently saying that Mabry was to be pursued regardless of any potential complications. According to his Threat Source Profile, Jordan was to be considered dangerous. He was someone to approach with caution, but his possible association with Mabry had not fazed D.J. Why?

"Before we go to the motel," offered Anderson smoothly, "why don't we swing by the Mabry house. We'll have a better feel for the briefing if we see the layout."

"Good idea."

"Go back to the highway. That's the same as Fourth on the street signs. Then turn right on Main and go down to Eleventh Street. The house is on the corner."

Turning on to Main Street, Francis asked, "Why does Fourth have all the businesses and Main have nothing but run-down houses and mobile homes on it? Don't they have it reversed?"

"Beats me. But a lot of the towns in the Inland Northwest are laid out like this. It does seem backwards. Everywhere else, Main has all the commerce."

Francis frowned as she drove slowly past the rows of small houses, uncut stacks of firewood and dozens of old pickup trucks.

"I think 'backwards' about covers it."

Yellow police tape encircled the Mabry's house. Francis pulled up in front of it and parked.

"This place is more than I expected," said Francis. "I was thinking a quaint, pink single-wide trimmed in rust. So, this is actually a step up."

Quietly, Anderson surveyed the littered front yard and then the windows of the house. He saw the crooked curtain and the trash but he also noticed that the window screens were not torn and the glass was clean. The shrubs were trimmed…and the lawn had been mowed.

Anderson rolled down his window. He inhaled the sweet smell of fresh cut grass. It had been mowed recently, likely that morning. So where did all the trash come from? If it were present when the lawn was mowed, everything would have been shredded instead of lying scattered about. And why would anyone take such good care of his landscaping and then litter it with paper wrappers?

Pointing to the empty field behind the house, Anderson said, "He must have cut across there and gone up into the mountains. They're less than a quarter-mile away. He would have made it in a matter of seconds."

"Bloodhounds should be able to track him easily enough," said Francis. "Maybe this won't take so long after all."

"I don't know. Lightening Creek is a half-mile to our left and is a major drainage for this range of mountains. If he gets in the water, we'll probably lose him. And even if he doesn't, look how steep those mountains are. Do you think any of our men can go up there and last more than an hour?"

"Then we'll get a helicopter and use infrared."

"Too many people are in the mountains. We'll have a hell of a time telling who's down there. There are hunters, loggers, woodcutters, mushroom pickers, hikers—you name it. Infrared won't be of much use and these people have been known to shoot at low-flying helicopters. Some of them are fiercely private and independent. And everybody, and I do mean everybody, owns a gun.

"D.J., you're used to large cities and flat, open countryside. This is mountain range after mountain range, thousands of square miles of timber and rock. You could hide a dozen armies out there."

"So, what do you suggest?"

"Just give him time. He'll come in on his own if he's like most people. He'll get tired and hungry or homesick and just walk back home. Then we reason with him and let the system handle the rest. Quietly."

Francis gazed at the rugged mountain range to the north. "Maybe you're right, John. But I've been given this assignment by the assistant director to end this ASAP, and I will carry out my orders.

"Are you ready to go to the motel or do you want to go inside?"

"I think the inside of the house has been…gone over already. I've seen enough for today."

As Francis backed out onto Main Street, Anderson noticed a full-sized pickup with a camper, driving slowly past the Mabry house. The camper was white but the truck was painted in non-glare army green. Three men with beards were in the cab.

On the way back to the motel, Anderson analyzed what little he knew. Someone high up in the Bureau, perhaps even higher than the assistant director, wanted Mabry brought in quickly, even if it meant a run-in with Luke Jordan. And, for the sake of the news media, the house where Mabry lived had been deliberately trashed. The Bureau elite wanted to present Mabry to the public in a negative way and had started with his home. What would they do next and why do it to Mabry?

Before Francis opened the door to their motel room, Anderson had postulated at least a partial answer to one of his questions. The Child Protection Act had always been a cornerstone of President Stark's agenda and now was to be part of her legacy. Mabry was standing in her way. It was possible that his refusal to surrender his son was threatening to embarrass her in front of the entire country and for that reason alone, the situation was receiving top priority. Or perhaps with the right orchestration, Mabry's highly publicized arrest would garner enough support from the voters to assure the President of the United States a second term. Either way, the stakes were high, and the deck was stacked against the schoolteacher.

When Francis opened the door to their motel room, the agents were met with the smell of hamburgers, French fries and coffee. The joining door to the adjacent room was open and Degan was standing near it.

"Come on over, you two. I'm Agent Degan and that's Flin and he's Jones," he said, pointing to two brown sacks and two Styrofoam cups on top of the TV. "We bought dinner for the both of you. How was the trip from Boise? Or should I say D.C.?"

"Long," replied Francis, as she set her suitcase down. "Where did you come in from?"

"Seattle," said Degan, as his eyes scanned Francis' long legs. Then, glancing at Anderson, he said cheerily, "John, it's been a while. How are you?"

"I'm the same as always," replied Anderson.

His casual response was meant to be a warning for the men who had altered Mabry's house in an attempt to mold public opinion. John Anderson and Phil Degan had met before. Each knew the ethics of the other.

After being introduced to Agents Jones and Flin, Anderson dropped his suitcase on one of the double beds as Francis went next door. Francis insisted on gender neutrality and for that reason alone they had slept in the same room on numerous occasions. And, except for one regrettable incident, their conduct was always professional.

Francis was ambitious, but he never doubted her integrity or devotion to duty and they worked well together. For more than two years, he had enjoyed her brand of friendship, but something about this assignment was unusual. Since the closed-door meeting with the A.D., there was something different about her. For the first time, their relationship was shrouded in a fog of distrust.

Francis was brilliant. She possessed a near photographic memory but ironically had an astounding lack of intuition and could not see what others found to be obvious. Unexplainably, she was unable to detect subtle changes in the eyes and tone of voice. She could not read body language or understand the importance of minor fluctuations in a person's mannerisms, including her own. These things she could not grasp, but as far as being an FBI agent was concerned, it was her only weakness.

When Francis first looked at Degan, Anderson saw in her a flicker of recognition, betraying some sort of prior association. Then he noticed Francis take a second, more subtle glance at him. This time, what he saw in her eyes sparked a twinge of jealousy.

Anderson took the brown bag from the television, then sat down on the edge of a bed. He was odd man out and he knew it.

Listening to the others next door, he ate in silence. He hoped Francis might join him for at least a few moments. It was an indicator, a subtle test of loyalty, but Anderson finished his meal alone.

Wadding up his paper bag, he tossed it in the trash and took a deep breath. It was time to be professional again, and the longer he stayed away from them the worse it would be. Picking up what was left of his fries, he went through the doorway and yawned.

"Almost fell asleep in there. What's the latest on Mabry? Anything come in from Quantico yet?"

Degan was sipping coffee from his cup. His eyes shifted slightly before he took it from his lips.

"Not much from Virginia, but our field office in Sacramento tells us he just went through a nasty divorce. Cocaine was involved. His ex-wife says he's prone to violent outbreaks."

"Is that all they have?" asked Anderson. "No unusual affiliations?"

"No. Why do you ask that?"

"John is worried," broke in Francis, "that Mabry has connections with a Luke Jordan, a right-wing extremist that lives here."

Anderson did not miss the look in Degan's eyes when he heard Jordan's name. He, too, knew who Jordan was.

"Well," responded Degan smoothly, "our initial reports are sketchy. Mabry kept a low profile. We'll get more on him by morning.

"But you know, I used to work in Domestic Terrorism. The name of Luke Jordan does sound familiar."

Degan took another sip of coffee, then another.

"Maybe we can kill two birds with one stone," he said with an impudent smile. "This could be a good hunt."

"Could be," Anderson agreed, then took a bite of cold French fry.

As he chewed, he casually studied the faces in the room. The men were all west coast operatives and seemed to display the brand of camaraderie that only came from a long association. Yet less than a year ago, Degan was in Domestic Terrorism. And from the appearance of Mabry's residence, it was likely the trio had planted more evidence than they had recovered. It was an established tactic of what the Bureau termed "low- intensity warfare," but it was normally reserved for extremist groups. Mabry was a lone citizen. He posed no threat to national security.

"We went by the suspect's house on our way in," said Francis. "Those mountains behind his house look rough. We need an Operation Plan that takes that into account."

Degan nodded. "I've been working on that."

"You have?" Francis said.

Degan put his hand to his forehead and smiled.

"Oh, I forgot to mention it. The assistant director called this afternoon and appointed me Assistant Special Agent in Charge."

If Francis was surprised, she covered it well.

"What does the OP look like so far?"

"First of all," replied Degan, "we have a cop posted at the house. And I asked for tracking dogs from the Bonner County Sheriff's department. The handler can't come until tomorrow morning, but he says the dogs can pick up a scent that's three days old if they have to. Five U.S. Marshals will arrive at seven tomorrow morning and accompany the dogs and the handler.

"According to the local deputy that was on scene when the assault took place, the suspect took Agent Brown's pistol with him when he escaped. The Marshals have been advised to consider Mabry armed and dangerous.

"We checked with the phone companies. He has no cell phone. According to our preliminary psychological profile, there is a high probability that he will attempt to call someone for help or advice tonight. Since he is now a federal fugitive, he's likely to use a pay phone instead of asking someone in town to use their home phone. There are only two pay phones in town, and we'll have both under surveillance from dusk until daylight. If he shows, we take him down. Otherwise we'll run him to ground with the dogs."

"He has his boy," Anderson interjected. "Maybe he'll say the heck with it and try for Canada."

Degan shook his head.

"The profile says no. He's a law-abiding citizen, at least on the surface. Not so much as a traffic ticket. He'll want to straighten things out. No. He'll come into town tonight because he believes he can beat the charges against him."

"And what does the profile say about this law-abiding citizen's propensity to abuse his child?" asked Anderson, but immediately wished he had kept the question to himself. He had expressed a dissenting opinion in favor of the fugitive. Now his commitment to the OP would be suspect, and perhaps his loyalty to the Bureau's plan as well.

A smirk twisted Degan's lips.

"That's right. You're the Supervisory Agent aren't you? Well, when the detailed profile comes in, it may address that issue. But that's not our concern. We are pursuing an armed federal fugitive."

"So far," returned Anderson with an edge to his voice, "you're after one fugitive. But your OP is incomplete. There's nothing in it about Luke Jordan."

The smirk on Degan's face melted slowly as the statement sobered him.

"Yeah. We'd better work on that. I'll notify the assistant director."

"That's my prerogative" interrupted Francis. "I'll contact Washington when I feel it's necessary. Until then, we'll send a team to the Jordan residence. If Mabry tries to get there, we can intercept him before he has any chance to interact with Jordan.

"Agent Degan, I want a second team of our agents, well armed and camouflaged, surrounding Jordan's house as early as possible tomorrow morning."

"You're risking escalation, D.J.," cautioned Anderson. "What if the team is discovered?"

"They will have orders to stay back. They're to observe and intercept only."

"It could be," suggested Agent Flin, "that the kid is already there at the Jordans."

Everyone in the room was surprised by the comment, but it was Degan who spoke first.

"Why do you say that?"

Flin pointed at the screen of his laptop computer.

"I was just re-reading Brown's report. According to Brown, Deputy Anson told him that the boy left the house first and then Mabry left, and they didn't go in the same direction. The boy was angling more to the north and the father northeast. I think they went to different places. And if Mabry was planning on running, a twelve-year-old would only slow him down. I think he sent the boy to a safe place to wait for him."

Francis glanced at Anderson.

"What would the boy run into if he kept going due north from the house?"

"Lightning Creek Road," answered Anderson grimly. "It's the only road that goes through the mountains from here. It follows the creek. There are only a few roads that branch off of it for several miles."

"How far up is the Jordan place?" Degan asked.

"I've never been near it," said Anderson, "but I've seen maps. It's seven or eight miles from the Mabry house, but most of those miles are on narrow mountain roads."

Degan glanced at Francis. His eyes narrowed and danced with eagerness.

"If the kid is there already, Jordan could be considered an accessory. If Mabry shows up too, Jordan could be charged with harboring a fugitive."

"Tomorrow morning we'll clear this with the Idaho State Attorney's Office," Francis said. "I want all the paperwork in order if we need it. No screw-ups."

Anderson sighed. He knew it was pointless, but he was the Supervisory Agent.

"I advise against any—I repeat—*any* contact with Luke Jordan. And if Mabry is at the Jordans', my advice is to wait until he comes to town or leaves the Jordan property to get him. The last thing this part of the country needs is a confrontation with someone like Jordan."

Degan thought for a moment. Setting his coffee down, he stuck a toothpick in the corner of his mouth.

"We've heard nothing unusual from our snitches or undercover operatives on the west coast. We have all the radical groups throughout our region isolated and unable to organize. We're monitoring everything—phones, e-mails, CB transmissions—you name it. We even open their mail. They can't fart without us knowing about it. I don't think Jordan, or anyone like him, can pose a significant threat. At the most, we'd be dealing with one more man and maybe a few sympathizers. I assume, Anderson, that you're not picking up anymore than we are?"

"It's the same in the inland area," agreed Anderson, "but even quieter than normal. And that bothers me. I have the feeling they've become more sophisticated. Or they've figured out who our snitches and covert agents are. I don't like the sudden lack of transmissions."

"We talked about this yesterday with the assistant director, John," said Francis. "You're making too much of it. They can't possibly have identified *all* of our coverts. And if we do have a situation arise that involves Luke Jordan, we can control it before it gets out of hand. Our tactics have been working for decades on these domestic groups, and they'll continue to work. These people are ignorant, paranoid and predictable. And that makes them easy to manipulate.

"We'll send the team to the Jordans' cabin. We want Mabry, but if we get Jordan as well, then all the better."

Chapter Seven

June 17th
7:48 PM (PST)

K elly Anson took a quick shower but spent fifteen minutes drying and combing her hair. Instead of wearing it up as she did for work, she let the sandy blond waves fall down around her shoulders. After looking in the bathroom mirror several times, she pulled her hair back and clipped it into a ponytail.

She stood in front of her open closet for several minutes before finally selecting a plain white blouse to wear, then pulled on a pair of jeans and cowboy boots. As an after-thought, she unbuttoned an extra top button then pumped a fine mist of her favorite perfume on her neck.

She looked into the full-length mirror and shook her head.

"Kelly Anson, you're making a fool of yourself. You've only met him twice, and one of those times you should have arrested him."

Turning sideways, she continued arguing with herself.

"But one thing's for sure. He's different than the men around here. Oh, he's good looking all right, but that's not it. Not all of it. Even if it's just for a few minutes, we need to talk. I need to explain…no, I need to…oh, shut up!"

Anson closed her closet door and turned her back on the mirror. As she left her bedroom, she re-buttoned the top button of her blouse.

"He won't be interested," she said flatly. "He's in serious trouble and I'm going to help him."

Grabbing the keys to her pickup truck, she checked the time. It was almost eight o'clock and it would take twenty minutes to drive to Clark Fork. She should be there in plenty of time, if Mabry was even going to show up.

Heading east on Highway 200, Anson tried to think of what she would say both to Mabry and to anyone that might ask why she was back in town…and in civilian clothes.

Maybe she was just curious to see what had happened since she got off duty. Or perhaps she was on her way to see Mr. Hickey, to ask if he had seen anything from his house across the street. Yes. It would be easy to explain her presence in Clark Fork, but what would she say to Justin Mabry? Would he recognize her out of uniform? Would he get into her truck? Would he trust her?

As Anson rounded the last curve and slowed to cross the Lightning Creek Bridge, she glanced to her right. A Dixie flag flew in front of a log house. A sign along the driveway read "Slow down or die fast." Clark Fork had some rough characters, and most of the residents were notoriously independent. The presence of federal agents here wouldn't go over well.

The sun had just dropped beyond the mountain peaks when she passed the first pay phone on the corner of Fourth and Main. Across from the phone, she spotted Agent Jones and on impulse she looked away. When she got to Eighth Street, she turned right and a block further down, she pulled over. There was no doubt another FBI agent would stake out the phone on the other end of town.

Anson knew the mountains around Clark Fork and had hunted them with her father. Mentally placing herself on the ridge overlooking the town, she tried to imagine which approach Mabry would choose to re-enter town.

There was more cover to the east than any other direction, with a ditch and thicket of trees along one side. To the west was Lightning Creek and fewer trees to conceal his approach. Coming in from the south side of town would be too risky for similar reasons. No. Mabry would try for the phone on the east end of town and he would eventually have to walk down Staci Street to get there.

Anson drove down Eighth again, slowly turned onto Staci then came to where the drainage ditch intersected the street. She parked in front of an empty lot and sat back to watch the intersection. If she guessed wrong, Mabry would likely be caught by the Feds and, if Jeff Brown was right, be convicted of assaulting a federal officer. The sentence would be severe, even though his actions were merely those of a desperate man in the heat of the moment. Even if it was the law, it wasn't right.

The next half-hour went by slowly and daylight gradually faded into evening. It would be difficult to recognize faces at a distance now, but she knew how Mabry was dressed. Degan had not asked for those details and Anson had not volunteered them. It was a small advantage.

She was watching the grass at the edge of the ditch when a figure appeared a hundred feet north of her, walking on the side of the street. A few seconds later she could see it was a man, and from the width of his shoulders and the way he carried himself, she could tell he was athletic. It was Mabry. He had cut behind some houses and found his way onto Staci ahead of her, but it was him. And he was coming her way.

Nonchalantly, Anson opened her door and stepped out of her truck. Pretending to search for her keys, she crossed to Mabry's side of the street and timed her steps to come close to him before she looked up.

"Good evening," she said pleasantly. "Nice to see you again."

Mabry froze.

"I'm sorry," he said politely, "but I don't recognize you."

Anson smiled and extended her hand.

"Kelly."

As Mabry took her hand, she firmly held onto his.

"We met at the donut shop yesterday. When you were with your son."

Mabry's eyes flared with shock as a jolt of adrenalin shot through him. He had the look of an animal that had been decoyed then trapped in a cage.

Mabry did not move for several seconds, but there were no loud shouts, no handcuffs. Still he waited, but there was only silence. His eyes slowly began to focus on the sincere face in front of him.

"Officer Anson?"

Still holding his hand, Kelly Anson said gently, "Don't worry. I'm not on duty tonight. I'm here to help you, if you'll let me."

Mabry eased his hand away from Anson's. For several seconds in the fading light, he studied her.

"I don't know what to say. But you can't. You'll get in trouble. I can't let you do that. I...I'm deeply thankful and totally confused but... no. I've messed things up enough without getting you involved, too. All I need to do is make a phone call to my attorney.

"I can clear this up. But thank you...very much for offering. Again...I...don't know what to say."

"Mr. Mabry, you don't understand. You cannot do this on your own. Both the town's pay phones are being watched by FBI agents. They'll arrest you if they see you."

Squinting at Kelly Anson, Justin Mabry repeated the words slowly.

"FBI agents?"

"Please, Mr. Mabry...Justin, we need to get off the street before some-one sees us. Please, we can get in my truck and talk about this, but we need to get away from here. They may be patrolling the streets already. Please, for Billy's sake, trust me and let me help the both of you."

Mabry took a deep breath and let it out slowly.

"I have no choice...but are you sure about this? You're risk-ing...more than I can ask anyone to risk on my account."

Placing both hands on Mabry's shoulders, Kelly turned him to-wards her pickup. "I'm very sure. Now, let's go."

Inside the truck, Anson asked the question that had been troubling her all afternoon. She had to be absolutely certain before she went any further.

"What did you do with Brown's pistol?"

Mabry shrugged.

"I threw it out in field behind the house. The only reason I took it was because I didn't know how long he would stay down. I didn't want to chance a bullet in the back."

"That's what I told the FBI when they showed up at your house," Anson muttered, then started the truck. "But the agent, Degan, didn't want to believe me."

With her headlights on, Anson drove back up Eighth then took a side street back to Fourth.

"We'll go towards Sandpoint, but when we pass Main act like you're looking in the glove box. And keep your head down. I saw an agent by the gas station earlier."

"Did he see you?"

"No. And he won't this time, either, so don't worry. I wasn't born yesterday."

"I still need to make that phone call," said Mabry. "And I guess they can trace just about everything these days. A pay phone is safest."

"Then we can stop in Hope. There's one there and not too many people will be around at this time of evening. Can I ask who you want to call?"

Mabry shook his head.

"My divorce attorney. He's the only lawyer I know, and he knows me as well as anyone could. He can at least put me in touch with the right peo-ple, people that can untangle this mess before it gets out of hand."

Anson put her lights on bright and kept an eye out for deer.

"I'm afraid I have some bad news. Your story was on the news tonight. Channel six. And they're slanting it against you. The station has political ties."

For several miles there was no conversation as Mabry grappled with the latest development. The FBI was already involved and the media had the story. Yet it was only a Spokane area broadcast. It was still a local concern. And since Agent Brown worked for a federal agency, it did make sense that the FBI was called in...or did it? He didn't know. He was a history teacher, and if he knew anything at all about the law, it was that only lawyers could understand it.

On the outskirts of Hope, Anson turned into the parking lot of a closed market. She stopped in the shadows and tuned off her lights.

"Do you need any change?"

"No, thanks. I'll call collect. He'll accept the charges."

Mabry went to the phone and turned his back to any traffic that might be on the highway. He gave the operator the information and waited. His heart began to pound. This was his only hope.

He heard the operator speak.

"Will you accept the charges?"

A familiar voice agreed, then asked excitedly, "Justin, is it you?"

"Yes, Bruce. Unfortunately. I'm afraid I have a serious problem."

Bruce Nason responded anxiously, "I know, Justin. It was on the news tonight."

"In Sacramento?" exclaimed Mabry. "What the hell is going on?"

"It's gone national already, Justin. What are you going to do?"

"That's what I need you to tell me. This whole thing is all a mistake."

"You mean you didn't assault the officer? Because that would be..."

Mabry interrupted.

"No, I hit him. But he grabbed Billy. He was going to take him away without letting me explain anything. I know who made the false accusation against me and why.

"I can prove I'm innocent. Shouldn't that make a difference?"

"I knew you didn't hurt Billy," said Nason. "But I'm not qualified to advise you on a criminal matter. Let me make some calls tonight and call you back. I have some connections in Boise. Is there a number where you can be reached? No, forget that. Can you call me again in…say, an hour, about ten o'clock? And from a pay phone again."

"I can do that. And Bruce…I can't thank you enough."

Nason swore.

"I've never seen such damned bad luck as yours, Justin. Try to hang in there. I'll do my best."

Mabry got back in the pickup. For the first time in an agonizingly long day, he felt relieved. He forced a smile as he glanced at Anson.

"He's going to make some calls. He knows people in Boise. He's a good man."

Kelly Anson smiled and touched Mabry's hand.

"That's good news. What's next?"

"I'm to call him back in an hour or so, and from a pay phone. He'll let me know what he finds out."

"Good. That's good, Justin. Have you eaten anything since…since today?"

"No, I haven't. Until now, I had no appetite."

"Then we'll go to my apartment and I'll find something for you to eat. We can use a phone in Sandpoint when it's time. Or better yet, we can use my cell phone. Since he's your attorney, there would be nothing unusual about a call on my phone record to him. He would have pertinent information about the investigation."

Mabry took a long look at Kelly Anson. He wanted to ask her why she had intervened but he decided against it. When she was ready, she would explain.

"You are an exceptional person. I'm fortunate, very fortunate, to have met you, Officer Anson. But I don't…I feel bad for having involved you. You're taking a terrible risk. But I do need your help. All can say is that I am extremely grateful, for whatever that's worth."

"You are welcome," replied Anson, simply. "And I value your gratitude very much. Let's leave it there for now. But please call me Kelly."

Mabry smiled and shook his head in disbelief. Among other things, Kelly Anson had integrity. It was a quality that was missing in too many people and totally lacking in his ex-wife. And the young woman was as courageous as she was beautiful. Under different circumstances…if his life were not in chaos…

"I know you can't tell me very much," said Kelly, as she interrupted his thoughts, "but how is your son? Is he safe where he is now?"

Mabry smiled as he thought of Billy.

"Yes. He's safe. But I hope he doesn't worry too much. My divorce was very hard on him. He's gone through more than his share of heartache and misery."

"Do you want to talk about it?"

Mabry frowned.

"Not really. It's over and I don't want to look back."

"Sure, I understand. But can I ask you one question? Of course, you don't have to answer, but I was just curious. I've been kind of wondering about it all day."

"Fire away."

"Jeff and I went into your house today on a search warrant. He found a box of your trophies in the garage. It looked like you put them in there a long time ago, like you didn't want Billy to see them. Wouldn't you want him to know how well you did in sports, since he's playing baseball? He would be proud of you."

Leaning forward, Mabry looked up into the western sky. The sunset had turned it a brilliant red-orange.

"I didn't want my son trying to live up to my accomplishments. I was afraid that if he didn't do well himself, he might feel inadequate...or he might feel too much pressure to succeed. I wanted him to enjoy sports for what they are, to learn the lessons they can teach without worrying that his shelves weren't full of shiny plastic."

A warm smile brightened Anson's face.

"I thought it was something like that. You are a good dad."

Mabry glanced at Anson but his eye caught the color of Lake Pend Oreille as it reflected the sunset. He studied it curiously for a moment then said, "Did you ever see that old movie, The Ten Commandments?"

"Yeah. Charlton Heston was Moses. Why?"

Mabry pointed to the lake.

"That made me think of it."

After seeing the unusually red color of the water, Anson said, "You mean where the water turned to blood."

For several seconds Mabry was quiet. When he spoke again, his voice was distant. "The Pharaoh of Egypt wouldn't let the people go.

His pride and stubbornness caused a lot of misery. He shouldn't have chased after them. They just wanted to go back home."

Anson looked again at the lake then thoughtfully back at Justin.

"The lake is very calm and it picks up the color of the sky like a mirror," offered Kelly. "But it won't last long. Sunsets, like a lot of things, never do."

Mabry chuckled.

"You're good at reading people, aren't you?"

Nearing the outskirts of Sandpoint, Kelly slowed her truck to just under the speed limit. They couldn't chance attracting the attention of the city police.

"I used to think everyone could read people, but I know better now. It just comes naturally. And, speaking of such things, I didn't like that Agent Degan, today."

"Who?"

"Agent Degan. He was one of the FBI agents that came to your house. There's something not right about him. I definitely wouldn't buy a used car from him."

Mabry rubbed his face with both hands then folded his arms.

"I can't believe I'm being chased by the FBI. I thought Clark Fork would be the most peaceful place in the country. A small community, all alone in the Rocky Mountains. It sounded like the perfect place to raise Billy. And now look at me."

Coming to a stoplight, Kelly put her hand on Justin's shoulder.

"Your lawyer will figure something out for you. You know they always do. The law can work for you as well as against you. Anyone can see you're not a criminal. When your story gets out, people will understand."

Justin Mabry felt the warmth of Kelly's hand. It was a comfort he hadn't known for nearly two years. Feeling encouraged by her words, he patted her hand before she took it away.

"You know, if you feed a lost puppy it may never leave you alone."

The light turned green and Kelly giggled, "Is that so?"

"Yes, it is. And do you know what else?"

"What?"

"You made quite an impression on Billy yesterday in the donut shop."

"Kids are always impressed with cops and badges."

"Actually, he asked me if you were considered pretty. I was surprised. But he is twelve years old. I guess it's starting."

There was a long silence that Mabry enjoyed. With a faint smile, he waited for Kelly to ask the obvious question.

This time, Kelly poked Justin in the shoulder with her finger.

"Well," she demanded, "what did you say?"

Mabry rubbed his shoulder. It was quite a jab.

"I said...yes."

"Why, thank you," said Kelly. "Your son is such a bright child."

Thankful for the lighthearted diversion, Mabry responded, "I'm not sure how bright he is but he undoubtedly has good taste."

Kelly kept her eyes on the road, but they were wide.

"Oh?"

"Yes," answered Mabry, then looking once more at Kelly, his eyes narrowed with realization. "He takes after me more than I thought."

Kelly smiled and glanced playfully at Mabry then turned onto a side street and then into a parking space.

"This is it. It's only a one-bedroom apartment, but it's enough for me and my cat, Weasel."

"Can't wait to meet him," said Mabry, as he got out of the truck and followed Kelly to the front door. While she turned the key, a thought came to him.

"You know, I didn't think to ask if my being here would cause you any...well, personal problems."

Stepping into her apartment, Kelly reached back and took Justin by the shirt sleeve and pulled him inside. After looking to see if anyone had seen them arrive, she closed the door and turned on the lights.

"Don't worry about that. I haven't had a serious 'personal problem' since I broke up with Vince Tagwell my senior year in high school."

Kelly went to the kitchen and opened a cupboard door.

"Looks like it's canned stew or canned spaghetti for dinner. It's too late to start cooking."

"Stew is fine," said Mabry, as his eyes searched the living room and then the kitchen for a clock. He had left his wristwatch in his house and Bruce Nason would be expecting his call at ten. The clock on the stove read 9:32.

Mabry sat at a bar that divided the kitchen from the dining area and watched Kelly going about her tasks. She moved easily, not in a jerky or careless manner and there was no wasted movement or loud clanging of pots and pans.

"What was it about that FBI agent you didn't like? You said his name was Degan?"

Kelly emptied two cans of beef stew into a pot and turned on the burner.

"He seemed dishonest. And arrogant, too. Most of the time he wore a smirk on his face."

"How many agents came with him?"

"Two. But they sure made a big mess for just three people. When they showed your front yard on the TV news, it looked like white trash lived there. There was litter all over the lawn. And I could see they were busy inside, too, because the front curtain was crooked. I know it wasn't that way when Jeff and I went in."

"What did they say about it on TV?"

Holding a spoon in her hand, Kelly leaned back against the kitchen counter. "The reporter, Steve Spence, was obviously slanting the tone of everything against you, but it just covered the basics. The only part I really found disturbing was when Spence said you were armed and dangerous. That made you sound like a common criminal.

"I told the FBI agent I saw you throw Jeff's gun out in the field. I guess they haven't searched for it yet, and they're just being cautious until they find it."

Mabry stiffened.

"What is it?" Kelly asked.

For several seconds, Mabry stared blankly at nothing. His chest rose and fell as his breaths grew deeper and longer. He slowly shook his head.

"When I left home today, I didn't go far. I went straight up that first mountain behind the field and stopped. I could see the house and cars…and the spot where I tossed the gun.

"I saw a white van drive up and leave. I saw another car stop and three men get out and go inside. Your car left. Then, quite a bit later, I saw the van come back and could tell it was a news crew."

Mabry paused and looked hard at Kelly.

"Between the time you left and the news van returned, the three men searched the field. I watched them with binoculars. They found the gun."

Kelly's face flushed red.

"So they did know you didn't have the pistol. I knew it! They had to be the ones that told Spence you were armed, because neither Jeff nor I said anything about it when Spence was at your house the first time. And now everybody that saw the news thinks you have a gun."

Tapping his finger on the counter top, Mabry thought for a moment. One of the subjects he taught in high school was U.S. history, and a few of his lectures dealt with national security. Some agencies of the government were devoted to foreign threats while others dealt with domestic concerns. The FBI was largely involved with radical domestic groups that threatened to destabilize the country. Their work had helped maintain social stability on numerous occasions and they, for the most part, did a superb job. But there were notable exceptions, some even resulting in criminal convictions.

The main weapon employed by the Bureau was termed "low-intensity warfare."

It was a simple strategy, easy to employ and almost one-hundred-percent successful. Even though it helped protect the freedom of U.S. citizens, it was an un-American tactic based on lies, deception and the planting of evidence.

The kitchen was silent, except for the simmering stew, as Kelly Anson and Justin Mabry attempted to decipher the new information. Kelly spoke first.

"They're trying to turn public opinion against you. That would explain the condition of the house, too. Someone wants you to look bad, but why?"

"The FBI has nothing to gain by lying at this point," surmised Mabry. "They're likely just following instructions from someone higher up, someone that has something to lose if…if what? If I'm not hated by the public? If I'm proven not guilty?"

Kelly turned off the burner under the stew and took down two bowls from a cupboard.

"Maybe both," she said, as she poured the stew into the bowls. "Someone or some group is worried. That sounds more like politics than law enforcement. Maybe this is more of a political ploy than a criminal case."

Mabry took a bowl and slid it towards him. He was no longer hungry but logic told him to eat.

"It's starting to look like I'm at the bottom of a very powerful food chain. Not many people can enlist the FBI to do their dirty work."

Glancing at the clock, Kelly said, "In a few more minutes you can call your lawyer. Maybe he'll have some good news. I'm sure there are a lot of things going on that we know nothing about. And no one has heard your side of the story yet."

Mabry stirred his stew with a spoon.

"My side doesn't amount to much. I just refuse to allow anyone— and I mean anyone—to take my son from me. That's all there is to my side of the story."

"You left out one very important thing, Justin. You are not a child abuser. You are a good father, one of the best. That's why I'm helping you. The law can't be allowed to just come into a home and take a child. Not from good parents and not on the say-so of one person. No matter what the intentions started out to be, anyone that condones that kind of behavior is a barbarian."

Mabry glanced up.

"In essence, you're talking about the president. Or someone close to her."

Kelly folded her arms and thought for a moment.

"I know."

Chapter Eight

June 17th
10:01 PM (PST)

After eating dinner, Mabry reluctantly checked the clock. He looked solemnly at the young woman seated next to him.

"It's time, Kelly. He should know something by now."

Handing Mabry her phone, Anson stood and pointed to another room.

"Would you like some privacy?"

Mabry shook his head while he punched in the numbers.

"You know as much about this as I do," he replied, then motioned with his hand for her to sit. "Please, stay."

The phone rang on the other end.

"Bruce, this is Justin. Were you able to find out anything?"

"Hi, Justin," said Nason. His tone was tense. "I made some calls but didn't find out too much because it's so late. But I don't like the feedback I'm getting."

"What kind of feedback?"

"Like something's going on behind the scenes...something unusual. My friend who works for the Idaho State Attorney General's Office said there were a lot of closed- door meetings going on today. She got the idea the meetings concerned your case. I'll know more tomorrow.

"She's going to test the waters and see how likely it is that you could plead to a lesser crime or get mitigating circumstances. She'll be discreet and keep my name out of it but try and get all the information she can. At this point, I wouldn't worry too much. But stay out of sight."

"What time should I call back tomorrow?"

"Try nine. No, Boise is an hour ahead of us, so call me at eight our time. That will give her an hour to check things out. That's the earliest I would expect to know anything. And don't give me any information about where you are or what you are doing. The less I know the better."

"Understood. And Bruce...thank you."

Handing Kelly her phone, Mabry leaned back in his chair.

"He says not to worry too much. But he sounded worried to me. And his source tells him that I may be the focus of a lot of attention at the state level."

"What level was he referring to?"

"The highest ranking federal officer in Idaho," Justin said, then sighed heavily. "The U.S. State Attorney General."

Kelly anxiously looked at the time. It was six minutes after ten, less than an hour before the last television news broadcast.

"I know that Jeff Brown was speaking directly to the Attorney General today. He called his supervisor and shortly afterwards, in maybe half an hour, he was talking directly with the AG. Right after that, Jeff told us he was certain you would get the maximum punishment for the assault."

Mabry suddenly felt tired.

"It sounds like the AG is taking directions from someone in Washington D.C. Add to that, the FBI deliberately misleading the news crew and the trashing of my house...I would say that my chances to smooth things over don't look very good."

"There'll be more news at eleven," offered Kelly optimistically. "We could learn more then. They could admit they made a mistake and you aren't armed after all."

Mabry glanced awkwardly at Kelly.

"Yes, they could do that. But it's getting late...and I'm putting you out."

Kelly put her hand up.

"Don't say anymore about that. You can sleep on the couch. I don't have to be on duty until four in the afternoon, and you'll need to call your attorney in the morning. Besides that, I can...oh, I just remembered something."

"What?"

"The FBI asked for tracking dogs for tomorrow. They're supposed to arrive at seven. If they pick up your scent, they'll follow every step of your trail. Will that be a problem for your son? Did you meet up with him anywhere?"

"No. But they will find my backpack."

Mabry paused thoughtfully then sighed.

"It can't be helped now. It was only full of camping gear. Billy and I were going to go fishing for a few days. We were only minutes away from leaving when everything went sideways.

"And I need to get word to Billy as soon as I can that I'm safe. But the people he's with don't have a phone up where they live, and they don't use a cell, either. After I call Bruce in the morning, maybe I should go up there and tell him I'm all right."

As Mabry took time to think and eat, Kelly Anson was busy putting a puzzle together. Without realizing it, Mabry had told her that Billy had not gone to some predetermined location like a campground or a particular bend in the creek or favorite fishing hole. He was at a residence. And Mabry had said "they."

Evidently, Billy was staying with a group of people, not a single person. Most likely, that meant a family, a family that lived off the power grid. So, he was with hill-people that lived only a few miles away, close enough that a twelve-year-old boy could walk there easily. And Billy had headed due north. There were only a handful of families that lived like that...and they were all fiercely independent.

"Justin," she said gently, "you have to consider the tracking dogs. You can't take a chance that they'll pick up your scent. They might even lead the Feds to Billy...or to whomever he's staying with. That could lead to serious trouble."

Mabry put both palms to his eyes and rubbed them.

"You're right, of course. I'll have to figure everything out tomorrow. Right now, I'm too tired to think."

Kelly stood up and gathered the bowls. As she placed them in the kitchen sink she said, "I've already taken a shower. If you like, go ahead and use the bathroom. There are extra towels on the rack. There are some disposable razors in the top drawer if you want to shave. But I don't have anything for you to sleep in or change into."

A smile brightened Mabry's mood.

"I've slept in my clothes lots of times. But I will take you up on the shower. I think I lost five pounds in sweat climbing those mountains. Sorry if I'm..."

Kelly shook her head and rolled her eyes.

"Don't apologize, Justin. I grew up in sports, too. Girls sweat all the time. Now go take a shower and try to relax."

Mabry scratched his jaw.

"All right," he said uneasily. "But it seems…kind of strange…we don't know each other. You, especially, don't know me."

Kelly laughed and shook her head in disbelief.

"You can lock the door if you're afraid of me. Now, get going!"

After Mabry closed the bathroom door, Kelly tiptoed down the hall and listened closely for the sound of the lock, but she heard nothing. The silence made her smile. But a moment later, when the shower was turned on, she felt her skin grow warm.

"Knock it off, Kelly," she whispered, "He needs your help. He doesn't have time for anything else…or anyone else."

Walking quietly back to the living room, she turned on the television as a distraction. Before returning to the kitchen, she glanced over her shoulder toward the bathroom door. After taking a deep breath, she let it out slowly and wiped a pair of sweaty palms on her jeans.

Six men sat around Luke Jordan's table. A kerosene lantern in its center flickered yellow light across their somber faces. They spoke in low tones. Their words were solemn and deliberate.

"I talked to Smitty," said a man wearing a stained ball cap. "I told him if he showed up with his trackers, we'd kill the dogs. He won't be telling the Feds until tomorrow morning that he ain't going to show up. He'll tell them his dogs come down sick."

Jordan tapped the eraser end of a short pencil on the table.

"They'll ask for more dogs. But the next time, they'll go out of state. Not to Montana, because they know better, but to somewhere in Washington. One way or the other, sometime tomorrow the Feds will get dogs here. Then they'll get Mabry tracked down and we don't want that yet. We need more time."

"There's one way to put that item to rest," said another speaker. "If the house burns down, the dogs won't have anything to get a scent off of, no clothes, no bed sheets, no nothing."

The men looked at one another. They were in agreement.

"We'll need the incendiaries set tonight," said Jordan. "Enough fire fudge for a quick burn. And remote ignition. They can be set on the back of the house. The cop is out front sitting in his car and has no reason to do anything else. He'll be out of harm's way, but it'll be safer to fire the house in the morning when all the neighbors are awake. If the fire jumps, we don't want anybody asleep if their house catches fire.

"As close to 0700 as possible, when it's all clear of any people, we ignite."

"I'll get right on it," offered a third man. "The voluntary fire crew won't respond for at least ten minutes. With the fire fudge, it'll be too late to save."

Jordan's eyes were hard.

"According to my son, Matt, all the man has to his name is in that house. If it can be done without detection, I want the pictures of Mabry and his son taken off the walls of the house before it burns. It'll mean a lot to him.

"I don't see any other option but to torch the house. It'll be hard on him. But it's the only choice we have to help Mabry. And it's him we need, gentlemen. Justin Mabry is the key to everything."

Another man at the table spoke up.

"Without a hot trail to follow, the Feds will have to backtrack. If they go to Kal Burns like you figured, Luke, there's no doubt they'll come sniffing around here figuring Mabry is headed this way. Of all of us sitting here, you are the only one that the Feds know about for sure. You are on their Sensitive/Select list."

Jordan nodded.

"We've known that for years, men. And we've studied and prepared for every strategy the FBI or BATF can initiate. I'm ready. All of us are ready."

A man sitting at the far end of the table said, "They could have spies or snitches up here right after the Mabry house is burned down. But most likely, they'll send a sniper-observer team instead. They'll come prepared to use lethal force if they have an excuse. Up in these mountains, our men can run circles around theirs, but are we going to have enough time to get our units here and in place?"

"Our first cell started arriving this afternoon," answered Jordan. "Some of them are in the field now. The rest of the local cells will be in tonight. Montana's are due in tomorrow.

"It gets light at 0430. We'll send word tonight to have the available cells move into position then. That'll give them at least a three-hour head start. They'll be set before the Feds make their first move up the mountain.

"Unless they're needed, all of the teams will be directed to stay back far enough to be undetected. The Feds won't be concerned about their rear exposure. Once they pass our positions, we'll have our cells close the gap so they can observe and respond rapidly if needed. I'll be all right."

A man with a thick beard spoke up.

"We need the rest of our people to start our rendezvous in the field to the Southeast and as far back as possible from where we calculate the Feds' staging area will be set up. We don't want them telling us to move our camps. We've got to stay out of their way until all the units are here."

"That's Walt Hickey's land and I've cleared it with him," agreed another. "And make sure no weapons are visible anywhere, at any time. We don't want to tip our hand or give the Feds any excuses to push us back. We've got to have that field if this is going to turn out the way we've planned.

"All of us have studied FBI tactics. Now we will use that knowledge. It's time they're taken down a notch and taught a lesson. It's time to defend this country. Strict discipline, men. Our rules of conduct for rendezvous will be enforced absolutely. Get rid of anyone suspected of spying or being a snitch."

After a long silence, Jordan stood up slowly.

"Then we are in agreement.

"I call this meeting to an end. And no matter what happens, gentlemen, remember that Justin Mabry is the key. He is our lamb, but I guarantee you, he is also our lion! May God bless America."

Agent Anderson sat in his motel room staring at his laptop computer as his printer published a hard copy of what was on the screen. The updated background check on Justin Mabry had just been e-mailed. Anderson chewed the inside of his lip as he re-read the report but this time only skimming the highlights.

Born in Memphis, Tennessee, adopted, father unknown, mother registered one- quarter Cherokee. Moved with adoptive parents to Sacramento when ten years old, conservative churches, Boy Scout, high school and college athlete, college degree with teaching credential. Recently divorced, reason for filing: wife with alleged cocaine addiction and infidelity. One child, twelve-year-old male. Recent magazines subscribed to—*Outdoor Life* and *National Geographic*. Prolific reader (emphasis non-fiction), history, computer usage, an academic. Financial status: minimum checking, no savings. Three months prior, moved to Clark Fork, Idaho. Criminal record: none.

There were other details in this latest profile but it was essentially no different than the one received earlier. The Bureau had extensively searched Mabry's past and come up with nothing. The man was squeaky clean. He was what the agents derisively referred to as a "Boy Scout." But in Mabry's case, the title fit him like no other.

If a man like this had indeed assaulted a federal officer, he must have been provoked. This was the "all-American male" they were after...and for what? Not allowing the government to take his child.

Anderson thought of Degan's boast that this would be a "good hunt." He was as small-minded and arrogant as ever. And what was Degan doing on the Evidence Recovery Team when he had worked his entire career in Domestic Terrorism? And why, instead of showing concern, did he seem pleased when the name of Luke Jordan was introduced?

Looking up from the computer, Anderson checked his watch. It was almost eleven and Francis had been in the next room with the other three agents for over an hour. Were they socializing? Or were they working on some type of covert operation, an operation outside the law?

Earlier in the evening, he and Francis had been briefed by Degan about the day's events. The conversation then digressed into telling dirty jokes and Anderson had returned to his room. They were east coast and west coast personalities and he did not fit the mold. Idaho and Montana people were more to his liking, but in Washington D.C. genuine people were few and far between. There, no one was what they seemed, and politics was the life-blood that pulsed through every institution in the city.

Anderson logged off his computer and took the paper report from the printer. It had been a long and disappointing day. The assignment was less than twenty-four hours old, and he was already weary of the case and of those running it. He needed a vacation.

Before joining the Bureau, his life had been simple. In the summer, he swam in the lake near his home. In the fall, he hunted deer and elk.

Then it would snow, and he would go skiing. How long had it been since he sat in front of a fireplace in his stocking feet and simply read a good book?

And what had come over D.J.? For two years he had hoped to see in her something more than raw ambition and intellect, to discover at least one trait that would explain his attraction to her. Until recently, the two of them had cultivated an increasingly good relationship, but now she seemed distant. She always despised Bureau politics and sexism, yet she readily accepted being appointed Special Agent in Charge merely because of her gender.

D.J.'s area of expertise was limited to large cities in the southwestern region of the country. She had been assigned a case she could not possibly understand without his help, but had not once asked for his advice. Even worse, when he did offer his opinion, she continually dismissed it.

Anderson's thoughts drifted back to the fugitive, Justin Mabry. The man was financially destitute, recently divorced, and now had been driven from his home. What was he thinking tonight? How did it feel to be alone in the woods with his world crumbling to pieces?

Anderson pulled the photo of Mabry from his briefcase and stared at it. They were almost the same age, both of them divorced, and neither of their lives had turned out like they expected. They had a lot in common. Under different circumstances, they might have been friends.

Picking up the profile report with his other hand, Anderson looked back and forth from the photo to the profile. After several minutes, he carefully placed the sheets of paper back into his briefcase and snapped it closed.

"Justin Mabry, you deserve better than this. We both do."

Kelly suddenly remembered the T-shirt in her drawer and went to get it. As she passed the bathroom, the shower water stopped running. She paused and leaned toward the closed door.

"Justin, I have a shirt that might fit you if you want a clean one."

"Ah, yes," replied Justin. "I could use one if it fits."

"I think it will," said Kelly, as she scampered to her bedroom then quickly returned with the shirt. "It's so big I use it for a nightgown."

There was a moment of silence.

"It's not pink is it?"

Kelly swallowed hard and felt her pulse jump.

"Open the door and see."

"Hang on a second."

A few seconds later the knob turned and the door opened. Steam billowed out, the heat of it engulfing Kelly as she stood in the hallway. Mabry stood in front of her dressed only in his jeans. There was no doubt why he had a box full of trophies in his garage.

Before she could stop herself, Kelly glanced at the muscular chest that glistened with moisture and then at the powerful shoulders. Flushing slightly, she made eye contact, hoping he had not noticed her indiscretion.

Handing him the folded shirt, she said, "I won this at the Idaho state archery contest last year. All they had left was extra large."

Mabry took the T-shirt and unfolded it. Holding it to his chest he smiled.

"What?" asked Kelly, looking at his grin.

"I was just picturing you running around your apartment in an over-sized camouflage night shirt. But it should fit just fine."

"Nobody sees me in it but my cat," said Kelly, realizing she liked the thought of him wearing her shirt. "The news is on in a couple of minutes. We can see if they report anything different."

Closing the door, Mabry replied, "I'll be out in time. And thanks for the shirt."

Kelly adjusted the sound on the television. She sat down on the small couch. Unless he stood, they would watch the news side by side. The broadcast would, at the very least, be sobering for both of them. Yet, the last hour had been...pleasant.

The commercials were still running when Mabry walked into the living room. The humor in his eyes was gone.

"It doesn't seem real," he muttered staring at the TV. "None of this seems possible."

"I can't imagine how you must feel, Justin. But you have the moral high ground and no one can change that. Eventually, you will win this. One way or the other, you will win."

Taking his attention off the television, Mabry turned and looked at Anson. Her eyes met his.

"All I want is my son. I couldn't...I won't be separated from him for any length of time. I'll go to Canada first, if that's what it takes. But thank you. Your support means more to me than you can know. I needed to hear those things from someone other than myself."

Kelly only nodded and deliberately scooted to one side of the couch.

"Have a seat," she said, then pointed to the television. "Here it comes."

Sitting down on the couch, Mabry leaned forward with his elbows on his knees. Unconsciously, Kelly changed her position and did the same as both glared intently at the screen. Their shoulders brushed, then parted, only to come together again. This time they did not separate.

"Again, the top story tonight concerns the manhunt taking place in the small town of Clark Fork, Idaho. It was there, early this morning, that a federal officer attempting to enforce the new Federal Child Protection Law was brutally assaulted.

"First on the scene this morning with that exclusive report, and still at the site of the investigation, reporting live, is our own Steve Spence. Steve, what can you tell us this evening?"

"Well, Stanley, there have been some new developments since our six o'clock broadcast. We reported then that the suspect, Justin Mabry, was armed and dangerous but now it appears he is also an expert in martial arts, which makes him even more dangerous. The FBI, too, wants us to warn people not to pick up any hitchhikers in the area. They're concerned that the fugitive may try to escape in that manner and, of course, the driver and any passengers would be in danger.

"Also, there is every reason to believe that Mabry is a member of an ultra right-wing militia group. I am told by my sources that this information is based on evidence discovered inside the Mabry residence, the house that you can see just behind me."

"What precautions are being taken to protect the townspeople, Steve?"

"Well, Stanley, most of the people here are very fearful. They'll be locking their doors tonight and every night until this manhunt comes to an end.

"But tomorrow morning, I am told, tracking dogs will be delivered. The FBI says the dogs will be escorted by an Idaho State Police SWAT team."

"Is there any word on Mabry's son, Steve? Is there any concern for his safety?"

"Again, Stanley, the fate of that child is unknown tonight. All we can do for him, until tomorrow morning, is hope and pray.

"Until then, this is Steve Spence reporting live from Clark Fork, Idaho, Channel Six News."

"Thank you, Steve, for that exclusive report for Channel Six News. Now in other news tonight, do transsexuals have the right to teach sex education in our middle schools? Today in Spokane..."

Kelly pressed the MUTE button on the remote then sat back in the couch.

"I saw the punching bag, but where did they get that militia stuff? Do you know karate?"

Mabry thoughtfully cocked his head to one side.

"I've never even had boxing lessons. The bag was just to help me get through my divorce. And as far as the right-wing militia goes, that is absolute nonsense. I can't see how they could have come to that kind of conclusion, unless it was an intentional fabrication. But you'd think they would need some sort of hard evidence before leaking something like that to the media. If this ever goes to trial, that lie will be totally disproved."

"More important is the SWAT team they said was coming tomorrow. The FBI would have to have convinced the State Police you were armed and a real danger or they wouldn't be sent. Idaho's economy is suffering. Budgets for law enforcement are extremely tight. There's no doubt the FBI is repeatedly lying about that gun. Is there any chance at all you could be mistaken about them finding it?"

"They found it, all right," Mabry said as he stared at the silent TV screen. "It was just where I threw it, and they had metal detectors with them when they looked in the grass. What else would they have been looking for? I saw them bend over and pick something up."

"Then you're being set up," said Kelly. "And that includes the claims that you're in the militia and martial arts."

"Are you the only witness who saw me toss the gun?"

"Yes."

"If they ask you again, I think it's best you start second-guessing what you saw. So much of what they are doing hinges on that fact. They won't like being contradicted.

I don't want to worry about you getting hurt on my account."

Kelly Anson forced a smile. She patted Mabry on the back then let her hand rest there.

"I can take care of myself. You don't have to worry about me."

"Tomorrow morning I'll talk to my attorney. But the way things are shaping up, it looks like the best thing to do is get Billy and go north. I don't see that I have any other choice. The FBI and the media are making sure of that."

Kelly felt a knot growing in the pit of her stomach.

"How far north are you talking about?"

"Canada. We can hike that far in two or three days, a week at the most. It won't be hard to stay out of sight if we keep to the forests and use the logging roads."

Kelly took her hand down and laid it in her lap. She swallowed hard, but knew he was right.

"Until it's all worked out," said Kelly, trying to sound at ease, "I think you would be wise to go. But when you're settled...I want to come see you."

Still staring straight ahead, Mabry was silent for several seconds. Without moving, he said, "I would like that. I would like that very much."

Chapter Nine

June 18th
7:20 AM (PST)

Sandpoint Daily Bee
Front page, Column 8
President Signs Roadless Act, 43 Million Acres Closed

Police blotter, back page
Suspect Assaults Officer in Clark Fork

Spokesman Review
Page A1, Column 1
Governor's Conference highlights political polarization

Page A3, Column 6
Idaho Fugitive Sought in Child Protection Case

egan paced back and forth across the cramped motel room as the faint wail of a siren seeped through the walls. Anderson and Francis sat on the couch while Flin and Jones could be seen through the window standing next to an unmarked panel van.

Degan angrily looked at his watch for the second time in the last minute.

"Where the hell are those dogs?" he snapped. "That hick, Smitty, was supposed to call twenty minutes ago."

Francis was deep in thought, but Anderson merely observed. On this case, that activity regrettably comprised most of his responsibility. He had been watching Degan closely since seven o'clock that morning. His swagger had disappeared. Now his stride was short and his spine stiff.

Anderson guessed Degan had a short temper and chose his words carefully. "What time did the State Police call?"

Degan snorted with disgust.

"Five-thirty this morning."

"What reason did they give for refusing to send their SWAT team?"

Looking out the window at the van, Degan said, "They claimed that the Child Protection Act didn't provide funding for its enforcement. And they said the state's budget was already too much in the red."

Degan stopped to swear before continuing.

"You know as well as I do, that's a bunch of bull. It's just the governor's way of thumbing his nose at the president."

"What time did our SWAT team get in from Denver?"

"They landed in Sandpoint just after four a.m. and they've been in the van since then. Without the state SWAT team to help, I'll have to split our men and send some with the dogs and the others to observe the Jordans."

Before Anderson could ask another question, Degan's cell phone rang. A few seconds after answering it, he began to swear again. But this time his profanity was laced with rage.

"What is it?" asked Francis, startled by the outburst.

Degan shoved his phone in his pocket.

"The dogs aren't going to be here either. The owner claims they're sick. All three of his dogs are sick at the same time!"

Anderson's eyes narrowed but he said nothing. In Bonner County, tracking dogs were privately owned by volunteers of Search and Rescue. The governor of Idaho would be unlikely to exert much influence on an individual at that level, and it was extremely unlikely the dogs were sick. If, as Anderson suspected, pressure was put on the dog owner not to cooperate, it would have come from the locals. Someone had surmised that the county dogs would be requested and then successfully outmaneuvered the FBI. And one thing was certain. It was not Justin Mabry!

Looking at her watch, Francis said mechanically, "If Governor Fulton is uncooperative, we'll get the dogs from the Spokane area. They can be here by this afternoon.

"We'll immediately deploy our entire SWAT team to the Jordan residence as planned and bring in a second team later for the tracking. We need surveillance on Luke Jordan as soon as possible. Nothing in the operation is altered except the time table."

For the time being, Anderson chose to keep his suspicions to himself. If they asked for his opinion, then he would offer it.

"I would expect," he said coolly, "more reporters are going to start showing up. And since this was on the news last night, there'll be more traffic from people who are curious. It's going to get crowded around here."

"What's your point?" Degan asked.

"If the State Police aren't going to assist us, I guarantee you the county cops won't for long. They don't have the funds, either. We're going to have to bring in more federal personnel. You can forget local support from law enforcement. And the only motel in town may not have enough room."

Degan glanced expectantly at Francis.

"He has a point."

With only a moment of hesitation, Francis responded.

"We'll set up in the field behind the house and tape off all the land we need. That will become our operations headquarters. I'll have the Coeur d'Alene field office deal with the owner of the property. I'll bring in ten field agents to set it all up. That should be sufficient for now. If we need more, we can call in all we need. We won't be deterred by minor difficulties."

A knock at the door interrupted the operational planning. Degan opened the door to see a pot-bellied deputy sheriff lazily chewing a piece of gum.

"Now what?" demanded Degan.

The deputy chewed a few times before responding slowly, "I'm Officer Jacobson. I was watching your house this morning."

Jacobson deliberately paused before going on. It was clear to everyone the officer did not like the tone of Degan's voice.

Degan glared at Jacobson.

"And?"

Jacobson sniffed and rubbed his nose.

"The house just burned down."

"What?" barked Degan. "It caught on fire?"

"Yeah. It burned to the ground."

"How? Where were you?"

"Don't know how. But it was quick. By the time the fire department got there, the roof already caved in. You might as well tell Smitty to stay home. There's nothing to get a scent off of now."

"Well, be sure and thank the sheriff," Degan drawled sarcastically, "for sending one of his finest to watch the house!"

Jacobson smiled. Before Degan could shut the door in his face he said, "My pleasure."

The motel room was silent for half a minute before Francis looked to Anderson. "Coincidence?"

Anderson answered impulsively, but not honestly.

"Probably. You saw how old the house was. When the Evidence Team trashed the inside they must have loosened an old wire or left something on. An electrical short maybe."

Francis studied Anderson for a moment. Her eyes held unmasked doubt.

"What do you think, Agent Degan?" she asked with her eyes still on Anderson.

Degan started to pace.

"First, the state SWAT team, then Search and Rescue, and now what could be professional level arson...I say the governor is responsible. He was a ringleader in that Western Governors Conference they just had in Coeur d'Alene. Who else could have that kind of power?"

"That is a possibility," said Francis flatly. "But where does that leave us now?"

Anderson knew but he let Degan answer.

"We still have Luke Jordan," offered Degan. "If the kid is there, we don't need the house or the dogs. But we need SWAT in position ASAP. Mabry may be there now or he could have already taken his kid and run. But if he hasn't and the kid is there, we'll have the perfect trap to get Mabry when he shows up. And then get Jordan."

"Agreed," said Francis. "So we will still send them in as planned. But just in case that fire was not accidental, I'm bringing in twenty field agents. If someone in this town set that fire, they'll think twice about doing anything else."

"Good idea," echoed Degan. "I'll get right on it."

When Degan took out his phone and started pressing numbers, Anderson stole a glance at Francis. Her eyes flickered with intensity as her fingertips danced rapid-fire on the keyboard of her laptop. He was Supervisory Special Agent, yet neither she nor Degan had bothered to ask his opinion about the operations plan. In fact, the two of them agreed much too quickly on an OP that involved complex maneuvers and the use of SWAT personnel.

Or had the basic framework of the OP been predetermined from the start, even as far back as Boise when she spoke privately with Assistant Director Berger? And why had Francis apparently recognized Degan when they were first introduced at the motel? Did they know each other already? Or was it just name recognition, a name she was expecting to hear once she got to Clark Fork?

Anderson leaned forward and stood up. They were very possibly making a huge mistake. He should say something, warn them of what could happen, but his instincts told him to wait until he and Francis were alone.

Casually, Anderson went back into his room and brought up a satellite photo of the Jordans' property. It was heavily wooded and the house was on a high point of rock. There were a few small outbuildings and several trails visible through the forest, likely old logging skid trails.

Walking through a forest that dense was difficult and noisy. The easiest and most direct path to the Jordans' would be the logging trails. The SWAT team would surely use them until they got close enough to make visual contact with the house. And that would take them too close. They would have an unacceptably high probability of discovery. And if they were discovered by Luke Jordan, all hell would break loose. The mission should be scrubbed!

Glancing up as Francis came in, Anderson motioned for her to close the connecting door to the other room.

Francis raised an eyebrow but did as she was asked. As she laid her computer on the bed she sighed.

"What is it, John? What now?"

Anderson hesitated. Lowering his voice, he replied, "Off the record?"

Now raising both eyebrows in surprise, Francis pushed a strand of her red hair back behind her ear. It gave her a moment to think.

"Okay, off the record."

Keeping his voice low, Anderson's eyes were steady.

"I'll put it to you straight. I think you're out on a thin limb, D.J., and you're being set up."

Francis paused for a moment and stared blankly at Anderson.

"Set up for what, John?"

"You were told something in the meeting with Berger. You were given some directives. I have no doubt they were verbal, or if they were written, they were intentionally ambiguous. And I believe you and Degan are working together, using the same or similar directives. And I think you are about to do something illegal.

"If it goes wrong, they'll sacrifice you and Degan. Or they may just come after you, since you're Special Agent in Charge. The buck stops with you, D.J. Unless you have documented orders that point directly to a superior, you'll be held liable.

"You're a good agent and a friend. I don't want you hurt, but that's the least you'll get if you're involved in dirty politics. And everything about this case adds up to exactly that."

For several seconds the tall redhead said nothing, then a faint smile betrayed her stoic demeanor.

"Thanks for your concern, John. But I don't need anyone looking out for me. You should know that by now."

Anderson shook his head.

"I told you once how I felt about you, D.J., and that hasn't changed. So, like it or not, I *am* looking out for you. You're a brilliant woman but you have a blind spot. You don't know people. And you especially don't know the kind of people that live in North Idaho.

"In my estimation, you and Degan are making a grave mistake in sending in the SWAT team. The risk is enormous, to you… and to the president."

"John," said Francis, as she patted him on the head, "you worry too much. And you're too old-fashioned. We have every conceivable type of surveillance system available to us. We can, and do, eavesdrop on every potential dissident in this country. We know more about them than they know about themselves. And there's nothing unusual going on. If there was, we would know it long before it happened and easily put a stop to it. You know our capabilities, and the procedures we employ are flawless.

"I'll take the surveillance technology; you go with your 'people reading.' We'll see who gets the job done."

"Even if our systems are not picking up anything, whether or not our implants and snitches are hearing anything, *something* is brewing out there D.J. I know it. You could be headed for a disaster. And if there is one, you can count on a congressional investigation. They'll ask me to testify—and I will testify—as much as I would hate to do it."

Francis placed her hand on his shoulder and said, "You're a relic, John Anderson. Fifty years ago you would have been a great agent."

In the room adjacent to Agents Francis and Anderson, Phil Degan took the vocal surveillance receiver from his ear. The rest of the private conversation between the two agents, he would record and play back later. Now, he had to think. John Anderson could get in the way. He would have to be watched.

Kelly Anson awoke in the morning to the smell of coffee. As her eyes slowly opened, a smile crossed her face. Justin Mabry had found the coffee and helped himself. A man like him wouldn't have done that unless she had succeeded in making him feel comfortable and welcome in her apartment. And, naturally, he would have made enough coffee for two!

Throwing off her covers, Kelly quickly slipped into her robe. Looking into a mirror, she ran her fingers through her hair. A comb would have been better but it was too pretentious. She would act the same as if they were good friends...or knew each other better.

Walking down the hall, she saw Mabry pouring coffee into two cups.

"Heard you moving around in there," he said. "I make it strong, so you may have to water yours down."

Wiping the sleep from her eyes, Kelly grinned.

"The blacker the better. How did you sleep?"

Mabry handed Kelly her coffee.

"Good thanks," he said, but the darkness under his eyes said different. "The couch cushions worked just fine. Does the newspaper come this early?"

Kelly took a sip of steaming coffee and glanced at Mabry. She took a seat across from him.

"Not until eleven or so. But we could try the radio. They'll have news at eight o'clock."

"It'll have to do then," said Mabry. "After we hear what they have to report, I'll call my attorney and see what he knows."

"What if..." asked Kelly, but her question was interrupted by the ringing of her phone.

"Hello."

"Hi, Kelly. This is Jacobson. I thought you might want to know, the house that Mabry was living in burned to the ground this morning."

"It what?"

"I was there, out front. I didn't tell that asshole Fed, but I think it was arson. The house went so fast it had to be. Somebody wanted that house gone before the fire department could get there. My guess is that Mabry did it somehow, to cover his tracks. You know, so the dogs wouldn't have anything to get the scent off of."

"What time did this happen?"

"About seven-fifteen."

"That *is* strange. Thanks for calling. See you at the station."

Hanging up the phone, Kelly Anson looked quizzically at Mabry.

"That was Deputy Jacobson. He was assigned to watch your house. He said it caught on fire this morning at a quarter past seven and burned to the ground. And he thinks it was arson. Someone set it to burn very fast."

Mabry set his coffee cup down.

"Why would the FBI do that?" he asked bitterly. "They had no reason to destroy what little I had left."

Kelly took another sip of coffee as she pondered the possibilities.

"Jacobson thinks the fire was set...by you."

Mabry glared at Anson.

"Why?"

"Because, and this is very clever, it destroys everything you own. Now there's nothing left for the dogs to get your scent. You can't be tracked and I can't see the FBI doing that. Can you?"

There was a long silence before Mabry responded.

"But who would do something like that in broad daylight. Someone would surely see them."

"But they apparently weren't," muttered Kelly thoughtfully. "There are no fences around any of those houses, and the field behind the house is flat with no cover. There is no way anyone could have gotten close to the house without being seen...unless they went at night."

After taking a sip from his coffee cup, Mabry's eyes narrowed.

"That would mean a delay of at least three hours from the time they were at the house and the fire actually started."

"That would require some skill and training. Like someone with a military background or someone in the fire department."

"I think," said Mabry, "the bigger question is, why? Why would someone who doesn't know me do that?"

Kelly looked into Justin's eyes.

"Someone either wants to help you or someone, believing you're a child beater, wants to hurt you."

118

Mabry nodded.

"Well, either way, now I can get my backpack and go see Billy without worrying about dogs."

As Kelly turned on the radio, Mabry added, "That backpack and Billy are all I have now."

Lowering the volume on the radio, Anson said softly, "Justin, you also have me. And before you know it, there will be others like me. I know people, and I especially know country and small-town people. They're the same wherever you go, and the western part of our country is full of them. They value family and integrity. You were fighting for your rights as a father, and you are one of the most honorable men I have ever met. Mark my words, Justin. You're going to have a lot of supporters when the real story gets told. And they'll be more than willing to help you get back on your feet. Just be patient. You'll see."

Mabry raised his head and forced a smile. He gazed into Kelly Anson's eyes.

"Where were you thirteen years ago?"

Understanding the inference, Kelly smiled.

"I think I was in the eighth grade."

"A little too young to be getting married," admitted Mabry.

"Yes," answered Kelly, but after a purposeful pause she added, "I was, *then*."

A country-western love song played on the radio and both paused to listen to the words. For a moment Mabry turned his back to the world and allowed himself a few seconds to appreciate the simple beauty of Kelly's smile. She was an attractive woman but one void of vanity. She was courageous and strong, yet remained feminine and compassionate. And...there was an unmistakable radiance about her, a rare emanation only sensed at the dawning of meaningful relationships.

She had helped him, and in doing so, aided and abetted a fugitive. She had risked her career simply because she believed in him. Now, before anything further developed between them, he had to tell her. She deserved to know.

"I need to tell you something, Kelly," he said, glancing uncomfortably at the clock on the radio.

"What?"

Mabry sighed heavily.

"I don't want you to get the wrong idea about me. Maybe I'm not who…or what you think I am."

Kelly's eyes blinked imperceptibly. The tone of Mabry's voice had suddenly changed.

"Whatever you want to tell me, it's up to you."

"It's about my divorce. You already know I got custody of Billy. And you probably wondered why his mother didn't take him from me.

"It was basically because my wife didn't want him. She was willing to give Billy to me if I gave her everything else. If I hadn't agreed, California law would have given her custody. But it's more complicated than that, and it's that part I want you to know about."

"Go on if you want, Justin. If you think it's important."

"We were married my senior year of college. I had already gotten the attention of several pro baseball scouts, so the future looked bright. After graduating, I was drafted and played minor league ball for a couple of years before injuries got in the way and ended my chances of going to The Show. My chances to play in the majors were over.

"The pay during those years was terrible, but I enjoyed playing more than anything, and it didn't bother me. But Linda, my wife, was not happy. She had expected a big contract and lots of money with a big house. She didn't know about the minor league system when she married me. She thought it was going to be one big party.

"Anyway, while I was living in cheap motels, riding around the country in cramped buses and eating peanut butter and jelly three times a day, she was calling and complaining about the small apartment we had and the credit card bills she had run up, things like that. She wasn't expecting a hard life, even if it was for only a few years.

"As tough as those times were for me and all the other ball players, we loved the games. And the attention of the fans. Even the minor leagues attracted a lot of fans, and there were girls waiting after almost every game. Most of them, I just flirted with and then went back to the motels alone."

Kelly raised an eyebrow.

"Most?"

Mabry nodded and looked down at his hands.

"There was one. She was different from the rest. She wasn't at all like Linda. She was a lot like you. For a short time, we were…together."

"My wife had started using what she called 'sleeping pills' while I was away on my trips. But when she found out about what I had done, she was devastated. The pills weren't enough after that, and so she started using cocaine. Billy was one year old.

"After she found out, I said goodbye to the girl. I never saw her again. I did my best to make things right with Linda, but nothing worked. It was like trying to straighten out an angry snake. Nothing seemed to make her happy except the cocaine she got from her boss at work.

"My baseball career ended not long after that, and I wasn't on the road anymore. But no matter what I did or said, she kept on using. Several times, I thought she had stopped. She even went to abuse programs and support groups, but she never did quit. Finally, she had enough. She was tired of me arguing with her about her addiction and tired of living on a schoolteacher's salary. Before the divorce papers were finalized she moved in with her boss. He was the one that hired her divorce attorneys and paid their fees.

"At the divorce hearing, she convinced everyone that I was the cause of her turning to drugs, that my indiscretion was at the root of all her problems. And, truthfully, I couldn't bring myself to say she was wrong. I had done all I could for ten years, but the damage I caused was irreversible. It was my fault."

Kelly's smile had disappeared, but she wore no frown of condemnation, nor did her eyes hold a scornful glare.

"How did your wife find out?" she asked evenly.

"I don't know what made her suspicious, but one day she just asked. I look back on it now and think how simple it would have been to just lie. But I wasn't willing to add that to what I had already done. So I told her the truth, hoping she would forgive me."

"Do you wish now that you would have lied?"

"No," said Mabry. "I broke one Commandment. I wasn't going to make it two out of ten. Telling the truth is easy if there is no cost. I failed one test and I wasn't going to fail my upbringing again, no matter what."

"That was a high price to pay," said Kelly.

"It was mine to pay. I was a young fool and I paid the penalty. Or at least I thought I had paid. But it seems that I'm not done paying yet. It never seems to end."

There was a long silence before Kelly spoke again.

"Ten years is a long time to live with a drug abuser. I've only been in law enforcement for a few years, but I've seen and heard a lot about addiction in that time. And I know several people that go to Al-Anon to get support and find help. Living with a spouse that's a user beats them down so much they get to a point they can't handle the pressure alone.

"They all tell the same story, Justin, whether it's drugs or alcohol. The users always try to blame someone else for their habit. Always. And all too often it's the spouse that isn't using who gets the blame. The users become experts in keeping old wounds from healing. There is always something in the relationship that the addict can use to make the spouse feel guilty. Some, like you, even start to believe it's their fault."

Kelly slowly put her hand out and placed it on Mabry's.

"You made a bad mistake, Justin. Everyone makes them. You did the right thing to tell the truth, and you did the right thing to try and save the marriage. But you aren't to blame for your wife using drugs. That is always the choice of the user. We all make choices when tragedy strikes. Most of us deal with it and go on with our lives without the use of chemical crutches. We just tough it out."

"I know," agreed Mabry, softly. "At least, I know that intellectually. But the other part of it-- that's not so easy. So I wanted you to know what I had done back then. I wanted to be the one to tell you."

Kelly took her hand from Mabry's. Placing both her forearms on the counter, she leaned towards him.

"Why?"

Mabry looked up. He tried to smile.

"When I was playing ball," he began slowly, "one thing I could do was recognize a pitch almost as soon as it left the pitcher's hand. I could pick up the angle, the spin of the ball, the thumb position of the pitcher and other things I can't really explain. It was like I could feel the pitch coming at me. And I could spot a really sweet pitch in less time than it takes to blink your eye. A batter didn't see one very often, but you were always waiting for one to come along, especially hoping for one in a tight game.

"Anyway, some things, not many, but some, I sense very quickly. You are a rarity, Kelly. I knew it the first time we talked. You are also someone I would very much like to know better, someone I would hope to see more of in the future...if I have one."

Kelly Anson smiled and blushed.

"Funny you should mention that," said Kelly sheepishly. "I felt the same way about you. In fact, I started thinking about you right after we met in the coffee shop."

"Well, with all that's happened in the last few hours, I kind of had a feeling, or at least I hoped I was reading things right. And if it was going to make a difference, if it was going to affect your opinion of me, I wanted everything out in the open so you wouldn't waste your time. That's why I wanted you to know about my past."

"That's what it is, Justin," Kelly said sincerely. "It's in the past. It was ten years ago. Now, let's both put it behind us and not mention it again. The here and now is more than enough for you to worry about."

For a moment, Mabry said nothing, then he began to smile. But this time he did not have to force it.

"When Billy is old enough to start thinking about finding a good woman to settle down with, I'm going to tell him to scout out the local eighth graders."

Kelly laughed.

"I don't think that would be a good idea. Even in Clark Fork."

There was a comfortable pause, a warm silence broken only by the faint tunes of another country-western song. Mabry shrugged.

"What about you?" he asked, changing the subject before the news came on. "How is it that you became a deputy sheriff?"

Kelly tucked a blond strand of hair behind her ear then toyed with her coffee cup. "My father was a deputy for thirty years. But, like he says now, that was back when cops were the good guys.

"Anyway, I was always a bit of a tomboy growing up. I was in sports and always liked that kind of fast-paced excitement. Back in high school, I thought law enforcement would be a good career. So, I went to a community college, played fast-pitch softball and studied enough law to get an AA degree.

"I worked as a dispatcher for three years before I made the force. This is my first year. I'm still a rookie."

Mabry briefly listened for the news before asking another question.

"What position did you play in softball?"

"Pitcher."

Leaning slightly forward, Mabry looked over the counter at Anson. He smiled out of one corner of his mouth.

"You're kind of puny for a pitcher, aren't you?"

Kelly sat up straight and filled her lungs.

"I'm five-four, mister," she said. "What do you mean, puny?"

Chuckling softly, Mabry said, "I won't ask how much you weigh, but I will ask how fast you pitched."

Kelly snorted as if insulted, then grinned.

"One hundred and eight and sixty-two."

Impressed, Mabry sat back in his chair.

"Sixty-two miles per hour! That's division-one speed. You could have played NCAA ball."

Kelly Anson frowned.

"A lot of times I wished I had, but life is full of forks in the road and most of them are one-way paths. You have to walk the one you choose."

The music stopped and voices could be heard on the radio. Kelly reached across the counter and quickly turned up the volume.

"...102.4 FM news brought to you courtesy of Bonner County Feed and Fence. Topping our news this morning is a report from the Bonner County Sheriff's department, where it appears that a resident of Clark Fork assaulted a newly appointed federal officer and is now the object of an FBI manhunt.

"According to a department spokesman, Agent Jeff Brown was knocked unconscious by the angry parent when Brown attempted to remove a child from the home of Justin Mabry. Mabry and his twelve-year-old son then escaped from the local sheriff's deputies and fled into the nearby mountains.

"According to FBI reports, Mabry may have connections with various militia groups and other extremist organizations. He is also believed to have set his house on fire early this morning in order to cover evidence that could have been used against him in a court of law.

"Mabry is said to be desperate and should be considered armed and dangerous. Anyone with any information regarding the case should direct their calls to the FBI field office in Coeur d'Alene.

"Agent Brown is an officer of the new Child Protection Service that President Stark signed into law just two days ago. He could not be reached for comment.

"However, FBI spokeswoman, Agent D.J. Francis, said early this morning in a phone interview that additional agents are being brought in to aid in the search and that they already have several promising leads. She also said she expects the operation to be completed in a couple of days.

"In more local news, county commissioners rejected a proposal to increase property taxes because the...."

Kelly turned off the radio.

"Well, I didn't think they would accuse you of torching your house, but I guess it does make some sense."

"It does," agreed Mabry, then said grimly, "But I still can't see how they came up with the connection to militias and extremists."

Kelly walked to the coffee pot and refreshed both their cups.

"Maybe it was something in the house. A magazine subscription or a book on the subject. The FBI doesn't need much to justify its conclusions. It could have been something in your background check that they're twisting to their advantage. With the computer files they have now, they can access records on your entire life in seconds."

"It's the same as yesterday, with the gun," said Mabry. "For some reason they're systematically putting out false information about me. They're building a straw man. At least, someone is. Someone at or near the top.

"The agents that are being brought in now will only know what they're told. They would have no reason to doubt anything that was just said on the news. The person they'll be hunting down is a child abuser, a martial artist, an arsonist, and an armed paramilitary extremist. They're likely to shoot first and ask questions later."

Kelly handed Mabry her phone.

"You'd better call your lawyer."

Taking the phone, Mabry stood up and pressed the numbers.

"I can already guess what he's going to tell me," he said, then pushed the speakerphone button and laid the phone on the counter. "You might as well hear this."

"Hello."

"Bruce, this is Justin. What have you learned?"

"Nothing specific, Justin, but enough. I'll be brief. They want you very badly. My suspicion is that the USAG is getting his instructions from Washington. They're saying there's no chance of a plea bargain. You are, unfortunately, to be made an example of, to...I don't know exactly.

"But Justin, I think this may be coming from someone close to the president, if not the president herself. The fact that it got on the Spokane news so fast and then spread nationally was the worst thing that could have happened. It has all sorts of political implications now. The president is counting on a lot of public support because of her Child Protection policy. If she gets embarrassed publicly, by you, she could lose her second-term election.

"And there are other political undercurrents in Boise that may be dragging you down with them. It's no secret how the governor feels about President Stark. And he could even be picked as a vice-presidential candidate for the next election.

"If the governor can use this case against her, my sources tell me he will. You're caught between the frying pan and the fire, Justin. And right now, and I can't believe I'm saying this, but my advice is to get Billy and go to Canada until you can get a decent trial.

"And another thing, very quickly. The FBI will be checking my phone records and they'll come up with the number you're calling from. You'll need to have a reason that phone called this one, so be thinking of that. It won't take them long.

"Justin, I'm very sorry this happened. After all you went through, all the abuse you took from your wife. I don't know how you did it, but I do know why. And now to be accused of child abuse—it's an irony from hell!"

"Thanks, Bruce," replied Mabry calmly. "If the FBI asks you any questions about me, or if anyone else does, go ahead and tell it all. There's no need to protect Billy now, and it could eventually help."

"It would be a pleasure, Justin. You are an honorable man, the last of a breed.

Goodbye and God's speed."

"Thanks, Bruce. Goodbye."

For several seconds, Mabry looked at the phone as it lay on the counter, then casually picked up his coffee as if nothing had happened.

"I better enjoy this while I can. It could be a few days before I get any more."

Kelly was speechless. She could not take her eyes off the man that had just received such devastating news. His breathing was steady. There was no agitation, no anger. He seemed strangely relaxed.

"I hope you'll come see me when I get settled," he said easily. "I don't think I'll get back this way for quite a while. I'll understand if you can't come. But I can't begin to tell you how much I enjoyed last night and this morning."

With both hands, Kelly pushed her hair behind her ears and stared at the sudden change in Mabry. He was smiling at her as if they had just met.

"You are welcome," she said, but her response was only a reflex. "What are you going to do now?"

Mabry took a sip of coffee and set his cup down.

"If I can get a ride back to Clark Fork, I'll get my pack and my boy, and we'll go on the adventure of a life time. We'll hike and camp all the way to Canada. We'll simply start over…for the second time."

"That simple?" asked Kelly. "You can do that?"

"People all over the world have been doing it for thousands of years. Like you said, life has a lot of forks in the road. Now there's no reason for me to be standing in front of one of them, wondering which way to go. That's usually the tough part. Now, I have no choice but to go north. So, I go north and tackle whatever I have to. It really is simple if a person's not afraid of hard work or the unknown. That's what makes it an adventure. Life is an adventure if it's lived right. There are always sacrifices along the way."

"This is crazy," said Kelly, rubbing her forehead with both hands and trying to think. "The sooner we get back to Clark Fork, the better. You should be on your way as fast as you can. And stay in the woods and off the logging roads, at least the newer ones. They'll send out helicopters.

"When you get across the border, try to get to Creston. My father has a friend there, a retired Mountie named McDougal, Ian McDougal. Find out where he lives, and go there if you can. Just mention my name. He's known me since I was a baby and he's old school. He'll take you in. Call when you get there, please. So I won't worry. If you have trouble before you cross…"

Mabry stood up and walked around the kitchen counter. Taking her by the shoulders, he gently kissed her.

"Will you come visit me?" he asked. "It will make leaving a whole lot easier if I know you'll come."

Looking up into Mabry's steady eyes, Kelly's face reflected a mosaic of mixed emotions.

"That, you can count on, Justin. I will come."

Chapter Ten

June 18th
9:12 AM (PST)

I n a truck stop café just outside Caldwell, Idaho, a man with a black snake tattooed on his forearm sat at a crowded counter and finished his breakfast. He sipped his coffee, and along with the others in the small diner, listened to the radio broadcast. As the commercial ended, the room became unusually quiet.

"Welcome back to the program, folks. If you've just joined us, we're talking about the manhunt that's taking shape up in Idaho, and the potential impact this could have on the upcoming election year.

"We're going back to the phones, and let me tell you, folks, the lines are busier than I've seen them in a long time. Most of our calls have been from the West, but now we have one from right here in New York City.

"Hello, Nancy. This is Hank Sprey. What's on your mind?"

"Hello, Hank. I was calling about that thing up in North Idaho. We didn't get the story here on TV but I did read about it in the *Times*. It sounds to me like the president's new law is doing just what she said it would do. That father up there has no right to treat his son that way. He shouldn't be allowed near that boy without some sort of supervision. That is, after he gets out of prison."

"Well, folks, here we go again. Nancy, why do you believe this man is an unfit father?"

"It was all there in the *Times* this morning. It said he was one of those right-wing nuts, one of those militia-type people, and that he beats his child. He attacked a social worker that was trying to rescue the boy and then took the poor boy into the mountains like some sort of animal."

"Okay, Nancy, let's look at what you just said. And believe me, you won't be the only one to react the way you have. But let's take a close look.

"You concluded the man was an unfit father, a child beater, a militia nut, an animal and finally a man that battered a social worker. You got your opinion from the way the *Times* worded its report, but the only thing that is factual in the whole article— and I read it this morning, too—is the fact that he decked the guy who tried to take his child from him.

"Everything else you said, everything else you now believe about the man, came from a highly prejudicial reporter and editor. I guarantee you that if you go back and re-read that article you'll see I'm right. And that is what I've been talking about for the last hour. The mainstream media is controlled by the leftist of this country.

"Thanks for the call, Nancy.

"Now, folks, it hasn't hit the news yet, but my sources tell me that early this morning, Justin Mabry's house burned to the ground. And that fire destroyed any evidence inside that might have been relevant to the case against Mabry. It eliminated any evidence that could possibly prove or disprove the allegations made against him in the *Times*. I find that very convenient, folks.

"It is my humble opinion that the FBI is pursuing a man that was merely protecting his child from a government-sponsored kidnapping.

"And I ask my self one question. Why? Why is so much attention being given to this relatively minor incident? Why did this story make all the west coast TV news broadcasts the very night it happened?

"And you people on the East Coast, take my word for it, you are going to see this story tonight. This is destined to have national attention. And, again, I ask myself, why?

"The answer, folks, is obvious. This is a political machination that has its origins in our nation's capitol. Someone is hoping to get a lot of political mileage out of this. The more attention this story gets, the more other important issues are ignored. This looks like a diversion, a vote-getting charade to show that the president is tough on crime and a protector of abused children. This is an image-making opportunity. It's all smoke and mirrors, folks, and Mabry is just a pawn in the game.

"This Child Protection Act got most of its support from the coastal states. It was very unpopular in the fly-over states where American values are still cherished. No, this whole thing is designed to bolster her support in the beach-nut states where the family unit is the weakest link in their fragmenting chain of civilization.

"Those people are so far to the left, so socialistic, that they think of children as a national resource, as property of the federal government.

Like everything else the lefties touch, they've now screwed up their own families so much, they want the government to step in and bail them out. They're more than willing to relinquish the authority to raise their children to the likes of Madeline Stark.

"I told you yesterday, folks, this Act was going to be big. But I even surprised myself just how right I was. This legislation is going to be bigger than the Super Bowl, and I have a gut feeling that Mr. Mabry may have just kicked off.

"This is Hank Sprey. I'll be back after another short break."

The tattooed trucker put his coffee down. Taking a cigarette from his shirt pocket, he spoke to no one in particular.

"Think I'll take a drive up to that Clark Fork town. I like the sound of this Bree character."

A trucker to the left of the tattoo grunted.

"I used to haul logs up there until Ma-*damn* President shut down all the mills. I got an empty trailer and no work, thanks to that bitch. I think I'll tag along."

From a table behind the two men, another spoke up. He wore a cowboy hat and worn-out boots.

"Thanks to Stark's environmentalist bastards, I can't haul enough cows to make a decent wage. The ranchers are going broke all over. Count me in."

Three truckers came to their feet. Their eyes were hard but each wore a smile. The cowboy grinned and stuck a toothpick between his teeth.

"Looks like we got us a convoy."

Mabry sat in the passenger seat of Kelly's truck wearing a pair of sunglasses and a baseball hat, both borrowed. He held a newspaper close to his face until they were well out of Sandpoint and heading east. When they crossed the Pack River Bridge, Mabry lowered the paper.

"When we get near the bridge at Lightning Creek, I think I better duck down out of sight."

Kelly glanced at Mabry's minimal disguise.

"Good idea," she agreed, but raised her eyebrows and smiled. "But the cab is kind of small. You'll have to lay your head in my lap."

Mabry shook his head then returned her smile.

"You are amazing."

Kelly huffed.

"Why?"

"You always seem to be in a good mood. Don't you worry about what could happen if we... if you get caught helping me?"

"Ah...no!" Kelly chuckled. "I'm not stupid. If we get stopped, if we're discovered—which we won't be—my story will be that you just turned yourself in to me. I'm the only one you trusted enough to surrender to, and I'm just now delivering you to the authorities."

Mabry lowered his sunglasses and looked over at Kelly Anson.

"When did you come up with that?"

"Yesterday. Before I asked you to get in my truck."

"Oh," said Mabry thoughtfully. "You did?"

Kelly shook her head.

"I was born at night, but it wasn't last night."

Mabry slid the glasses back against the bridge of his nose.

"Clever. I'm glad you're on *my* side."

Kelly smiled, showing a dimple in her cheek.

"So am I."

Too quickly, another mile was behind them and Mabry's mood began to darken. He had sacrificed everything for his son and had no regrets, but in doing so, he had lost a part of himself. There was an emptiness inside him, a void that sometimes turned into a quagmire of despair. He smiled often for the sake of his son, but the burden was a heavy one and at times overwhelming.

The last few hours with Kelly had kindled a spark of hope that he could, with her help, finally climb out of the collapsed ruins of his life. But now, he was being subjected to another dose of tyrannical injustice. He would have to retreat even further than before, and in doing so, leave behind the most unusual woman he had ever met.

"Did you mean what you said earlier?" asked Mabry, his tone suddenly somber.

Glancing at Mabry, Kelly said, "I'm pretty sure I did. But what exactly are you referring to?"

Mabry was silent for several seconds. He had no right to ask her. He was being a fool.

"I'm sorry. I was just...it's nothing."

Kelly waited for him to continue. Finally, as they rounded the last curve before Clark Fork, she spoke instead.

"I meant everything, Justin. Everything. Especially the part about wanting to see you again. And I *will* come see you, if you still want me to. I hope that's what you wanted to know.

"I know I've been very forward and sometimes I say too much, but I just tend to know things. That's all. And I know how I feel. Even though it sounds stupid to come out and say it, I know you and I like each other. So, there. Stupid or not, I said it."

Behind his sunglasses, Mabry closed his eyes and inhaled slowly. He wanted to cherish the moment, to remember what it felt like to be with her. When he opened his eyes again he did not smile. Staring at the road ahead, he swallowed hard.

"Thank you, Kelly," he said. "Thank you."

Kelly looked at Mabry. As they approached the Lightning Creek Bridge, she gently took his hand.

"You're welcome," she said tenderly. "You can do this, Justin. You can make it."

Mabry clinched his teeth and smiled.

"You've just made it a lot easier," he replied, then slid down in the seat of the pick up and rested his head on Kelly's lap. "I could get used to this."

Placing both hands on the steering wheel, Kelly raised one eyebrow and suppressed a giggle.

"You'll have time for that later, mister. First, you and Billy have to take a sixty- mile hike through the Rocky Mountains."

"A walk in the park," whispered Mabry. "The three of us will be having lunch in Canada four days from now. But you'll have to buy."

"Deal," said Kelly as she slowed to twenty-five and passed Main Street. "The town looks quiet. Nothing unusual. I think some of the Feds are in the motel up ahead. I'll go past it and let you out on the south side of the mountain. When you look down towards town, you'll see Mosquito Creek. Follow it, and you'll hit the drainage ditch near where I picked you up. From there you can get your bearings and find your way back to where you left your pack."

A few seconds went by and Kelly spoke again.

"There's the motel. I see two, no, three government plates. No one near the cars. That's good. We're going over Mosquito Creek now, but stay down until I check the traffic. When I say go, go fast. I won't be able to see up the highway too far, and the cars come fast. You'll have a good ten seconds to get into the forest. And call me as soon as you can."

"Yes, ma'am. I'll borrow a cell phone from the first red-coated Border Mountie I run into."

Kelly pulled to the side of the highway.

"Funny boy," she retorted, letting a car and then a pickup go by. "Now, go!"

Mabry sat up quickly, turned Kelly's head and kissed her.

"Worth the risk," he said as he jerked the door open. With amazing quickness and agility, he was across the road and out of sight with seconds to spare. No cars came by. It was quiet.

With the morning sun coming through the front windshield, Anson felt its warmth on her skin. She could see no sign of Justin, but still felt his kiss. Touching her fingers to her lips she said, "You shouldn't have taken the time to kiss me goodbye."

She smiled.

"But I knew you would."

Mabry tediously maneuvered his way around walls of rock and through thick stands of timber that grew at the base of Antelope Mountain. Patches of tangled brush and countless windfalls blocked any direct path to where he had cached his backpack, but compared to the last twenty-four hours, the rough terrain felt like a welcome mat.

His son was waiting just a few miles away in a remote cabin. After they were reunited, a three- or four-day hike would put them across the Canadian border where they would hopefully find refuge. There, in relative safety, he could respond to the charges against him and eventually clear his name. And in Canada, he would once again be able to see Kelly Anson.

As Mabry worked his way through the forest, he wore a smile. Kelly was tender and compassionate. Yet with a blend of determination and optimism uniquely woven into her femininity, she was also a woman of uncommon courage. She was one to stand beside a man and add her own strength to his.

Pausing in a small clearing, Mabry felt the sun's heat on his shoulders and inhaled the clean mountain air. He had almost forgotten what it felt like to be free of grief, and what exhilaration there was in simply being alive. It was the first morning of a fresh start and a good day for a hike. As he walked across the meadow, he realized that each step he took not only brought him closer to his son, it also took him toward another country and a new life. For the first time in ten years, the future looked bright.

A few minutes beyond the clearing, Mabry spotted the hollow Ponderosa log where he had hidden his pack the day before. He paused in the shade of a fir tree and studied the landscape around him. Nothing was out of place.

Taking a few steps closer, he stopped again. To his left, the trees were thin enough to see Mosquito Creek below him and Clark Fork less than half a mile in the distance. Just beyond the creek was a hayfield of perhaps one hundred acres, and connected to it by a gravel road was the pasture just north of where his house once stood. Four vehicles were parked in the hayfield, and what appeared to be a tepee was being erected nearby. In the northern field, Mabry could make out three vehicles, a large square tent and several people in dark clothing.

Going to the log, he removed a few pieces of bark and then hoisted the pack to his shoulders. Everything he needed for the trek to Canada was on his back and the weight of the load was reassuring. He and Billy would lack for nothing. They had plenty of food and enough equipment to make them comfortable along the way. It would be no different than other camping trips they had gone on together.

Keeping to the security of the trees, Mabry continued north for half an hour before approaching the western fork of Lightning Creek Road. Before crossing it, he listened for several minutes. When he was certain no one was near and no cars were coming up or down the mountain road, he sprinted across the gravel and quickly disappeared back into the forest on the other side.

After climbing for several more minutes, Mabry sat down on a ledge of rock to rest. Below him he could easily see the north fork of Lightning Creek Road as it wound its way up around the base of the mountain. He would parallel that road as he hiked above it and easily stay out of sight. Eventually, he would find the turnoff that led to Jordan's cabin. In an hour, or two at the most, he and Billy would be together again.

Behind the ruins of Mabry's house, three government cars and one unmarked van were parked in the center of an empty field. Next to the vehicles was a large military style tent. Ten men were inside, dressed in full camouflage and body armor. Eight sat in metal folding chairs. Francis stood behind them in a black business suit. In front of the group, Degan and Anderson stood next to a framed aerial photo of Luke Jordan's cabin. Surrounding the aerial shot were photos of Luke Jordan and each member of his family. Anderson began passing out eight-by-ten photos of Justin and Billy Mabry while Degan continued the briefing.

"The psychological profile on Luke Jordan says he's willing to die for his beliefs. And he will not hesitate to fire on you or return fire if fired upon. Do not approach him unless he has been designated as a target, or it is absolutely necessary.

"His wife Rebecca is not considered dangerous but is as much a fanatic as her husband and wields a dominant influence on family decisions. She, too, is willing to die if she feels it's necessary.

"So far the profile we have on Mabry is sketchy, but we know he's armed and dangerous. He may be emotionally unstable due to his present situation. In an uncontrolled encounter, he could be very unpredictable. Use extreme caution here, men.

"Our mission is the covert surveillance of the Jordan residence. We are to ascertain the number of occupants and their identities. We also want to assess defensive fortifications, if any, and basic defensive capability of the cabin and outbuildings. This is information gathering *only*. We have no Operation Plan until we complete the surveillance. Avoid contact with anyone. Standard rules of operation are in effect should we have complications."

Turning to the aerial photo, Degan pointed to a structure.

"This is the Jordan cabin. These buildings next to the cabin are a woodshed and a chicken coop. As you can see, the cabin sits on a rise. They have the high ground but the woods surrounding the house are very thick. They offer excellent cover, but our snitches tell us they're hell to walk through.

"To avoid making excess noise, we'll be taking these two parallel logging roads here and here. We will continue on these trails until we reach this one that intersects right here. This will be called the 'intersection' and it is where Agent Flin and I will be stationed.

"Agent Anderson and his sniper will then go to the south, the other three sniper-observer teams will go to the north, west, and east sides of the cabin. If you are discovered, retreat immediately. But be prepared to return fire. Any questions?"

A seated FBI agent spoke up.

"Are the twelve-year-old males to be considered targets?"

Degan paused and glanced at the back of the tent. Seeing Francis nod, he answered, "Any armed person, male or female, is considered a legitimate target if you are fired upon. Any more questions?"

Anderson's eyes narrowed as he looked at Francis but he said nothing. The group was silent. They were ready. This was a routine mission.

Picking up his AR-15 rifle, Degan commanded, "Alright, then. Let's load up."

As Anderson and the other agents filed past him, Degan waited for Francis. As she came near, he asked, "Anything else?"

Francis stopped close to Degan and lowered her voice.

"You *did* read Mabry's Alternative Psychological Profile, the one that came in this morning? Did you see who they compared him to?"

Degan snickered derisively then swore.

"Pure fiction," he said and waved a disregarding hand. "He's never even been in the military. It sounds to me like Anderson had something to do with this new version of Mabry. There was no need to mention it in the briefing. It's just a bunch of bull!"

Francis' eyes hardened.

"Just the same, I don't want any mistakes."

Grabbing his helmet off a chair, Degan sneered.

"The first profile is the right one. This Mabry's a nobody. He didn't even fight back in his divorce. His wife took him to the cleaners, and all he did was whimper about his kid. He's just a damned Boy Scout."

While Degan strapped on his helmet, Francis gazed at a discarded photo of Mabry that lay at her feet. It was smeared with a dirty boot print, but something about the eyes of the man still disturbed her.

"We can't afford any screw-ups, Degan," she said uneasily. "There's too much at stake."

On the fourteenth floor of the Independence News building, Thomas Rico stared out his window at the New York City skyline. For several seconds, he thoughtfully tugged at the corner of his graying mustache before returning to his desk. He depressed an intercom button.

"Pete, do you have any more on that guy?"

"No, sir," came the reply. "I've hacked into all the usual computers and still no more than before. There doesn't seem to be anything else."

"Okay, Pete. But keep looking," replied Rico. "If you find anything, anything at all, let me know immediately."

Rico sat down in his chair and leaned back with his hands clasped behind his head. Looking at the wall in front of him, he muttered to himself.

"School teacher, militia, baseball player, divorced man who gets custody of his son then abuses him, never owned a gun, armed and dangerous. Nothing fits. Nothing fits at all."

Leaning forward again, Rico picked up his phone and hit the speed dial.

"Sam, this is Rico. Get the crew ready. Book us to Spokane or as close to this Clark Fork, Idaho as you can get a jet. I've got a hunch this is where our next story's going to be. I want us there by five o'clock tonight, local time. I want to do a telephone link for our ten o'clock broadcast for the East Coast. Thanks."

Hanging up the phone, the reporter studied the downloaded photos and reports scattered across his desk.

"So, Justin Mabry, who *are* you? And what's the real story out there? Why do they want you so badly? And which one of the FBI's profiles is the right one? Or can you just switch from one to the other whenever you choose? If you can do that, and things up in North Idaho get out of hand, God help us."

The driver of the unmarked FBI van wore plain clothes and drove slowly on the winding gravel road. Whenever an occasional oncoming car or truck would pass, he gave a friendly wave and received one in return. Inside, ten agents checked their assault weapons and smeared their faces with brown and green paint.

Three miles from the field tent command post, the van pulled to the side of the road. When the dust settled, the driver got out with a camera around his neck pretending to take pictures of Lightning Creek to the west. After waving to the driver of a flatbed pickup truck and certain no other traffic was near, he went to the side of the van and slapped it twice with the palm of his hand.

The rear doors flew open and in a matter of seconds, ten men scrambled up a twelve-foot embankment, then disappeared into the brush and trees.

Looking up and down Lightning Creek Road, the driver raised a radio transmitter.

"You're clear."

Working his way up a steep slope, Degan paused.

"Roger that," he said, then tripped over a snag and swore as he hit the ground.

Anderson saw Degan fall, and a smile came to his face. This wasn't the big city, and these men weren't raised in the Rocky Mountains. They would learn soon enough that moving quickly and silently at the same time was impossible in the thick woods. Their only hope in not prematurely announcing their arrival to the Jordans was to find the logging trails and stay on them. Their chances of being able to surround the cabin without being discovered were slim. But it wasn't his plan. He wasn't in charge of the mission, and they had not asked for his input. When they failed, they would come to him for advice. And then, perhaps, he could defuse the entire affair.

After several minutes of searching and whispered swearing, an agent stumbled onto one of the two logging trails; a few minutes later, the second was located. The observer-sniper teams divided into two groups and started up the mountain. They were expecting a simple hike to the Intersection trail less than a mile away.

On the aerial photos, the logging trails looked like narrow roads, but there was no bare dirt to be found. These were old skid trails, littered with fallen limbs and knee-high alders. The agents moved more easily on them and with less noise than before, but the snapping of dry twigs under heavy boot soles could still be heard eighty yards in any direction.

As a half-dozen FBI agents clumsily maneuvered up one of the trails, a green hand emerged from what appeared to be a dark pile of brush huddled at the base of a jack pine. In the hand was a camouflaged radio.

138

"This is Moose," whispered a man with green and brown paint streaked across his face. "I count six Feds coming your way. Over."

When the woods were quiet and still, the green-faced man pocketed his radio and stood up. An AK-47 rifle rested in his hand and on the shoulder of his camouflage jacket was a small red, white and blue patch that read "Idaho Militia." He wore knee-high moccasins.

A few hundred yards ahead of the hidden militia men, Degan led his men further up the skid-trail. As they neared where they thought the intersecting trail would be, the assault teams began to slow their pace. Five minutes later they found the trail just as the aerial photo had shown it.

Bringing his men to a halt, he motioned for Anderson and two other agents to go to the south. On his radio headset, he ordered the other agents to take their assigned positions. From the intersection, nothing but dense forest was visible. The cabin was no more than two hundred yards ahead, and as yet, there was no sign they had been discovered.

Degan took a step closer to Agent Flin.

"I thought we would be able to see the parallel trail from here," he whispered. "The trees are too thick so just find a place up ahead and take a position in the woods. I'll cover our back trail here."

Flin nodded and started carefully forward. A faint gust of wind blew then the air was still. A moment later another gust stirred the tops of the trees, slightly bending the branches.

Luke Jordan's radio was on the kitchen table where Rebecca was sewing a patch-work blanket. It had been quiet all morning and when the baby cried, she went to get her. She was gone only a few seconds, but it was long enough to miss the abbreviated alert message.

Jordan was splitting wood by the woodshed. His Ml Garand rifle was leaning against a nearby tree, but after years of working with heavy logging equipment and chainsaws, his hearing was slightly damaged. At first, he did not hear the dog barking.

Matt had seen the family dog lift his head and sniff the incoming breeze, and then watched with interest as Buster trotted down an old skid-trail with his hackles up. When the dog started barking, Matt ran to his room and took his twelve-gauge double-barreled shotgun from the wall and scooped up a handful of shells. Jamming them into his pockets, Matt threw open the back door of the cabin and called to his friend, "Come on, Billy! Buster's found a deer or maybe even a bear!"

As the two boys ran past the chicken coop and down toward the intersecting trail, Matt opened the twelve-gauge and shoved in two rounds of double aught buck shot. After running full speed for half a minute, the pair of twelve-year-olds slowed to a walk, then stopped and listened to the pitch of the dog's barks.

"Got to be a bear," whispered Matt, "or maybe even a cougar. Buster don't bark like that unless it's something big."

Wide-eyed, Billy nodded and let Matt take the lead. The jack pine on either side of the narrow skid-trail were dense and alders grew in patches where there was enough moisture. Buster was barking less than fifty yards away, but in the deep woods he could not be seen.

Abruptly, the dog let out a high-pitched yelp. The barking ceased. A moment later Buster exploded through the brush twenty paces in front of the boys. The dog turned towards them, took one leap and fell on his face. His tongue dropped out of his mouth and his side was drenched in blood. After one last breath, there was no more.

Before Matt could react to the death of his dog, the crushing of twigs and snapping of branches filled the forest from the direction Buster had come. Something large, something that had killed his dog was charging towards them from the darkness of the forest.

Matt saw the alders shake and the heavy branches bend as something huge fought its way through the brush. Raising his shotgun, he fired the left barrel then immediately emptied the right into the creature.

"Run," he screamed, as he turned and bumped into Billy. "Run!"

The boys started running, but they had only taken a few steps when a rifle cracked behind them and Matt suddenly spun and hit the ground.

Billy slid to a stop and went back for Matt as another rifle, this time in front of them, exploded four deafening rounds in rapid succession.

As Billy helped Matt to his feet, the boys looked up to see Jordan covering their retreat.

"Get home, boys!" he bellowed. "Get home, now!"

Matt's elbow was shattered and bloody. He held his arm to his stomach with his good hand, and with Billy at his side, the boys ran for home.

"We're going, Dad," yelled Matt. "I'm hit!"

Jordan roared at the top of his lungs and fired off two more 30-06 slugs into the brush. Then the forest went completely silent.

Degan lay behind a log. He had managed to get off one shot before Jordan suddenly appeared and opened fire on his position. For several seconds he kept his head down and did not move. He knew he had hit one of the boys as they ran away. Finally, he spoke in a soft but urgent tone.

"What the hell just happened?" he said into his helmet transmitter. "Flin, what's your status?"

Flin did not answer.

"All units, hold your positions," ordered Degan, then, after making certain the trail was clear, started cautiously in the direction of the dead dog.

Flin's rifle was equipped with a silencer. There was no way to know if he had opened fire or returned fire. But one thing was certain. Flin was not answering his radio.

Mabry had to traverse the western side of the mountains keeping Lightning Creek Road in sight. He knew no other way to find the Jordans' house than to follow the same route he used when he had driven Matt home from baseball practice. He was turning up the road that branched off Lightning Creek when he heard the shooting and then the bloodcurdling yell of what had to be a very large man.

Mabry had no idea how far up the road the Jordans' lived, but he was certain they had no neighbors nearby. The shots had to have involved the Jordans, and the sound of the man's yell raised the hairs on the back of his neck. Billy was up there, too!

After taking a quick look up and down the road, Mabry stepped out onto it, and with much less caution, hurried towards his son.

Degan stood over the body of Agent Flin. He had fallen out of the brush onto the trail and lay sprawled in the grass. Buckshot had hit him in the leg then in the side of the neck. He was facedown in a pool of blood that glistened in the midday sun. A few feet away lay the dog he had been ordered to silence.

Calmly, Degan hung his assault rifle on his shoulder then took out a pair of close-fitting black leather gloves and slid his hands inside. Rolling the body over, he then placed a stone under Flin's head to prop it up at a steep angle. Reaching into his inside vest pocket, Degan removed a plastic bag. From it, he took a small snub-nosed pistol.

Backing up two steps, Degan aimed and fired the pistol into the dead agent's temple. Methodically folding the plastic bag, he replaced it in his pocket then tossed the pistol onto the trail in plain view. When Degan turned to leave the crime scene he had created, he came face to face with Anderson's glaring eyes.

Hearing the nearby report of the pistol, Mabry turned off the road and headed blindly towards it. Cutting through the maze of trees as quietly as possible, he soon found another trail and started to climb. There was no sign of the Jordans' cabin, but the shot had to have been fired just ahead of him. Rounding a sharp turn, Mabry stopped suddenly.

One man, in what appeared to be military combat gear, lay on the trail a few steps ahead of him. Just beyond the prone figure, with his back to Mabry, stood another man. He had an assault rifle slung over his shoulder and was looking intently at someone or something just off the trail.

Catching movement out of the corner of his eye, Anderson looked down the trail beyond Degan and immediately recognized the intruder as Justin Mabry.

Seeing Anderson's eyes shift and then the surprise on his face, Degan crouched and spun in one movement. Immediately catching sight of Mabry, he jerked the rifle from his shoulder and fired recklessly at the fugitive as his target ducked into the forest and ran through the trees.

"Mabry sighted," he barked excitedly into his mouth radio. "Heading east from the Intersection. Teams three and four pursue. Teams one and two split up and surround the cabin. Mabry killed Flin. Repeat. Mabry killed Flin. All persons with or near a weapon are now legitimate targets. You have a green light."

Anderson gritted his teeth. An FBI agent was dead. Most likely, he had been shot by Luke Jordan, but thanks to Degan and what appeared to be a planted pistol, Mabry was certainly going to be blamed. More were going to die now. And there was nothing he could do to stop it.

Mabry had no idea in what direction he was running. The shots had narrowly missed him, one cutting two holes in the belly of the camouflage T-shirt Kelly had given him. Another bullet felt like it hit his backpack. There was no doubt they had tried to kill him.

For ten minutes he ran, stumbled, jumped and tripped. When he finally stopped to catch his breath, he could hear them close behind. Sometimes it was the crashing sound of sticks breaking. Sometimes it was the sound of voices, but he had not lost them.

He was tempted to discard his pack, but it was vital if he and Billy were to escape to Canada. And he knew he needed to make less noise as he moved through the woods, but he could not afford to slow down. If he were to survive, he had to put distance between himself and those who were after him. When he gained enough, he could slow down and then, perhaps, silently sneak away.

Taking a deep breath, Mabry continued across the face of the mountain, gaining in altitude. If they weren't in good shape, he would eventually outlast them.

For hours the chase went on. The pack grew heavier by the minute and Mabry considered trying to cache it. But he had no idea where he was and knew he could never find it again. He had to keep going with the near crippling load on his back.

It was late afternoon when his legs began to spasm. He was dehydrated and near collapse when he turned up a narrow ravine, hoping to find a shallow cave in the rocks to hide in. When he came to a solid rock wall, he was finished.

He gasped for air then heard a twig snap on the ridge above him to his right. Then leaves crunched above him to his left. He was trapped. He tried to sit down but his legs folded and he fell on his back unable to move. It was over.

Four men in full camouflage slid down the ravine. Their faces were streaked with green and brown sweat. On their backs they packed military weapons. They wore green berets.

"Finally!" bellowed one of the soldiers. "And look at the pack he's been carrying!"

Another man took a plastic canteen from his belt. After wiping the sweat from his forehead, he took a drink and let out a loud sigh of relief.

"Help him up, Coyote," he said, then reached in his pocket and took out a small white pill.

Two men took the pack off Mabry's back, then pulled him into a sitting position. The man with the canteen squatted down next to him. He offered the white pill to Mabry. "Salt tablet. You lost plenty and we want you able to walk back on your own."

Reluctantly, Mabry accepted the salt, then the canteen. As he took a second drink of water to wash down the tablet, he looked more closely at those surrounding him. They were smiling.

The squatting man grinned.

"You can call me Bobcat," he said, his eyes curiously studying Mabry's face. "That fella behind you is Coyote. This big one here is Bear, and that skinny one is Wolf. We're Idaho Militia."

Mabry blinked hard, trying to cleanse the stinging sweat from his eyes. These men tried to kill him then had run him to ground. Now they had captured him. There would be no Canada, no Billy...no Kelly.

"Why did you try to kill me?"

The smiles on the men's faces melted away.

"What do you mean?" asked Bobcat. "Who tried to kill you?"

"One of you," said Mabry pointing to his T-shirt, "shot these holes in my shirt. I think you'll find another one in my pack."

Bobcat took hold of Mabry's shirt and looked closely at it.

"That's a two-twenty-three caliber hole," he snarled. "That would be the FBI. We use AKs and they make a bigger hole. *We* didn't shoot at you. It was the Feds that were trying to drill you."

His mind was still foggy, but Mabry was growing curious.

"Then what will happen when they get here?"

All four men began to laugh.

"They got all tied up," howled Bear. "They won't be making it."

"Yeah," agreed Wolf. "They're kind of...chained to their work, you might say."

When the men stopped laughing, Mabry was ready with another question.

"What happened to my son? There was a lot of shooting. Is he all right?"

Again the smudged faces grew somber.

144

"We don't know," answered Wolf. "We came after you because Luke asked us to watch out for you. We haven't used radios all afternoon. They could triangulate in on us if we used them."

Mabry's mind sharpened.

"Luke? Do you mean Luke Jordan?" he asked incredulously.

"That's right," agreed Coyote proudly. "We're on your side. That's about all we can tell you. We are an independent cell."

"My side? You're on *my* side?"

"Yep."

"Then what happened to the FBI? I know they came after me…at least at first."

"When you're able, we'll take you to them," said Bobcat. "Another cell has them stashed away. They don't have any electronic devices on them anymore, but they were in contact with their commander long enough to know what happened early on. If you can get them to talk, they can tell you what all they know."

June 18th
5:18 PM (PST)

Officer Anson started work at 4:00 PM and had been on duty for less than half an hour when she got the call from dispatch to head for Clark Fork. An Agent Anderson of the FBI was requesting that the sheriff's department investigate a gathering of vehicles near their command center. He had asked for her specifically.

In a hayfield adjacent to the one cordoned off by the FBI, and nearly half a mile away, Anson discovered the cluster of vehicles to be the beginnings of an old-fashioned rendezvous encampment. The participants of the event were dressed in period clothing of the 1830s, duplicating in intricate detail the garments worn by traders and fur trappers of the Rocky Mountains.

They would be camping in tepees and trading homemade crafts. At night they planned to have dances and play fiddles. Hundreds of people were expected but the organizer of the encampment assured Anson that due to the heavy turnout, no flintlock rifles were to be allowed. It was to be a quiet and orderly rendezvous.

The FBI wanted the field cleared, but the sheriff of Bonner County decided against it. After all, the Feds had already taped off forty acres for themselves and they had insulted his deputies at the Mabry residence and at the motel. That was enough for the sheriff.

Anson was on her way to the FBI tent headquarters to report the sheriff's decision when her patrol car was stopped at the edge of the field by an armed agent. Dressed in black fatigues and dark sunglasses, he held up his right hand. In his left was an assault rifle, and on his head was a black cap with FBI printed in white.

Kelly Anson rolled down her window.

"I have a message for Agent Anderson."

"You'll have to wait here," said the agent gruffly, then relayed his own message via his headset microphone.

The command tent was one hundred and fifty yards away. A dust-covered white van was close by and three other cars were parked near it. While Anson waited, two trucks were waved around her. Border Patrol was painted on the doors.

Rolling down the passenger window, Anson heard a helicopter to the north. Leaning over and looking out the window, she caught a glimpse of the dark chopper as it rose above a distant ridge.

Her heart began to beat faster. They were searching the same area that Justin was now in. Had they somehow deduced where Billy had gone, or was the FBI merely making a general surveillance? If the Feds were hoping to find Mabry from the air, they would soon realize it was impossible. Once they viewed the impenetrable canopy of trees from above, the federal government would quickly get an education in what poor forestry management had created.

When Anson looked back, she saw a lone figure, also in black fatigues, coming towards her from the tents. On his hip was a pistol but he carried no assault weapon. His eyes were not hidden by sunglasses, nor did he wear a hat.

Opening the door of her patrol car and ignoring the armed guard, Kelly Anson stepped out. She wasn't going to be talked down to, especially on her own turf.

The federal agent stopped a few steps in front of her, purposefully beyond handshaking distance.

"I'm Special Agent, Anderson."

Anson did not introduce herself.

"The sheriff doesn't believe those people pose a threat to your operation. They are over half a mile away and only having a Rendezvous. That's when people…"

"I know what it is," Anderson interrupted brusquely. Glancing at the guard, he added, "I want to take a look for myself. Can you take me over there, Officer?"

Anderson's facial expression did not match his tone of voice, and Anson noticed his eyes lacked the impudence she had seen in Degan's the day before. For a federal agent, maybe this one wasn't so bad.

"If you want," replied Anson evenly, "but the sheriff won't change his mind."

Anson started the car and appraised Anderson. He in turn stared at her for several seconds.

Putting the car in reverse, Anson backed up then turned from the field onto Lightning Creek Road. She drove a short distance to the intersection with Main Street, stopped and looked to the west.

A news van with its antennae up was positioned along the side of the road that bordered the FBI field. A second van, from a competing Spokane television station, was parking just ahead of it. A crowd of people on the opposite side of the road watched as the news crews set up.

Anderson glanced at the vans then back at Anson. This time he extended his hand.

"Let me start over. I'm John Anderson."

After a moment's hesitation, Anson shook his hand.

"Kelly Anson," she said blandly, and then waited for Anderson to speak again.

"Have you been a deputy long?" asked Anderson.

Anderson's tone was genuine, so Anson took no offense to the question.

"I'm a rookie."

As Anson turned off of Main onto a side street, Anderson nodded approvingly. "You were the one on scene when Mabry assaulted Agent Brown?"

"Yes"

"Had you ever met him before? Had any run-ins with him at all?"

Driving slowly towards the rendezvous, Anson answered cautiously.

"Just the day before, we met in a donut shop. We spoke for maybe a minute."

"What impression did you get of him?"

Anson paused to think and chose her words carefully.

"He seemed close to his son. Very close, I would say."

Anderson considered Anson's response before he asked another question.

"Do you know Luke Jordan?"

Anson took her foot off the gas pedal and looked at Anderson.

"Yes. Is that what the helicopter was doing? If you're flying over his place he won't like it. In fact, a lot of people up that way won't like it."

Anderson sighed.

"It's too late to do anything about it now."

Anson tried to remain calm, to sound professional.

"Do you think Mabry is at the Jordans'?"

The silence from Anderson was enough of an answer. The helicopter was circling in the immediate vicinity of the Jordans' cabin and Billy had gone off in that same direction. And the Jordans had a twelve-year-old. It all added up.

Anson pulled off the road and stopped the car. Staring straight ahead, she spoke impulsively, passionately.

"No!"

It was only one word, but how she expressed it told Anderson the rookie cop could be trusted.

"I'm afraid it's already started," said Anderson, "and it's going to blow wide open. It's our fault, too. The Jordan family is barricaded in their cabin and the Bureau is to blame."

Anson's eyes were wide.

"What's happened?"

Pointing towards the rendezvous, Anderson frowned.

"We better keep moving. They may be watching."

For a moment, Anson stopped breathing. She bit her lip then eased her foot off the brake and continued on.

"First of all, Mabry's being set up," Anderson said bluntly. "And I believe the directive to do so is coming from D.C. headquarters. I don't know how high up it goes."

Anson's palms began to sweat.

"Why are you telling me this?"

Without hesitation, Anderson answered, "I checked your file. That's why I asked the county to send you specifically. And after meeting you I think I can trust you. I'm taking a chance, but I go with my instincts when it comes to judging people's character.

"And right now, the Bureau is a tangled maze of corruption. I can't take a chance on going to the wrong person. I'm already wondering if I'll get out of this with my job...or my life. As far as I know, I'm alone on this.

"And since you've been seen with me, you'll have to be careful who you talk to as well. You may be the only one who will know the truth after the evidence disappears into a pile of ashes and a knot of shredded documents.

"We don't have much time, and I don't know all the details yet, but an agent was killed today in a gun battle near the Jordans' cabin. It won't be reported to the media until this evening, but they will be told Mabry had a part in the agent's death. He did not.

"A bullet will be found in the body, a bullet fired from a pistol with Mabry's prints on it, but the agent was shot after he was dead. I can't prove it but Degan fired that shot then planted the gun near the body to frame Mabry."

Visually stunned by the news, Anson parked behind a pickup truck loaded with long lodge poles.

"This is terrible. It's much worse than we thought."

Anderson looked at Anson. She had said "we."

"Worse than you thought? What is?"

"I saw Justin throw the gun away. I even told Degan where he would find it. And then Degan tried to tell me I was mistaken. But all along I knew he was never armed and dangerous like they said. It was a lie they used to make Justin look like a criminal."

Anderson covered his surprise that Anson used Mabry's first name, as well as the news about Degan and the pistol.

"So, you already knew for sure about the gun?"

"Yes. There was never any doubt about it."

Anderson nodded.

"Good. That will help. But there's more."

"What?"

"Mabry is not at the cabin. He's on the run somewhere up in the mountains as best we can tell. The FBI spokesman will report to the media that he's holed up in the cabin with the Jordans. It's just another lie."

"Then they haven't caught him yet? Justin, I mean?"

"We don't think so. But headquarters hasn't heard from the four agents that went after him in several hours. In fact, all their tracking devices, radios, GPS systems—none of them are operable. We don't have a clue where our men are or what happened out there."

Anson's brow wrinkled with confusion.

"All he had with him was a backpack full of camping gear and he threw the pistol away. I can't see how Justin could have done anything to those agents."

"It could simply be equipment malfunction," said Anderson. "But Justin Mabry may be capable of more, much more, than anyone suspects."

Anson thought for a moment.

"I don't get it. Why are they saying he's at the cabin?"

"My superiors want to tie him to the Jordans. I can only guess what they have in mind."

Anderson opened the car door and motioned with his head.

"Let's take a walk through the crowd. I want a closer look at these people."

As Anson and Anderson worked their way around dozens of parked cars and trucks, they spotted another cluster of vehicles several hundred yards farther out in the field.

"Who are they?" asked Anderson.

Looking them over carefully, Anson answered, "Looks like a different bunch. They weren't there when I came by earlier. They must have come in fairly fast."

Anderson squinted.

"They appear to be raising some sort of a pole."

Anson pointed to her right as the two continued walking closer to the hub of the camp.

"A pole like that one?"

Encircled by a dozen tepees and a handful of canvas lean-tos, a fifteen-foot wooden pole stood perfectly erect. Fresh dirt was mounded around its base. Hanging from its tip, and waving in a gentle afternoon breeze was a red, white and blue 1830s flag of the United States with twenty-six white stars.

Anderson stopped to stare up at the flag.

"Patriotic, aren't they?"

"Most of the people around here are," replied Anson. "It's not considered naïve or simplistic to raise a flag in North Idaho. We're proud to be Americans."

"I realize that. I was born in Wallace and raised in Coeur d'Alene. That's one reason the FBI hired me. They wanted someone that knew the people from the grass roots on up.

"Officer Anson, do you notice anything about these people, the men especially, that strikes you as unusual?"

Anson glanced around the busy camp. All of the men were dressed in buckskins, fur hats and moccasins. Around their waists, wide leather belts supported leather pouches, knives and hatchets. And almost every one of the period frontiersmen wore a beard or mustache.

"It looks like a typical Rendezvous to me. I've seen several."

"So have I. But the men in this one are a little different."

Anson scanned the men of the encampment again.

"I don't see anything. What is it?"

"There isn't a big belly out there. They are *fit*. These guys look like real mountain men."

Anson took a moment and looked one more time.

"You're right."

Anderson took a step forward.

"Let's walk through their camp a bit. I want to see how they react to us, especially to me and my black fatigues."

As the officers emerged from the parking area and started for the tents, heads began to turn. But, without exception, the campers paused for only a few seconds, then went back to whatever they had been doing. When the pair entered the courtyard created by the circle of teepees, they were universally met with smiles and friendly salutations.

Walking casually through the heart of the camp, Anderson returned their smiles and nods, but under his breath he said, "Ever see so many friendly faces?"

"Uh-uh," Anson uttered, through an artificial smile of her own.

Anderson offered a courteous wave to a woman dressed in a buckskin dress that was beautifully decorated with beads and elk teeth.

"It's like a bunch of hungry cats watching two canaries."

After exiting the far end of the growing community of tents, Anderson and Anson circled back to the patrol car.

"What do you make of that?" Anson said, her hand on the door latch. "I haven't been on the force very long, but long enough to know that people generally aren't that glad to see cops at a social event. We're treated more like wet blankets."

"Exactly what I was thinking. Now let's go check out that other group that came in. Unless I miss my guess, they won't have anything to do with this Rendezvous."

With no road between the teepees and the distant gathering, Anson drove slowly, making certain not to bottom out on half-buried rocks or tree stumps. When the car finally came near the parked trucks and cars, Anderson spoke suddenly.

"That's close enough. Let's go back. I know who they are."

Without questioning Anderson's request, Anson started a gradual turn back to where they had originally entered the field. He did not offer an explanation until they turned back onto the gravel road.

"Those were skinheads. White supremacists. Luke Jordan is a separatist, not a racist, and the two groups rarely associate. The supremacists would definitely be sympathetic to Jordan *if* they knew what happened this morning. But nothing about Luke Jordan has hit the news yet."

"What are you getting at?"

"We've had Jordan under surveillance for years. We monitor every communication system he has and, as yet, he hasn't contacted anyone since the shooting. So the Aryans can't know anything about Jordan. The only reason they are here is to offer support to Justin Mabry. They're responding to what they've heard on the radio or seen on TV."

"Why? Mabry's not a racist. Or a separatist either."

"Yeah, I know," said Anderson grimly. "Mabry is as neutral as they come. And having the Aryans here worries me."

Anson shrugged.

"Why would that worry you? There are only a dozen or so of them."

"I have my reasons," answered Anderson, uneasily. "A lot of it has to do with Mabry's updated psychological profile that we received this morning. Our first report indicated he was just a little above the average guy on the street. But now I'm not so sure. People could rally behind someone like Mabry. All types of people. Aryans, separatists, loggers, farmers, ranchers, you name it. There are tens of thousands of very agitated people throughout the entire Inland West. He could be a lightning rod for the widespread discontent. And whether Mabry knows it or not, he has enormous potential as a leader."

"The more support he gets, the better," said Anson. "As far as I'm concerned, he needs all the help he can get."

When Anson came to Lightning Creek Road, she stopped and watched two more federal cars and another Border Patrol truck go by.

"You're bringing in more men?"

"At this point, only federal personnel. My partner, or at least she used to be my partner, is Special Agent in Charge. When Flin was killed and the Jordans barricaded themselves in their cabin, she asked Governor Fulton to declare an 'Extreme Emergency' so we could bring in the National Guard and their tanks. That's the way it's usually done when this happens.

"As you may know, Fulton is a leader among the western governors and there's no love lost between them and President Stark. So far the governor has refused to declare the emergency. He views this operation as entirely federal and wants us to back off. It's getting political now. Or maybe it always has been.

"But after all that's happened, if we back down now, the president gets embarrassed. It's her Child Protection Act that started everything. It's face-saving time and an election is coming up. So we're flying in more SWAT teams from back east and bringing in all the Border Patrol we can spare. At this point, all we can call on are federal employees. We don't have access to any heavy equipment if the Guard doesn't come in. Even your sheriff isn't cooperating."

"How many people do you think you need?" asked Anson indignantly. "The Jordans are only one family on a remote hilltop."

Anderson took a deep breath and let it out slowly.

"A federal agent has been killed. Now, they let loose the dogs and make a show of massive force and historically, it always ends in a slaughter. We always win…no matter what."

"Can't you do anything to stop it? You aren't one of them. You're not like most of them."

"I'm doing my best to keep the lid on, but I'm on the outside. From the beginning, I was reduced to an advisory role. And they have consistently ignored my advice.

"I don't know what you can do with all I've told you, but I had to tell someone outside the Bureau. I believe this mess could go as high as the assistant director, maybe even higher. I can't chance talking to the wrong person in Washington until I know whom I can trust.

"If for any reason I'm...silenced, maybe you can testify if it comes to that. And now you'll have to be extra careful as well. They'll know we at least had some contact and that will arouse suspicion."

Anson eased onto Lightning Creek Road. In a few seconds they would be stopped by the armed guard.

"Is there anything I can do for you?" asked Anson.

Shaking his head, Anderson stared icily at the guard.

"I'm in too deep. And besides, it may not be too late to stop this. But part of me wants it to blow up in their faces. Then there would at least be a token investigation, maybe even a purge. This country can't survive without the Bureau, but like everything else on the planet, it's only made of flesh and bone. It's corruptible."

Stopping next to the guard, Anson spoke softly.

"You're a good cop, Anderson. Good luck."

"I'm going to need it," muttered Anderson, then thoughtfully rubbed his forehead. "We're all going to need it. The love of a devoted parent for a child is one of nature's most powerful forces. Interfering with that bond will rip apart the fabric of our civilization. Split an atom and you get a nuclear explosion. If the government comes between a man like Justin Mabry and his son, I'm very much afraid we can expect nothing less."

Chapter Eleven

June 18th
6:23 PM (PST)

M att Jordan's arm had swollen to twice its normal size. For the first two hours after being shot in his left elbow, the twelve-year-old boy vomited repeatedly from the unbearable pain. Now, to help ward off infection, his mother was pouring peroxide on the wound and giving him cayenne pepper capsules.

The family, along with Billy Mabry, gathered in the kitchen. Billy was on his knees next to Matt, wiping his forehead with a damp cloth. The baby lay on a blanket underneath the kitchen table and Luke Jordan sat leaning against a wall with a rifle in his lap.

An electronically amplified voice had been bombarding the small cabin for over an hour. The same message, with minor variations, was monotonously repeated. Sometimes the speaker sounded sincere, sometimes callous and sarcastic.

"Come on out, Luke, and give yourself up. Think of your family, Luke. Do you want them to die? Their blood will be on your hands."

Rebecca smiled at her husband.

"Trust in Yahweh. He will deliver us from evil."

Jordan nodded.

"Amen."

"I didn't know it was a man. I thought it was a bear."

Matt had said this before but the confession seemed to ease his pain.

"You did nothing wrong, son," assured Luke. "If that agent would have seen you with the shotgun in your hands he would have killed you, and maybe even Billy. They came on our property carrying weapons. They came to get us. You did the right thing under the circumstances. God knows your heart, Matt."

For a moment the megaphone was silent.

"We have to have the patience of Job," declared Rebecca, then began to pray on her knees. Her words were soft and could barely be heard over the labored breathing of her wounded son.

As the droning mechanical voice of the FBI negotiator resumed, Jordan caught sight of a small shadow flickering across the drawn curtains of a kitchen window. Hearing the slapping of wing tips, he looked up expectantly. A few seconds later, a pigeon walked out on the rafters above his head.

Jordan crawled across the floor on his hands and knees until he was underneath the bird. Slowly standing to his full height, he reached over his head and gently grasped the pigeon. After removing a small tube from its leg, he returned the homing pigeon to its perch and crawled back to the wall.

He unrolled the tiny scroll and read it with a determined smile.

"They are praying for Matt. Our people are coming, Rebecca. From everywhere.

They have heard the call. We will be delivered!"

With her hands clasped together and her eyes closed, Rebecca continued to pray. "Praise the name of Yahweh Almighty and his son Yashua."

On a narrow blacktop road, just behind the remains of Mabry's home, a third Spokane news truck pulled in behind its two competitors whose dishes and telescoping towers were already at full mast.

Kelly Anson and Gill Jacobson were assigned to crowd control by the county sheriff. If the feds wanted more than two officers, they would have to provide them. The sheriff told them in no uncertain terms that Bonner County, unlike the federal government, had budget restraints.

The two officers stood to one side as dozens of curious onlookers gathered around the news trucks. Dogs barked at the news crews as they prepared to broadcast, while children swerved in and out of the crowd on bicycles. People were laughing and the smell of barbecues flavored the air. The sun was getting low in the western sky.

"Nothing like this ever happened in little old Clark Fork," chuckled Jacobson. "Look at them. It's like the circus came to town."

Anson looked out across the field at the FBI tents. Several more were going up and portable generators were already humming. Two men were unrolling electrical cable towards the news trucks.

"That's what this is, Gill. It's a circus."

"You sure can pick them, Kelly," taunted Jacobson. "All this caused by that guy you thought was so cute. He'd have made quite a catch if you could have landed him.

"Or should I say, arrested him."

Ignoring Jacobson, Anson said, "This is serious, Gill. This is not going to end well."

The section of barbed wire that Mabry crossed over the day before had been cut down. The break in the fence was designed to allow the reporters, news crews and spectators to enter into a fifty-by-fifty-foot square bordered on three sides by a thin but ominous yellow plastic ribbon. It was to be the official media outlet.

Jacobson watched the agents hook up the microphone.

"It won't be long and the whole town will be here. Look at all these rubber-neckers."

"It won't be just the town," muttered Anson. "This will attract people from all over. Even if the sheriff calls out the whole force, what good are a couple of dozen deputies going to do when thousands of people start showing up in and around town?"

Jacobson was suddenly grim. A frown began to form on his round face.

"We better hope that doesn't happen."

Someone tapped on the microphone and blew into it.

"Testing, testing," crackled through two speakers at the base of the stand.

Three TV crews and two newspaper reporters rushed into the square and flocked in front of the man who was about to speak. Behind the reporters, some of the more adventurous townspeople drifted in but most stayed along the fence. A few of the spectators were dressed in buckskins. Two had shaved heads.

An agent stepped to the microphone as one last reporter with a gray mustache maneuvered his way through the crowd and up to where the other reporters clustered elbow to elbow.

"This morning, while in hot pursuit of the fugitive Justin Mabry," announced the spokesperson, "Special Agent Craig Flin was fatally wounded in a brief firefight near the home of Luke Jordan, a longtime resident of this area.

"In this encounter, Jordan was observed firing repeatedly at federal agents. However, it is believed Agent Flin was killed by Mabry and not Jordan.

157

"Jordan and Mabry have apparently barricaded themselves inside the Jordan cabin along with Jordan's family and Billy Mabry, the twelve-year-old son of Justin Mabry.

"The FBI is calling on Governor Fulton to declare this an Extreme Emergency."

The FBI spokesperson paused and questions erupted. The first reporter called on was Steve Spence.

"Why do you believe it was Mabry that killed Agent Flin?"

"A pistol stolen yesterday by Mabry was found at the scene and his fingerprints were on it. Forensics is presently examining the evidence, but a preliminary investigation strongly implicates Mabry as the one that fired the shot that killed Agent Flin."

"Why would you want the governor to declare an emergency?" blurted another reporter. "Can't the FBI handle the situation?"

"It is unconstitutional for the federal government to use the military against citizens of this country. That is referred to as the Posse Comitatus rule. But a declaration of Extreme Emergency by the governor of any state allows the FBI to bring in the National Guard. We can then use those troops and their armored equipment to deal with the situation.

"The area immediately surrounding the Jordan cabin is believed to be booby-trapped and the cabin walls reinforced. We believe armored vehicles are in order. And we feel that a show of force is the surest way to bring this siege to a peaceful conclusion."

An angry voice from the crowd yelled out, "How do you know the place is booby-trapped? You've never been up there!"

A round of grumbling went through the townspeople, but the speaker was unmoved.

"The FBI has had Luke Jordan listed as a Sensitive/Significant person of interest for many years, and he has been under surveillance for quite some time. Our Threat Source Profile on Jordan lists him as a dangerous political extremist with ties to the White Supremacist movement."

Another rumble rippled through the crowd, but this one carried a less belligerent ring. Now, there was a mixed tone of surprise and doubt.

Another reporter barked out a question.

"What is the connection between Mabry and Jordan? Are they part of the same extremist group?"

"At present, we are unaware of any previous interaction between the two men, but Justin Mabry's house was found to contain several clandestine magazines and antigovernment pamphlets. We have these in our possession as evidence.

"Should we find evidence of interaction between the two men, Mabry will also be charged with conspiring to cause an armed confrontation with the government. But at present he is still considered armed and dangerous and wanted for the murder of a federal agent."

Holding out her own microphone, a female reporter asked, "Who are the agents in charge of this siege?"

"Agent Francis is Special Agent in Charge. Assistant Special Agent in Charge is Agent Degan. Agent Degan is also the on-site commander and will be heading the Hostage Rescue Team."

The woman fired a quick follow-up question.

"Why is the HRT involved?"

"Billy Mabry is considered a ward of the state. His presence in the Jordan cabin constitutes kidnapping, just as it does when an estranged father takes a child from its mother. Billy Mabry is classified as a hostage."

The last reporter, who had arrived late then forced his way through townspeople to the news platform, raised his hand.

Behind the FBI microphone, the spokesperson's face flushed red as he recognized a troublemaker. There was a slight pause, then he reluctantly pointed to the raised hand and acknowledged the man from New York's Independence News Network.

"Mr. Rico."

The news teams in front of Thomas Rico turned in unison to see the investigative reporter and national celebrity looking steely-eyed and square-jawed.

"I have a question and then a follow-up," said Rico.

"Go ahead."

"Did anyone actually witness Justin Mabry shooting Agent Flin?"

Without hesitation, the answer was offered.

"Yes. Agent Degan was present. And your follow-up question?"

"Are we then to understand the same man that was appointed Assistant Special Agent in Charge, *and* On-Site Commander, *and* head of the Hostage Rescue Team is also the same man that witnessed the alleged shooting of Agent Flin?"

The spokesperson stiffened.

"That is correct."

Several more questions were asked simultaneously, but the FBI spokesperson raised his hand.

"No further questions," he said, then turned abruptly away from the microphone.

As he walked back towards the tents, several agents with weapons dangling from their shoulders positioned themselves along the yellow tape. With blank faces and eyes shielded by reflective lenses, they planted their feet and stared defiantly into the crowd of townspeople.

Anson shook her head.

"What a load of bull!" she snarled. "One lie after the other."

"Who knows?" countered Jacobson. "But it's none of our business. We're just county cops trying to make a living. Like the sheriff said, it's their ballgame. Let's take a walk-through. I think these townspeople ought to at least know we're here."

Walking slowly past the TV crews as they prepared to link with their home stations, Anson spoke briefly with men and women she knew, as did Jacobson. When she neared Thomas Rico she watched him closely. He was shorter than she thought and a little older looking. He was a maverick but had a reputation for being unbiased and courageous. His very presence would cause the FBI to stop and think.

Steve Spence and most of the other reporters were in the pockets of politicians and more than happy to spin the news in whatever direction they preferred. Unlike Rico, they were in the business of shaping and molding public opinion, regardless of the facts.

For now, there was nothing she could do with the information she had been given. Agent Anderson undoubtedly told her the truth, but without any proof, who would even listen to her? The local and national news would report everything the FBI spokesperson said. Anyone hearing that news would be inclined to believe Justin Mabry was a murderer, an extremist and possibly even a racist.

And the spokesperson had made no mention of the four missing agents who had gone after Justin. If they had finally returned to their home base, they certainly had come back empty-handed. If they were still missing, what had happened to them? And why was that information being withheld?

One thing the FBI spokesperson said did ring true, however. Luke Jordan was always a bit of a mystery. He worked for a helicopter logging company and rarely showed up in town. When he did come in, he barely spoke to anyone. And his pickup always had a rifle or shotgun in the gun rack, even when it wasn't hunting season. It wasn't out of the question that he could indeed be what they claimed.

A few paces beyond Rico, Anson stopped suddenly. In a way, she did have some proof.

"Hang on a second, Gill. I'll be right back."

Rico was going in the opposite direction, but Anson quickly caught up.

"Mr. Rico," she said softly. "Four FBI agents went after Justin Mabry. He's not in the cabin like you were told. The four agents are missing. He did not shoot anyone."

Before Rico could react, Anson veered away from him, making it obvious he was not to follow. Hopefully, he would understand he had just been given a tip, a message from someone that wished to maintain a low profile. Being a real reporter, he would know what to do with the information. He would smell a story.

The distant sound of low-pitched air horns broke into Anson's thoughts just as she caught up with her partner. Turning to the west, she asked Jacobson, "Did you hear that?"

"Yeah, I did. And God help us if it's what it sounds like. That's all we need."

Listening intently as the horns blew louder, the officers looked at each other. "Trucks?" asked Anson.

Jacobson nodded soberly.

"Lots of them. It sounds like they're crossing the Lightning Creek Bridge."

Between the air-horn blasts, people could be heard cheering in the distance and then the dull roar of diesel engines rolled down the streets, echoing between the houses. Everyone nearby began to move to the side of the road. Some sort of convoy was coming down Main Street.

Jacobson raised his voice.

"Sounds like the National Guard finally got here. They must have brought an entire division."

The ground was beginning to shake. Above the rooftops, a long plume of black smoke blasted into the fading blue sky. A moment later a chrome bumper caught the brilliant rays of the setting sun, and flashed them back into the eyes of the awed spectators. Above the bumper and a small Dixie flag, a polished red cab with twin air horns rolled into view. A man with a black snake tattooed onto his forearm was waving vigorously.

As the big rig turned east on Main, the side of its trailer became visible to the stunned onlookers. A white sheet was fastened on both sides. On it, painted with spray paint, were the words "Bree, innocent until proven guilty."

A few feet behind, another big rig hit its horns. It was pulling an empty cattle trailer with another sheet reading, "Free Bree!" Behind the stock transport a third rig was decorated with "Impeach Stark" banners. Trailing it were lumber trucks, logging trucks, milk trucks, trucks with farm tractors and bulldozers on flat beds, hay trucks. One after the other, bumper to bumper, the trucks rumbled past.

Following the lead of the first semi, the rigs parked in a perfect line just beyond the Rendezvous encampment. When the last truck passed by, a cheer erupted from those lining both sides of Main as dozens of onlookers began walking out into the makeshift parking lot and camping area.

"I'll be damned," said Jacobson. "What in hell is that about? What is 'Bree' anyway?"

"I counted thirty seven rigs," beamed Anson. "They're here to take a stand. Don't you get it? Bree is short for Mabry. The truckers love nicknames and they've given that one to Justin."

"Take a stand for what?" demanded Jacobson. "You heard the same thing I did. Mabry shot an FBI agent. He's gone from bad to worse."

Kelly Anson glanced at Jacobson. He was passable as a cop and as a person, but he always tried to skate by, to take the easiest way out. For that reason, she could not confide in him.

"They're right, you know," offered Anson cautiously. "Being cops, it's easy to forget that people in this country are innocent until proven guilty. Right now, Justin Mabry is as innocent as you and me."

Jacobson shook his head and snorted.

"Rookies!"

"More people will come, you know," replied Anson.

"Afraid not, Kelly. When people hear what we just heard about Mabry, they'll turn against him. These truckers haven't heard the latest news yet. John Q. Public is notoriously fickle and short on memory.

When they find out what Mabry is, and what he did today, they'll change their tune. Clark Fork will be a ghost town by tomorrow."

Agent Anderson walked into the main tent. A large table had been set up in its center. A light was hanging from a tent pole over the table and papers were scattered all across it. Agents Francis and Degan were working on an operations plan.

"I know you heard the trucks," he said, barely able to suppress his anger. "But did you bother to go out and look at them?"

Degan had been leaning over the table, but now he stood up defiantly.

"We looked. So what? Rednecks always show up at these things. You know that better than anyone, don't you, country boy?"

Anderson looked hard at Francis, hoping to find a glimmer of support, any hint of friendship. He saw only irritation in her eyes.

"What are you two going to do if Governor Fulton doesn't declare a state of emergency? You think you can handle what's happening out there. Do you even know what's going on? Mabry's becoming a hero."

"Relax, John," said Francis. "We have it covered."

"Covered? How?"

Leaning back over the table, Degan didn't bother to look at Anderson as he spoke. "You saw the first truck in that parade didn't you? You know, the shiny red one."

"What of it?"

"The driver is one of our best snitches. We'll send an undercover agent in there tonight and get a full report. Then we'll deal with the rabble-rousers like usual. You know the drill. Now if that's all, we have an assault plan to formulate."

Again, Anderson studied Francis' face. She was at least maintaining eye contact with him. How much did she know about Degan? How involved was she in the conspiracy against Mabry? It was time to find out.

Keeping his eyes focused on Francis, Anderson said clearly, "You planted that pistol, Degan. Mabry didn't shoot Flin."

There was an almost imperceptible movement of facial muscles, but there was no question that Francis flinched. She had been caught off guard by what he said, but why? Was she surprised he knew about the pistol or surprised that Degan had planted it?

For half a minute no one spoke, but then Degan started slowly towards Anderson. When their faces were inches apart he stopped.

"Johnny boy," he smiled, "you've got no one here to watch your back. You're on the playground with the big kids now, and you're all alone. You need to rethink what you saw out there. When you do, I'm sure you'll remember it more accurately."

Anderson did not blink. His eyes were fearless and his jaw was set, but he was outgunned and outnumbered. To have any chance at all, he would have to fight this battle another day.

"Nothing to say?" goaded Degan. "That's good. Now, get out. We have work to do that doesn't involve you."

Staring into Degan's impudent eyes, Anderson chose to retreat. This was not the time and certainly not the place to take a stand. He spun on his heels and left the tent. His face was hot with rage, but he still felt the sting of being betrayed by Francis.

It was dark before Mabry and the four Idaho Militia soldiers made it to the militia camp. One of the men had carried Mabry's pack and when they walked up to the fire, Mabry was well rested.

Six men sat on logs near the flames. All of their faces were covered in camouflage paint. Behind them, four other men wearing only green underwear sat together with their hands tied behind their backs. All ten men looked up at Mabry when he neared the fire and the flames illuminated his sweat-stained face.

"So this is him," said one seated by the fire. "I hope he's worth all the trouble."

The militiaman carrying the pack slid it off to the ground.

"Well, he wore us out. It was a hell of a chase, though. Better than cougar hunting."

Mabry looked over the men at the fire, then at the prisoners.

"Are those the federal agents?" he asked.

"They're the ones that were after you," answered another at the fire as he observed Mabry closely. "We weren't far behind when the shooting started. We followed after you like we were ordered. You're supposed to be an important man. Or so we're told. Personally, I don't see anything special."

164

Slowly turning his head, Mabry looked hard at the speaker. When he did, the militiaman unintentionally dropped his eyes.

"All I want is my son," declared Mabry. His tone was even, almost subdued. But something in his voice or his mannerisms, something intangible, now commanded their attention. "And right now, I want to know what happened at the trail by the cabin. Can anyone here tell me? Did the federal authorities get him? Is my son all right?"

The man who had dropped his eyes again looked up.

"Once we started chasing you, we cut off all radio transmissions for security reasons. The last thing we heard was the shooting coming from the trail."

Pointing to the four bound men, he added, "They know what happened. They had their headsets on for quite awhile before we were close enough to capture them. We tried to find out what happened. But they won't talk."

Mabry stepped over a log and went to the seated men.

"I want to know about my son. He's all I care about. So, please, can any of you tell me? Is he safe?"

An agent nodded to Mabry. When Mabry squatted down beside him to listen, the agent spit in his face.

Mabry blinked as the saliva splattered his skin, but he did nothing else for several seconds. The militiamen watched and waited to see what this supposed leader would do.

"These Feds here are all former Delta Force," said another militiaman. "They won't talk...unless you think you can get them too." His voice carried a tone of challenge.

Wiping the spit from his face, Mabry came to his feet and slowly walked back to the fire. As he turned and looked back at the prisoners, the flame's soft glow turned his skin yellow-orange. He seemed unusually calm, but as the flickering light danced in his eyes, they darkened into a predatory stare.

"I have done nothing except protect my son. I hit the man that tried to take my son from me. And, for that, for *that*, you tried to kill me.

"Now, I'm no longer only interested in my son. I want to know why you tried to murder me. I'm going to separate the four of you. Then I'm going to ask you the same questions. If the answers don't match up *exactly*, I will ask again. If I don't like your answer, I will ask again. One of you will tell me what I want to know."

Mabry paused, then faced the men of the Idaho Militia.

"If you gentlemen will assist me, we can get some answers."

The militia soldiers looked from one to the other. One finally shrugged.

"What do you want done?"

Mabry pointed.

"Put one there. And one there, and the third one over there. Make sure they can see the spitter...Leave him where he is."

Several of the men got up and positioned the prisoners as Mabry requested. The rest stayed where they were but everyone, including the agents, wondered what would come next.

Calmly, Mabry said, "I need to borrow a pistol."

Only the crackling of the fire could be heard for a slow count of ten. Then a holster cover snapped open, and a hand offered Mabry a Colt 1911 semi-automatic.

Accepting the weapon, Mabry held it in the firelight.

"Where is the safety?"

"The lever by your thumb," said the owner. "But the chamber is loaded. All you have to do is cock the hammer and pull the trigger."

Thumbing back the hammer, Mabry walked up to the agent that spat in his face. Without hesitation, he pressed the gun barrel along the side of his head and fired.

The spitter fell to the side and landed with his face in the dirt, his body partially hidden by dancing shadows.

To the shock of everyone, he moved to the next agent and squatted down. He asked his questions quietly and the agent answered quietly. But he did answer.

Mabry went to the second agent and then the third. When he was finished with all three, he walked back to the fire. Flipping the safety back on, he handed the pistol back.

Ignoring the wide-eyed stares of the militiamen, he said, "Someone should attend to the spitter. He's going to have a deep cut in his scalp and one hell of a headache when he wakes up."

For a few heartbeats, what Mabry had said and done did not register. When it did, the men burst into laughter. Then, one by one, they stood and shook his hand.

"Hot damn!" blurted Bobcat as he patted Mabry on the back. "Luke was right! Luke said you were the one we've been waiting for. He said we'd see soon enough. He said we'd see and, man alive, was he right! You got what it takes, sure as hell's fire."

The man that challenged Mabry came up.

"I'm Owl. Sorry to have doubted you."

Standing in the firelight, Mabry looked into the eyes of the men that encircled him. The events of the last twenty-four hours had thrust him into a different world, surreal in the extreme, yet a world that was increasingly and unexplainably familiar to him. He turned to Owl and extended his hand.

"Don't be sorry. You should have doubted. It shows good judgment."

Owl smiled and nodded. Then he introduced the rest of his men. Each used an animal name. It was the same with all cells and none knew the true identity of the other. Their security, though crude, could not be breached by federal spies.

As the wounded agent's head was being bandaged, the other three were returned to their original location. Mabry sat down cross-legged at the fire. The militiamen waited eagerly for him to speak. They could sense in him the same charisma that Jordan had discovered. He was more than just a man living by his principles. He was calm, he was smart and when all else failed, he could be cunning and ruthless. This man was like none they had ever known. He was a leader of men.

"All their stories matched up," began Mabry solemnly. "These agents we have, and those that stayed behind, all communicated by radios built into their helmets. Before those four over there were ordered to follow me, they heard an agent given the command to shoot a dog that was barking and giving away their position. The agent that shot the dog had a silencer on his rifle.

"Next, they heard two shots very clearly, one right after the other. Then, voices could be heard but not the words. Another shot was fired a second or two later, but this one they knew came from an Agent Degan. After Degan fired, Luke Jordan opened up on Degan with six rounds from a big-bore rifle, but didn't hit him. Then, a minute or so later, they heard a pistol shot. That's when the Jordan family ran back to their cabin and that's also when Degan radioed to everyone that I had shot and killed an agent named Flin."

Mabry took a stick and thoughtfully stirred the fire.

"After I heard the shots, I went up the trail as fast as I could. When I rounded a turn, I ran into two camouflaged men. One was standing close to someone on the ground. The other one was a few more feet up the trail but off to the side. Both of them got a look at me before I ducked into the trees."

"Besides you," asked Owl, "who else were they shooting at? It sounds like Luke showed up late with that Garand of his, after three shots had already been fired."

"I was hoping one of you could tell me. How many people live with Luke?"

Owl shook his head.

"Nobody else. There's Rebecca his wife, and they have a new baby...and then there's Mathew and your boy. That's all I know of."

Mabry poked the fire sending up sparks.

"Does Matt know how to use a gun?"

Owl swore, then looked around at those by the fire.

"Matt's got a side-by-side twelve-gauge shotgun. And he can shoot the hell out of it."

Tossing the stick into the flames, Mabry stiffened.

"Then it was likely Matt who shot those first two shots and my son was probably with him. They heard the dog. Went to see what it was barking at, saw something, and fired both barrels."

Bobcat had been counting on his fingers.

"This Degan character said you killed that Flin fella. And he said Luke shot at him but didn't hit him. If you didn't kill that agent and Luke didn't, that means it was most likely Mathew that shot him. It seems to add up that way each time I count the shots."

Staring into the fire, Mabry said, "Then Agent Degan was shooting at the boys, after they had emptied both barrels."

Grimly, the men all agreed but it was Coyote who spoke up first.

"He would have been shooting at Mathew. He had the gun."

For several minutes no one said anything. The situation had taken a grave turn for the worse. Matt Jordan was possibly wounded or dead. The Jordans were surrounded by an unknown number of federal agents and may have already been captured or even killed. And Mabry was now wanted for the murder of a federal officer. It was anyone's guess what had become of Billy Mabry.

Mabry looked closely at the militia patches on the sleeves of those near him. "When this started," he said somberly, "all I wanted was my son. Now I have another family and another man's son to consider. What's happened to them is my fault. They have become my responsibility. I'll still do whatever it takes to get my son to Canada, but the Jordan family will have to be rescued first.

"The agents involved are corrupt and should be put in prison. They lied about me and tried to murder me. They've very likely trapped my son along with the Jordans and are trying to take him from me, and at this very minute they're almost certainly pointing guns in his direction. They are my enemies and anyone—*anyone*—who stands against them is my ally. But one thing should be clear from the beginning. I want no part of any organization or group. My fight is for my son and for the Jordans. Nothing else."

When Mabry glanced up from the fire to see the reaction of the militiamen, he was puzzled to see them smiling at him.

"Do you understand what I'm saying?"

Coyote scratched the back of his head as his grin broadened.

"Luke already told us you would say that. Yeah, we understand."

Mabry took a deep breath, let it out slowly, then came to his feet. He began to pace in front of the fire.

"How many men do the Feds have?"

"When we came up the mountain," said Wolf, "we counted about forty. But they're probably more by now. And they had a helicopter, too."

Mabry stopped pacing and looked up at a patch of star-filled sky.

"Then we have to get rid of the helicopter somehow. And we need to close Lightning Creek Road to the north beyond the Jordans' turn-off."

"Do you prefer bulldozers or dynamite for the road?" asked Owl. "We can do both."

Mabry turned back towards the men.

"Dynamite the road. The Feds will understand explosions better than dozers. The helicopter will be guarded. We'll have to think about the best way to deal with it. How many men do we have?"

"On the mountain, there's only us here and two more that are observing the cabin. But down below there will be one hundred to one hundred fifty men by morning. All of them disguised as mountain men at a Rendezvous. They will have their rifles hidden from view."

"Where is the Rendezvous?"

"They're setting up camp in the field just east of town. They're about half a mile from the FBI headquarters. The Feds wanted them moved out, but the county sheriff won't do it. That was a lucky break for us."

Mabry paced some more.

"If they call in the National Guard, we'll be helpless. But if we can get rid of the helicopter and pin them in before the Guard shows up and there aren't too many federal agents, we have a chance to end this peaceably. Is there any way to get word to Luke?"

"We got a way," said Owl, then nodded toward the four prisoners. "What do we do with them?"

Mabry glanced at the prisoners then back at the fire.

"Do we have any more zip ties?"

"Yeah."

"Tie all four together, back to back so each one faces a different direction. Take their socks off then put their boots back on. But don't tie the laces. With all the tripping and the blisters they'll get, they won't cause us any more trouble. Just tell them to keep going downhill, and they'll find their way home in a day or so.

"How long will it take us to get to the Rendezvous camp from here?"

Bobcat took out his compass and looked at it in the firelight.

"In the dark, I'm guessing three hours, maybe four by night travel."

"We don't have much time," said Mabry, as he went to his pack and lifted it. "If you can get us there by first light, it could all be over by noon."

"That's doable," said Coyote. "But you should have a weapon. They already shot at you once. You don't want to be caught unarmed."

"All right. What's the simplest one you have?"

"Simplest?"

"Yes. Until tonight, I had never fired a gun."

The militiamen were stunned. Some swore good-naturedly, others whistled. Grinning broadly, Wolf asked, "Where the hell did you grow up?"

"The suburbs."

Coyote pointed to Owl.

"You're going to need his backup, then. We make fun of Owl for carrying it, but I guess we can't do that now."

170

Owl stood up and removed a pistol from its holster. He shook his head.

"If I ever had need of a gun in the middle of the night, I'd always grab this one first. Especially if it was dark. This is the most natural-handling pistol ever made, and it's perfectly balanced."

Mabry accepted the pistol.

"What is it?"

"A single-action Colt .45 with a four-and-three-quarter-inch barrel. It was patented in 1873. At the time, it was the most powerful handgun in the world."

Palming the pistol, Mabry nodded.

"It does fit the hand well."

"You cock and fire each shot," continued Coyote. "If you're in a hurry or it's dark, you can just point it like you would your finger, or if you have time you can use the sights. If you do, make sure you see just the tip of the front blade in that rear groove. You can empty the chamber and dry-fire it, to practice.

"When you practice dry firing, remember to squeeze the trigger. Don't jerk it. And for new shooters like yourself, always aim a shade to the right. The trigger pull for a righty will push the pistol to the left. Say, for instance, if you're fifteen feet from somebody and you have time to use the sights, and you wanted to hit him between the eyes, you'd aim at his left eye. Your trigger push would likely put the bullet dead center."

Mabry looked down the barrel and into the flames of the fire.

"If I have to use this, I'll be very, very close."

Coyote glanced at Owl, then at Bobcat.

"Well, then remember this. You'll have time for one shot. The Feds are trained to triple-tap. That is, to shoot twice in the heart then once to the head. If you're planning on being that close, we had better fit you with a vest."

Chapter Twelve

June 18th
9:41 PM (PST)

F ollowing Degan's orders, Special Agent Jones took a leisurely stroll along the barbed-wire fence that separated the FBI field headquarters from Main Street. The summer night air was cool. The campfires of the Rendezvous sparkled in the darkness a half-mile away in the adjacent field. Jones had been called upon to contact an embedded agent and relay a message.

Agent Jones casually spoke to a posted guard as he walked past him, then lit up a cigarette. Pausing to inhale the smoke, he watched the shadowy figures of several townspeople pass by. He checked his watch and waited for his undercover contact.

A man in a red ball cap crossed the blacktop to the fence line. The floodlights powered by the distant FBI generators dimly lit up his face as he grew closer. With no one near enough to hear, he said, "Are you, Jones?"

"Yeah. And you are?"

"Baker. What's the assignment?"

"Get to your snitch. Tell him he's to start spreading negativity about Mabry. We want to undermine his popularity. A lot of the people out there didn't hear the latest news we put out. Emphasize the killing of Flin. And the child-beating, too. Tell your snitch to use his imagination. You know the routine. And we want to know what the skinheads are up to. Got it?"

"No problem," quipped the undercover agent. "Routine."

Agent Baker walked quietly into the darkness. Worn out jogging shoes and jeans had been his uniform for months. He worked part-time as a diesel mechanic and was in charge of several snitches in the Coeur d'Alene area. One of them, with a black snake tattooed on his forearm, was already here. If a snitch did not cooperate, Baker had the authority to send him back to prison. His job was easy and he enjoyed the power.

Baker started for the parked semi trucks. He had worked with Slade many times. The informant was loosely associated with the Aryan Nations and knew the whereabouts of a dozen methamphetamine labs. And facing twenty years for armed robbery, he was always willing to do what he was told.

Spreading rumors and starting arguments in the ranks of extremist groups invariably weakened them. Infecting such organizations with disunity and mistrust was easy with the right set of lies. Agent Baker recruited Slade from San Quentin prison, and then trained him in low-intensity warfare techniques. Slade loved his freedom and was one of the best snitches in the business. By morning the truckers and those few who had joined them would be thoroughly disillusioned, ready to go home and resume their boring lives.

It took half an hour for Baker to locate Slade. When he finally spotted him, he was sitting around a campfire with a dozen men dressed in animal skins. They were drinking beer and listening to a woman play her fiddle.

Baker was angry but hid it well as he approached the fire. Slade should have been with the Aryans instead of wasting time with these buffoons. And he'd better not be drunk again.

When Slade glanced up, he recognized his FBI contact. A sneer twisted the pockmarked skin on his bony face, but when Baker motioned for him, Slade responded obediently.

"Let's take a walk," said Baker with an artificial smile. When they had taken a few steps away from the others, he whispered sternly, "You were told to stay with the Aryans."

Coming away from the heat of the fire, Slade rolled down his long sleeve shirt. "It's cool out this evening," he said, then belched out the stale odor of beer. "The skinheads ain't up to nothing tonight. I was just making a friendly visit and bumming a beer."

The men walked between two fifty-foot trailers where it was almost pitch-black. The starlight above was barely enough to illuminate their faces and Baker's dirty white T-shirt.

"What is it this time?" asked Slade.

"You are to undermine and then destroy all support for this Mabry guy before it gets out of hand. Tell them they missed the latest news, that he murdered an FBI agent today. Make sure they know he beat his kid. Tell them he's bisexual. Tell them whatever the hell you want, but get the job done. You know how it works. I want these trucks cleared out of here by tomorrow morning at the latest."

"I kind of thought you'd be the one that showed up," quipped Slade. "You federal boys don't like it when somebody stands up to you, do you? You afraid of one man now?"

Baker tried to see the expression on Slade's face, but it was too dark. He didn't like the insolence in his voice. But if Slade gave him any trouble, he would put him in his place.

"We're not afraid of anybody. Now, do you want to do your job or do you want to go back to the pen?"

Reaching behind his back, Slade's eyes filled with contempt.

"Neither one," he said coldly.

It was too late for Baker to react. The ice pick pierced his heart. He tried to call out, but a hand was over his mouth.

It was close to eleven p.m. and Deputy Sheriff Jacobson had gone home early. The town of Clark Fork was quiet, and it was time for Officer Anson to take her dinner break. She missed the six o'clock news, but the gas station on the corner of Fourth and Main would have the TV going, especially tonight.

Parking her squad car under a streetlight, she started for the station. Through the large glass window, she could see several older men sitting around a small, yellow Formica table. They were drinking coffee from Styrofoam cups and watching a small illuminated screen.

Walking through the open door, Anson immediately recognized Walt Hickey. She hadn't seen the old logger since the morning Justin had knocked Brown out and escaped. Other than her, Hickey was the only other witness to what happened that day.

"Good evening Mr. Hickey. How are you tonight?"

Hickey took a pipe from between his yellowed teeth.

"Been better."

The others around the table looked up at her with faces full of suspicion. She was local, but she was still the law. And at this moment in the city of Clark Fork, that was reason enough for caution.

Going to a refrigerated glass cabinet, Anson took out a sandwich.

"Dinner," she said, smiling at the men. "The coffee still hot? I was hoping to catch the eleven o'clock news, if you don't mind my company."

Hickey pulled out an empty chair.

"Me and the boys just made a fresh pot. How's it looking down at the Fed camp?"

"It's quiet," said Anson, as she took a seat next to Hickey. "Lots of bright lights, though, along the fence. The TV people are gearing up to broadcast.

"Anything happening on this side of town?"

Hickey replaced his pipe and glanced slyly at the men seated near him.

"Well, rumor has it that the Feds shot Matt Jordan this morning. Shot him in the arm."

Anson was stunned, then her shock instantly turned to doubt.

"How did that rumor get started?"

Standing to get a cup, then filling it, Hickey handed the coffee to Anson. When he sat back down he said sternly, "Believe it."

Looking over the lip of the coffee cup as she took a sip, Anson stole a quick glance at the other men. They knew something. This wasn't idle gossip. Somehow, word had been sent from the cabin or someone had overheard an agent talk about it. But, as yet, the FBI hadn't publicly admitted to shooting Matt Jordan.

"We were just talking," continued Hickey, "about what Bree might do about it. If he's done all they say he has, he'll sure as hell fire do something to them Feds."

Another old man spoke up.

"The Jordans are a respected family. Luke is from a long line of Swedes and they've been here for generations. When this gets out about Luke's son, people around town are going to be fighting mad. A lot of them ain't made up their mind about this Bree fella, but they know Luke and his boy."

Anson tried to remain neutral.

"That nickname is sure catching on. I heard the truckers gave it to him way down in Boise. They started out with just three trucks, then got on their CBs and others kept joining in. I hear most all of them are out of work."

`Hickey smiled knowingly at Anson and took a puff on his pipe.

"I saw Kal Burns this evening."

Anson flinched.

"Oh?"

"Came in here, all nervous-like just after the six o'clock news and filled up with gas. He had suitcases in the back seat of his car. Somebody told me he was leaving town and wasn't coming back. Seems a mighty *odd* thing to do, don't it?"

Anson eyed Hickey over another drink of coffee. Did he know Burns was the one who filed the false report on Mabry? Was he making a connection between the announcement that Mabry was now a killer and Burns' hasty departure? How much did the old logger know? And how was he getting the information?

"What channel are you on?" asked Anson.

"Two," answered Hickey. "We don't trust but one newscast. The Independence News Channel is where you get it the straightest. Especially from Thomas Rico."

When the news anchor came on, the man nearest the TV turned up the volume.

"Our top story tonight continues to be the siege at Clark Fork, Idaho, where FBI agents, along with reinforcements from the U.S. Border Patrol, have surrounded the cabin of Luke Jordan and the fugitive Justin Mabry.

"As we reported on our six o'clock broadcast, Mabry allegedly killed an FBI agent early this morning. At any moment we are expecting Governor Fulton to respond to the FBI's request for a declaration of Extreme Emergency. We may have to cut away to that news conference at any moment, but now on the scene in Clark Fork is our own Thomas Rico. Thomas, what's the latest from Idaho?"

"Good evening, Rita. Late this afternoon, that truck convoy you can see over my shoulder roared into this tiny town and parked in this huge open field where I'm standing now. But since then, everything has been relatively calm.

"You can also see, to my left, several campfires going. Those are from an old-fashioned Rendezvous where, I would guess, two hundred men and women have gathered. I can hear music and laughter from both the truckers' camp and the Rendezvous. There is certainly no sign of Extreme Emergency here.

"Most of the activity from the FBI camp has come from their helicopter. It has made several trips since I arrived late this afternoon. I can only conclude that it is hovering over the Jordan cabin. Perhaps it's being used to help in surveillance, or perhaps, just to intimidate those inside."

"Thomas, what is the feeling of the townspeople? How are those North Idaho people taking the arrival of so many federal officers?"

"Rita, the reaction is mixed. When Mabry first escaped, it was the consensus of opinion that he and his son would try and make it to Canada where he would be safe. This region of Idaho is known for its freedom and independence and for that reason alone, he initially had a lot of sympathy and support. But the announcement this evening that Mabry allegedly shot and killed Agent Flin has really confused a lot of people. But the incident is complicated by other factors, Rita.

"As everyone knows, Idaho, like many western states, is very big on states' rights. And the policies of President Stark have not gone over well in the west. In fact, if you recall the dead wolf and grizzly they found on the front steps of the Federal Building a few days ago, you'll realize her policies have now been met with open hostility.

"At first, I think the people were ready to rally around Justin Mabry as a symbol of their dissatisfaction with the administration's policies. But these are good people. I think they have to draw the line with the shooting, *if* Mabry did indeed shoot Agent Flin."

"You sound as if there is some doubt about that, Thomas."

"Rita, with all the information that's available through computer networks, it's possible to do a thorough background check on just about anyone. We've taken a very hard look at Justin Mabry, and I have to say, some things don't add up. He just doesn't fit the profile of a desperate killer.

"More importantly, since I've been here on the scene, I've had contact with what I would call a very credible source. This source told me that, in fact, Justin Mabry did *not* shoot Agent Flin. The same source told me that Mabry is also *not* inside the cabin."

"That would certainly be big news, Thomas. Is there any way you could corroborate that information?"

"Actually, there is, Rita. There is one additional piece of information that I will not divulge at this time that, if true, would absolutely cast doubt on the accuracy of the FBI's account of what happened this morning. Right now, I would say there is a lot of confusion, if not actual misinformation, being disseminated about this case."

"Hang on Thomas, the governor of Idaho is about to make a statement. We're cutting directly to the State Capitol."

Governor Fulton walked to an outside podium. He smiled at the cameras.

"The Federal Bureau of Investigation has requested I declare a state of Extreme Emergency in and around the cabin of Luke Jordan in the city of Clark Fork.

"Upon extensive review of the situation in Clark Fork, I have decided no actual emergency exists. I have also concluded that the FBI, under the direction of the administration in Washington D.C., has unnecessarily aggravated a relatively benign incident.

"Considering the current anti-federalist atmosphere that exists in all the inland western states, I am formally requesting President Stark order the withdrawal of all federal officers and allow local law enforcement to defuse the situation.

"I am also calling for a full investigation into what initiated this incident and what actions the FBI took that eventually led to the death of one of their own agents, allegedly by Justin Mabry, a man with no criminal record.

"I also call upon President Stark to review her Child Protection Act, to discover why it failed so miserably the very first time it was tested. Why, instead of protecting our children, it has led to her request that I spend hundreds of thousands of taxpayer dollars to chase one man that fled from his home, and to force another man and his family from theirs."

Governor Fulton turned and walked from the podium.

"That of course," said the somewhat startled news anchor, "was Governor Fulton here at his press conference at the State Capitol. Thomas, I'm sure you were watching the governor on your monitor. What do you make of that? What do you think the reaction of the FBI there is going to be?"

Rico rubbed the back of his neck then looked into the camera.

"I have to admit, I am shocked, Rita. But I think he's right not to send the National Guard. I don't see any reason for such a show of military force. There is only one family up there and there is no rush. My feeling is, if they give it time, things will calm down.

"As far as the rest of the governor's comments go, they were purely political, Rita. As you are aware, Governor Fulton is hoping to win his party's presidential primary, and I think he was taking a big swing at the president's policies in general. The two of them have very different ideas of just how much the federal government should be allowed to intervene in state issues.

"But I do solemnly believe that what the governor said will have a tremendous impact on what happens here tomorrow. Rita, back to you."

The camera switched back to the main station.

"Next, a meth lab blows up in..."

Hickey tuned down the volume on the TV and refilled his coffee cup.

"Damn! It's going to hit the fan now. Without the Guard, I wonder what the Feds will do. They won't have a tank to back them up this time."

"They won't be getting those armored personnel carriers they like to use, either," sneered another old man. "I can't recall that ever happening before. No governor ever stood up to them and said what Fulton did."

"The governor is right," Anson said matter-of-factly. "These are just ordinary people up there. They don't need troops and tanks to handle them. The FBI doesn't need snipers either. In fact, they should go home and let us handle our own affairs. This was a screw-up from the very start and it was political from the get-go. The whole thing started with a lie and it's being fueled by more lies."

The men at the table grew strangely silent, but Anson continued eating her sandwich as if she did not notice. Hickey had somehow received information about Matt Jordan, and that meant he was connected in some way with the family. If the Jordans trusted him, she wanted him to know she could be trusted as well.

"Those four agents the FBI is missing, haven't been heard from since early this afternoon," offered Anson. "I'm told they went after Mabry."

Eyeing Anson intently as the smoke curled from his pipe, Hickey's eyes narrowed into slits.

"I wonder who that 'source' is that Thomas Rico has been talking to?" questioned Hickey slyly. "Maybe she ought to tell him about Mathew being shot."

For a second Anson stopped chewing. After she swallowed and took a quick sip of coffee, she said smoothly, "Maybe she should."

A one-hundred-watt bulb illuminated the tent of FBI headquarters, as diesel generators with twenty-foot high floodlights cast a blue-white light over the entire commandeered field. Degan was swearing under his breath and pacing. Francis sat at a table tapping her slender fingers. For the first time, she was beginning to worry.

She was in charge. Her orders from the assistant director were verbal, and though the actual instructions had intentionally been vague, the meaning was profoundly clear. She was to bring an obviously guilty Justin Mabry to justice, as quickly as possible. The administration was expecting the eminent and highly publicized arrest of the first federal child abuser, but no one had counted on doing it without the aid of the National Guard. Using them had always been the tactic employed by the federal government to get around Posse Comitatus, and their armed presence was the best means of imposing extreme intimidation. To make matters worse, Thomas Rico, the maverick reporter, was on scene and already in possession of sensitive information.

Francis was considering a late-night phone call to Washington when Degan suddenly stopped pacing and blurted, "That's it!"

"What?"

"The governor won't give us the Guard, so we bring in the ATF. They can give us another hundred officers by morning. Maybe even more."

"How are you going to justify their presence to the media?" asked Francis. "Not to mention the U.S. District judge."

Degan smiled.

"All we have to say is, we thought we heard a fully automatic weapon up there today. That gives us enough suspicion to investigate, and that will get us a federal warrant. It worked years ago in Waco, Texas. And there is no record of Luke Jordan ever applying for a permit to posses any machine gun. He's now in violation of federal gun laws. And we get the ATF in here by morning."

Francis nodded approvingly.

"Good plan, Degan. And the judge is only one hour behind our time zone. If he's in bed, he won't have been there long. And besides, he's been briefed by the AD and some of those in the administration."

"He'll give us the warrant immediately. I'll call him while you get hold of the ATF and get them mobilized. We'll have to work fast to get them all here by morning. And I want this entire operation wrapped up by noon tomorrow."

Anderson turned off the motel TV and opened his brief case. Wondering how Francis and Degan would react to the governor's news conference, he took a single sheet of paper from a leather pocket. Sliding onto the hard mattress, he leaned against the bed board with a pillow behind his back.

Their plans would have to change now that the National Guard was unavailable. They should have listened to him from the beginning, but now it was almost too late. He would formally make his recommendations in the morning, but if they wanted his input tonight, which they clearly did not, they knew where to find him.

At the top of the sheet of paper was "Mabry, Justin Lee, Second Opinion Profile."

Anderson skimmed the report as he had done several times before.

Reading out loud, he muttered, "Introverted, does not like crowds, few friends but extremely loyal to those he has. Decisive, capable of leadership, though reluctant to accept it. Similar types: Old West gunfighters, Mafia hit-men. Personalities matching: General George Patton, German Field Marshal Erwin Rommel."

Anderson stared at the paper as if it were alive.

"A man who shines brightest in the darkest hour. Is this really you, Mabry? Do you know, yet? Do you even have a clue *who* you are? Or are you evolving by the minute?"

Chapter Thirteen

June 19th
3:45 AM (PST)

Spokesman Review
Standoff Continues in Clark Fork
Front page, column 2
Canadian Prime Minister snubs Stark;
Mabry welcome in Canada

New York Times
Separatists Defy FBI
Front page, column 1
Idaho Governor Swings at Stark
Front page, column 2

Boston Globe
Idaho Extremist Kills FBI Agent in Standoff
Front Page, column 3
Idaho Governor Sides with Protestors
Front Page, column 4

Nevada Tribune
Fulton Slams Stark in Standoff

Missoula Mountaineer
Mabry, Jordan Focus of Unrest

Cody Review
Fulton Exerts States' Rights

The stars had faded away and the sky was a clear gray-blue. The sun was an hour from rising and the valley below was cold and dark. Ten men sat on a solid rock bluff letting the cool air dry their sweat. They had traveled all night but none of them were tired. What lay ahead consumed their thoughts and erased their fatigue.

For as far as they could see, on every road, scattered headlights could be seen as they approached Clark Fork. Some came alone, some in pairs and some in small groups, but the stream of traffic was constant.

Bobcat sat beside Mabry on the point of a flat rock.

"What do you make of it?"

The floodlights of the FBI compound were still running. Mabry had been surveying the headquarters with his binoculars for the last ten minutes.

"Most of the headlights are onlookers but some are federal reinforcements," said Mabry. "Lots of activity. I estimate between two and three hundred armed men are down there. Most of them are outside the tents and meandering around or eating.

"The Rendezvous field is too dark to see much. A few fires are starting up and dozens of cars and trucks have pulled in and parked, but then they turned off their lights. I can't tell how many people are down there. The streets of the town are jammed with cars."

Bobcat billowed his shirt back and forth to let the heat out.

"All our men would have been there already. Maybe a few stragglers would be driving in, but not this many."

"Then they're likely just curious people," said Mabry, "or maybe they've come to show support in some way. We'll have to wait for daylight or...how long until Coyote gets back?"

"I figure it's a good hour down there and then an hour and a half back up here. He'll report in and get the latest from our camp. That's another ten or fifteen minutes, maybe. Looks like two hours before he's back, unless he thinks it's safe to use the radios. Then we'll know in about an hour. Just about sun-up."

"One thing is for sure," said Mabry. "The National Guard isn't down there yet. But we're out-gunned by at least one hundred men, men with semi-automatic and most likely fully automatic weapons. *And* they have the helicopter."

"Coyote will check on the helicopter," assured Bobcat. "I think your idea to get rid of it will work, and like you said, it can pass as an accident. And by then, the men on the dynamite can use their radios. That part we can handle. What we need is more guns and people with the grit to use them if they have to."

Raising his binoculars again, Mabry looked at FBI headquarters and the surrounding terrain.

"Not many people are willing to die for something they don't believe in. Especially if they are outnumbered."

"Our men down there in camp," replied Bobcat confidently, "are the best of the best, sir. They aren't weekend warriors or blowhards. They're the real deal. Every bit as good as the men up here with you. They won't turn tail and run. You can count on that. They are true militia. But more than that, they are patriots."

"I believe you, Bobcat. Your men here are proof of that. But I was referring to the Feds down there. Right now, most of them are cocky and strutting around like barnyard roosters. They believe they have everything on their side—numbers, firepower, the law and the moral high ground. We need to reduce that by seventy-five percent."

"Sir?" questioned Bobcat.

"Do you know your Bible, Bobcat?"

"Pretty well."

"Do you know the story of Gideon?"

Bobcat thought for a moment, then scratched his head.

"Yeah, I know it, but how does that work here?"

"Gideon won the battle over the Midianites by appearing to outnumber them and convincing them they were going to die. It was psychological warfare. And the Midianites knew they were only a bunch of thieves and trespassers. They didn't want to die in a foreign land taking what didn't belong to them in the first place."

Bobcat said nothing. Mabry had extracted information from Delta Force-trained FBI agents in a matter of minutes. His plan to trap the federal agents had been simple, yet cunning. If Mabry had a plan that involved Gideon, it had to be a good one.

After a moment Bobcat's curiosity got the best of him.

"You said seventy-five percent. Out of the four things they have going for them, which one do you leave them with?"

"The law. But, as both of us know, the law was made for man. Man was not made for the law. And the law will only be on their side for a little while longer. When the truth comes out, it will be used against them, too. The men down there basking in those flood-lights and bragging about how tough they are won't risk their lives for the sanctity of our legal system. They know too much about it to die for something so corruptible as that."

"There's a whole lot more Feds down there than yesterday," offered Bobcat as he gazed at the distant lights. "Do we still aim for today at noon?"

Mabry took the binoculars down.

"I'll let you know after we hear back from Coyote. Everything could change then."

Bobcat nodded and stood up.

"Whatever you decide, the men are with you. We can disappear back into the woods, or we can go toe to toe with them down there. But we've waited a long time for this. We'd prefer a face-off, sir. We want to put teeth back into the Constitution and the Second Amendment and let those in Washington know this country is run *by the people*, not a bunch of elitists in black boots. You and your son are the lightning rod, but this storm has been brewing for decades. It's way overdue."

As the eastern sky gradually brightened, Mabry sat alone on the bluff staring thoughtfully at the valley below. Now there was ample light to see both the Rendezvous and FBI camps, as well as the entire town. His plan was almost complete.

The city streets and the highway that ran through the center of town were blocked with hundreds of cars and trucks. The Rendezvous field had become a huge parking lot dotted with scores of small encampments. In backyards, on the streets and in the field, as far as the eye could see, small fires and propane stoves were glimmering as two to three thousand people began cooking breakfast. No one could get into, or out of, Clark Fork unless they walked or flew.

The FBI had positioned forty officers around the perimeter of their field station, where four dozen tents had been erected with military precision. Two to three hundred heavily armed agents loitered in front of the tents waiting for something to do.

A twig snapped on the trail beneath the rock ledge and nine militiamen grabbed their weapons. Then a soft whistle rolled through woods and was quickly retuned. A moment later Coyote climbed the ridge and stepped into view and went directly to Mabry. He was sweating and breathing heavily.

"We got company," he said, as the other men expectantly gathered around. "There's more than just our militia down there."

Mabry let Coyote catch his breath for a moment, then asked calmly, "Do you know who they are?"

Accepting a canteen of water, Coyote nodded and took a quick swallow. "Farmers, ranchers, hunters, loggers, Aryan Nations, Ku Klux Clan, church groups, truck drivers, you name it. They're all here for you and the Jordans, but they're mad as hell about a bunch of other things, too. And I'd say more than eighty percent of them are carrying some sort of gun or have it in their rigs. It looks like the Old West down there!"

Coyote took another drink form the canteen then continued.

"The highway has even more people. It's backed up for miles in both directions. CBs are buzzing all over. People are walking into town from as far away as Hope. And traffic is heavy coming down from Bonners Ferry and up from Coeur d'Alene. Thousands of people are coming this way. The license plates are from every state in a thousand miles. Nobody's ever seen nothing like it.

"They told me there were three or four news trucks down by your house. And Thomas Rico showed up last night."

"Then we must act quickly," said Mabry. "We only have a few hours. The time for us to make our stand is now. I want no misunderstanding. When you go down to the town, be honest. Tell them what I expect...and what the ultimate cost might be. I need everyone we can possibly recruit, but I only want those that are willing and capable to help our cause. Get the leaders or representative from each group you can identify, and set up a place where I can talk to them all at the same time.

"And I am going to need someone down there who can use a computer or write well. That person will be calling my attorney as soon as possible and then drawing up some legal papers. The document will have to be airtight because it will be served on the FBI agent in charge. And we need the document finished before noon."

Squatting down, Mabry smoothed out a place in the dirt. He dug his finger into the soil.

"This is the FBI headquarters. We need this street cleared. Drive the cars up on the lawns or in the ditches. I want a ten-foot wide path from Fourth Street to the fence line, here. I want the first line of people stretching from here..."

When another pigeon flew into the Jordans' cabin, the sun had crested the mountains to the east. The agents had been on the loudspeakers nonstop throughout the night, and a third-generator floodlight had been brought in. No one had slept. The baby had cried for hours but finally stopped. Matt groaned occasionally from the pain, but there was little conversation. They had been waiting and praying.

Luke Jordan eagerly slid across the kitchen floor then retrieved the message from the bird's leg. Kneeling quickly, he unrolled the message.

"Start negotiations. Stall, then surrender only to Thomas Rico at 9:30 AM today. When get to field, stay behind cover."

Crawling to a nearby window but staying out of sight, Jordan handed the note to his wife.

"I'm ready to talk," he yelled, then winked at Rebecca. "But how do I know you won't shoot us if we give up? I don't trust you. I need to talk to someone I trust."

What little sleep Kelly Anson got was in her squad car. A few other deputies were in town, but they were scattered and isolated. Without warning, thousands of people had flooded into the small town. They slept in campers, tents, trucks and cars. They rolled out sleeping bags in backyards and roadsides, any place they could find space.

It was the brink of chaos, yet it was not. Guns were everywhere, yet none that she knew of had been fired. There were no reports of theft, vandalism or fighting. The people had come to vent their anger against a common enemy, an enemy that threatened not only their livelihoods but their God-given rights.

They came to support a simple backwoods family, but galvanizing the anger and mosaic of hopes and beliefs into one community was the one they called "Bree." Mabry refused to be intimidated and was fighting the way they wished they had fought. Spitting in the face of death, he alone had rebelled against injustice and tyranny. When there appeared to be none left, when hope was fading, these people believed they had discovered an American hero.

After eating at the gas station the previous night, Anson parked in front of Mabry's home. From there she and Jacobson had circulated among the crowds gathered in the vicinity of the news trucks and the

FBI's taped-off microphone. Jacobson's truck was now somewhere in the field of the Rendezvous and Anson's car was stuck where it was. No one was going to drive anywhere now.

Anson was leaning against her car door when Walt Hickey came out of his house. "Come on in, Officer Kelly. I got eggs and coffee going. And some information for you."

Glancing at the rising sun, Anson felt her stomach growl.

"You don't have to ask twice."

Hickey held the door open for her. He glanced around, then smiled slyly.

"Got a few visitors in town, don't we?"

It had been a long night but smelling the fresh coffee lifted Anson's spirits. Before she could ask, Hickey pointed out the bathroom. When she returned to the kitchen area, the old logger was sitting at a small round table. For some reason, he was still smiling.

"Help yourself to some eggs there on the stove. There's toast next to the coffee pot."

Anson filled her plate, then poured a cup of strong coffee.

"What did you have to tell me, Mr. Hickey? You said there was some information."

Hickey took a sip of coffee and raised his gray eyebrows.

"Word is, that Luke Jordan is going to give hisself up this morning at nine-thirty. But he'll only do it if Thomas Rico is there as a witness. That way he'll be sure they won't shoot him down in cold blood and claim it was self defense."

Nodding as she chewed, Anson swallowed a mouthful of eggs.

"That's great news. What about Billy, Mabry's son?"

"Oh, he'll be with them, too. But we need some insurance that this happens just at nine-thirty. That's where you can help."

"Me? How?"

"Thomas Rico will listen to you. He'll believe a cop, especially you. He has to be told that Luke is asking for him. The FBI may not want to let Rico up there. But if Rico announces on the air that Luke will surrender *only* if he is there to witness it, the Feds will have to agree. But don't tell Rico that Luke will give up at nine-thirty. Luke is negotiating his surrender right now. Soon he'll start asking for conditions, then he'll mention Rico and that he'll only surrender to him."

For a moment, Anson ate and drank in silence but her eyes never left Hickey's face. This was obviously part of a plan, but whose? And how were they able to communicate?

"How do you know all this?"

Hickey laughed.

"A little birdie told me."

"Did that birdie tell you anything else?"

Savoring his coffee, Hickey smiled.

"Bree is coming!"

Anson froze.

"Justin is all right? They didn't catch him?"

The old man's eyes flickered with curiosity.

"Justin?"

Feeling her face flush and trying to hide her reaction, Kelly Anson took a sip of coffee. "All he wants is his son."

"That's true enough. But he'll have to take him from the Feds. They won't give him back once they get hold of him. Not unless they're forced to. And that will take a lot of doing!"

"With all these people here," said Anson, "the governor will eventually have to send in the National Guard to straighten out the mess. They'll have to fly in because the roads are backed up. They're blocked all the way to Sandpoint to the west, and east to the Montana border. But there's no doubt now that an Extreme Emergency is developing."

"They won't be able to get here until noon," agreed Hickey, "even if the governor declares an emergency by seven o'clock. That's already been calculated, too."

Anson continued eating. This was getting out of control...or was it? How was Hickey getting information, and how was Luke Jordan getting his instructions? The FBI would be monitoring every conceivable type of communication system. No matter how sophisticated it was, they could break into it. Yet, some form of counter intelligence was operating under their noses.

And where was Justin? How had he escaped and how could he ever get Billy back from the FBI once they had him? In a matter of minutes, they would have him on their helicopter and he would be stolen away. Justin would be helpless.

Coming to her feet and taking one last gulp of coffee, Anson said, "I'd better find Rico. And I think he may need some protection, too. He shouldn't go up there without backup."

Anson crossed Hickey's front yard and then Eleventh Street. She worked her way between the vehicles and in a matter of minutes was standing next to the news trucks. The sun was clearing the mountain peaks when Steve Spence stepped out of his van and started combing his hair using the side mirror.

"Have you seen Thomas Rico?" asked Anson.

Spence turned slowly. Recognizing Anson, Spence sneered, "What do you want him for?"

"Police business."

Spence pointed to a gray house and muttered.

"Unlike the rest of us, he got invited to sleep inside last night."

Weaving through the cars and stepping over sleeping bags, Anson went to the front door of the house and knocked.

"I need to speak to Thomas Rico, please."

A woman wearing a plaid robe eyed her suspiciously, then closed the door. A minute later Rico stepped outside and closed the door behind him.

"What is it?" he whispered.

Anson glanced back over her shoulder then spoke in a low tone.

"Luke Jordan is going to give himself up, on the condition you are there as a witness and I'm there to protect you. The FBI is unaware that we know what Luke is asking for at this very moment. You need to apply pressure to make sure they comply with his conditions."

"What kind of pressure?"

"Announce the story on your news station, that Jordan is asking for you."

"Can't. We're not scheduled to broadcast this early. Maybe this afternoon."

"No!" exclaimed Anson. "It has to be soon...very soon."

Rico thought for a moment, then took out his cell phone.

"I know how to do it," he said, as he quickly pushed his speed dial.

"Hello, this is Thomas Rico. I need to talk to Hank on the air, immediately. It concerns the Clark Fork standoff and it's urgent."

While Rico waited, Anson asked, "Hank who? Who are you calling?"

"Hank Sprey. The radio talk-show host. He's on in New York right now. He's talking to ten million people, coast to coast. And they'll be listening to him in Washington D.C. and the Hoover Building."

Anderson had to walk from the motel to the FBI headquarters. When he entered the main tent, Francis and Degan glanced up from what they were doing. Anderson was visibly shaken, his eyes were open wide and his face was flushed red.

"What is it?" asked Francis, somewhat startled by the agent's appearance.

"Don't you know?" barked Anderson. "We're trapped...and outnumbered!"

Degan's brow wrinkled, then he shook his head.

"By what? A bunch of backwater blowhards? Come on, Anderson, you're losing it!"

"Blowhards? Does your snitch think so? What did he say about what's out there? I just walked through those people getting here. We are in trouble and I'm sure your snitch will concur. These people are seething with hatred for the federal government."

Degan shrugged.

"We haven't heard back yet from our informant. It's early. We should have the report soon enough. Anyway, Jordan started negotiations this morning. He caved in earlier than I thought. Some tough guy he turned out to be."

Caught off guard by the news, Anderson took a moment to think.

"Luke Jordan is already surrendering? On what conditions? What is he asking for?"

"He's a typical right-wing paranoid," said Francis. "He's afraid we'll murder him if he shows himself."

Anderson's eyes narrowed into a scorching glare.

"Like Degan tried to do to Mabry?"

Francis groaned, but Degan smiled.

"Your word against mine, Anderson."

Another agent entered the tent.

"What is it?" asked Francis.

"Thomas Rico's on the radio with Hank Sprey. He's saying that Jordan should give up to him, that he is volunteering to go up and talk to him. And that Jordan is, in fact, asking for him to do just that."

Picking up a radio transmitter, Degan put it to his mouth.

"This is Degan. What's the progress with the negotiations?"

A metallic voice answered, "He just asked for either the governor or Thomas Rico. He wants one of them to be present to witness his surrender. He's waiting to hear our response. So far, we've stuck with our stance of 'no deals', sir."

"Keep it up for now. Over," replied Degan, setting the radio down on a nearby table. "So, Jordan has a radio, at least. It figures he would listen to the likes of Hank Sprey. He'll be asking for the reporter, now that he's heard Rico is volunteering to go up there. So do we agree to Jordan's demand?"

Francis folded her arms as the corners of her eyes wrinkled with concentration. "We would get Billy Mabry. Then the father would have nothing to fight for, no reason to hold out. His profile says that if we get the boy, he's washed up. All the fire will go out of him. And we would make Governor Fulton look bad, too. That would go a long way in fulfilling our directives."

"It sounds good to me," agreed Degan. "We can deal with Mabry later."

Anderson spread his arms wide and swore.

"Have you two even looked out there this morning? You couldn't get out of here if you tried. What if you do get the boy? So you'll put him on the helicopter and fly him out. What if Mabry decides to go after those who took his son? Someone tried to take him once already and he fought back; he knocked that guy out cold. What if he does it again and the people fight along with him? There are thousands of people out there. I just rubbed elbows with them. They're mad as hell about all sorts of things, and there are plenty of guns to go around. These are gun people. This is gun country, and they sure as hell know what they're for. Most of them, including the women, can outshoot half the men we have."

Francis sighed patronizingly.

"We've been over this before, John. You're talking about the unwashed masses. It's all bluster. It's always bluster. The only real threat is Jordan, and he's all but finished. And with the influx of so many sympathizers, Governor Fulton will have no choice but to send in the Guard to escort them out of town. There is nothing to worry about. No one is going to get in our way. They know what would happen if they did.

"When Jordan and his family quit resisting, the party will be over. All those people you're so concerned about will light a few cigarettes, drink a six-pack or two and drive their pickups back to their trailer parks."

"You should know that, Anderson," ridiculed Degan. "D.J. tells me that these are *your* people; you're from these here parts."

Anderson looked from Francis to Degan. Both of them wore a smirk.

"Your arrogance is only surpassed by your ignorance. If Justin Mabry shows up before the National Guard gets here, that ignorance is going to cost you. If he sparks a fire, it will burn everything in its path, from here to Washington D.C."

Ignoring Anderson as he stormed from the tent, Francis went to the radio.

"This is Agent Francis. We agree to bring up Rico. We will transport as soon as we locate him. Hold your positions until we arrive."

Replacing the radio, she took out her phone and dialed.

"This is Special Agent in Charge, D.J. Francis. I need to speak to the governor immediately."

Anderson went to the news trucks. Mabry was a desperate man and, whether aware of it or not, possessed the soul of a warrior. Should he discover his hidden potential, his innate ability to lead men in battle, he would stop at nothing to get his son back. Rico's presence would protect the Jordan family from the FBI, but if Mabry were near and discovered what was happening, Rico could be in danger.

After asking a few questions, Anderson was directed to the house where Rico had spent the night. As he approached, he saw the reporter talking with the young female deputy. He nodded at Anson.

"Mr. Rico, I'm Special Agent John Anderson. I need to speak with you before you go up to the cabin."

"Then the FBI agrees to let me go up there?"

"Yes. They'll be here any minute to give you that message. I'm here off the record, but Officer Anson can hear what I have to say."

Rico glanced at Anson, then back at Anderson.

"I see. What is it, Agent Anderson?"

"I believe you could be in danger if you go up to the Jordans' cabin. Mabry is desperate. And based on what we know, he's a man of uncommon abilities. He could be dangerous to anyone that gets between him and his son. He might try and take him by force after you leave the cabin. On the road, maybe. The woods are thick all along there. He could be anywhere, just waiting for his chance to strike."

"Mr. Rico will be safe as long as he's with me." Kelly Anson's voice carried the unmistakable ring of confidence.

Anderson paused. The woman was young and undoubtedly inexperienced, yet her eyes communicated more than naïve self-assurance. She *knew* something.

"Why do you say that?"

"Because, I personally drove Justin Mabry back to Clark Fork yesterday morning."

Anderson and Rico looked at each other in amazement, but neither spoke for several seconds. Anson forced a smile.

"And I will meet him in Canada when this is all over."

Rico chuckled, not with humor but astonishment.

"That's good enough for me. I'll insist you come with me."

"Me, too," added Anderson, then hearing the rapid approach of footsteps he glanced behind him. Another agent was coming.

"I'll make sure you're included, Officer Anson."

Turning to the approaching agent, Anderson waved his hand.

"I've already told him. We'll be at HQ in five minutes."

After the agent left, Anderson checked his watch. It was eight-fifteen. Two TV helicopters had been circling high above the town for half an hour, but as far as he could tell, everything seemed quiet...unusually quiet.

"The three of us will go up. I want to make certain the HRT doesn't get trigger- happy. This whole affair is close to being an illegal operation, and part of my job is to keep it from going over the line."

As they started for FBI headquarters, Anderson offered some last-minute advice. "Say as little as you can to Agents Francis and Degan. I'm not sure about Francis, but Degan is dirty. And he's dangerous."

Two vans were waiting with engines running when the trio arrived at HQ. Degan was standing next to an open sliding side door. Degan pointed angrily at Anson.

"What is she doing here?"

"She's with me," returned Rico. "I want her along."

Before Degan could object, Anderson added, "He insisted. And it won't hurt for the Jordans to see a local cop, either. The sooner we get their trust, the sooner they'll come out."

Degan grunted.

"Fine. Get in."

With a cloud of dust billowing from the rear tires, the vans drove quickly up Lightning Creek Road and fifteen minutes later pulled in behind a dozen other federal vehicles. Degan and Anderson wore their helmets and headsets.

Degan stepped out of the second van and quickly took the lead of his unit.

"This is Degan. Tell them in the cabin that Thomas Rico is here. He'll be coming to the front door to talk in two minutes."

Walking behind Degan and Anderson, Kelly Anson tried to locate the positions of the snipers, but their camouflage was too good. Guessing from the number of cars and trucks, there must have been at least a dozen men poised and waiting to get a clear shot and a green light. Or perhaps, they already had a green light.

"I should go up to the door with you," she whispered to Rico. "Should anything go wrong, two witnesses would be much harder to refute than one."

Sensing the unseen eyes of hidden riflemen, Rico shuddered.

"I could use the company. I can only imagine what those folks in there must be feeling."

Rico looked to his rear and motioned for Anderson to come close. When the agent was near, he said adamantly, "I want the deputy with me all the way up to the cabin."

Anderson merely nodded. As he walked on ahead, he replied, "I'll clear it with Degan."

Fifty yards from the parked vans, the cabin came into view. In a small clearing, a square house built of foot-thick logs stood like a small fort. The roof was steep and made of metal to shed the snow. It would be almost impossible for a man to stand on it without sliding off, and it was resistant to fire should a helicopter drop fuel on it. The doors were made of heavy timber and steel. All the windows had the curtains drawn. There was evidence of some sort of basement under the house.

Anson took off her pistol and laid it on the meager grass that covered the front yard as a loudspeaker announced their arrival.

"Thomas Rico and a local deputy sheriff are coming to the door, Luke. Mr. Rico wants the deputy with him."

Degan and Anderson watched the pair go to the front door. For several minutes Rico and Anson spoke through the door in low tones, but despite their efforts to maintain secrecy, the conversation was monitored by listening devices concealed in the trees. A message from a hidden agent came through Degan's headset.

"They're about to come out. Luke Jordan has agreed to come out."

"If Jordan has a weapon, you have the green light," advised Degan coldly. "The green light is on for anyone carrying a weapon."

Anderson clenched his teeth.

"You're hoping aren't you, Degan?"

"You're too soft, Anderson. This is what we train for."

Billy Mabry was the first to come out, followed closely by Rebecca and the baby. Behind them, Luke Jordan emerged carrying his son in his massive arms. With Rico and Anson in front of them, the family moved in a tight cluster to the middle of the yard.

The weeds at the edge of the lawn seemed to come alive as an agent, covered from head to foot in artificial grass, stood up in front of them. Another, wearing what looked like an entire tree, came out of the shadows. Snipers hatched from every log and shrub within sight and pointed their weapons at the defenseless prisoners.

"My boy needs a doctor," said Luke.

It was not a humble request nor did the big man hang his head. Even Degan noticed the lack of humility and was about to put the rebel in his place when he remembered Rico's presence.

"As soon as we get back to HQ," replied Degan with a burnished smile.

"We'll have our doctor look at him."

With the camouflaged snipers looking on, three more armed agents in black fatigues and helmets emerged to search everyone for hidden weapons. Anson offered to search Rebecca, but her offer was refused and Luke Jordan's wife was given a thorough frisking as Degan continued to smile.

"I thought a big tough man like you would have lasted longer, Jordan," chided Degan. "Your followers down there aren't going to be very impressed. What was it, a whole day?"

Behind a heavy beard, Jordan tried to suppress a smile.

"One day is like unto a thousand years, and thousand years like unto a day."

Deliberately choosing the words most offensive to Christians, Degan swore the best he knew how. The insulting tirade lasted half a minute. He was in control now. They had defied the federal government, and they deserved degradation.

196

Rico started to say something, but recalling what Agent Anderson said about Degan, he held his tongue. Officer Anson was not as cautious.

"That kind of talk is unprofessional," said Anson. "Even for a federal agent."

Degan swore again and looked at Anson.

"Hell, Mabry's a Boy Scout and you're a cute little Brownie. You two ought to get together."

Anson glared back at Degan, full of defiance.

"I'll send you an invitation when we do. I'd like to see what a brave man like you would say to him face to face."

Anderson was only half listening to the argument. Luke Jordan had quoted from the Bible and would not have done so lightly. And why had he smiled? Something wasn't right.

"Let's get out of here," interrupted Anderson. "The sooner they're on the chopper, the sooner this is all over."

Staying in a tight group, the Jordans and Billy got into the first van along with Rico and Anson. Anderson picked up Anson's pistol off the grass and took the passenger seat in front of them. Degan and a half-dozen black-clad agents took the rear van. In a matter of minutes they were descending the last quarter-mile of Lightning Creek Road. Just as the vans leveled off, the sound of a powerful explosion rattled the metal skin of both vehicles.

Degan grabbed his headset.

"What the hell was that?"

Anderson was listening on his own headset, but no one had an answer. Those still at the Jordan cabin said the explosion was definitely between them and the field headquarters; that was all they knew for sure. But it sounded to them like a charge of dynamite had gone off, on or near Lightning Creek Road.

The lead van came to a sliding stop in front of the central HQ tent. Degan shoved the passenger door open and jumped out. Just as he started to slide open the side door and order the Jordans out, he caught sight of something that made him hesitate. Thousands of spectators formed a wall of people stretching from the base of the mountain to the east all the way to the bank of Lightning Creek to the west. Facing the townspeople, more than three hundred armed federal officers were positioned at forty-foot intervals from one end of the line to the other.

Degan placed his hand on the door latch and spit. He had nothing but contempt for such people. As the van doors flew open, he turned his back on the town.

"Get the Jordans and the kid into the main tent and get the chopper ready," he ordered. "I want all of them out of here in five minutes."

What at first sounded like distant thunder suddenly echoed off the mountains and down into the valley below.

"What now?" roared Degan. He began to swear but his profanity was quickly drowned out by the deep rhythmic beat of a large engine somewhere over his head. Looking up, he saw a twin-bladed helicopter crest the mountain to the north. Suspended by a long cable was a fifty-foot log. The logging helicopter was less than one hundred feet off the ground and coming fast. As is neared the field, it slowed.

The massive machine momentarily hovered in a cloudless sky. Dangling below, the two-ton tree swayed gracefully back and forth. Without warning, in what seemed like slow motion, the log dropped through the clear morning air and landed squarely on top of the FBI helicopter. The sounds of collapsing metal and shattering plastic were engulfed in cloud of dust. For a moment the crowd was completely silent. Then, as if one collective breath had been taken, a triumphant cheer erupted from the line and then reverberated across the town with unseen thousands joining in the celebration.

As the logging helicopter disappeared over the mountains and the dust surrounding the mangled chopper cleared, the wall of exuberant spectators settled down. Without any apparent signal, they suddenly grew quiet.

Anderson stepped away from the van and handed Anson her pistol.

"He's here."

Recovering from the shock of seeing the helicopter crushed into ruble, Anson asked, "Who?"

"Justin Mabry."

Anson felt a chill go down her spine.

"Where?"

Anderson sighed.

"He's coming. It won't be long. I can feel it."

With her perpetual stoicism erased, Francis ran from the tent where she had been finalizing what she thought would be her final report to

Washington. With lips parted in shock, she stared at the twisted metal that was to have taken the prisoners away and brought an end to the crisis. Slowly, she turned to Degan, but he was too stunned by the loss of the helicopter to notice her. Everyone inside the FBI compound began listening to the eerie silence.

A gentle breeze drifted down from the hills, ruffling the long black sleeves of the federal agent's uniforms, but the huge crowd of sympathizers stood motionless. Several seconds passed, then five hundred feet east of the tents, something moved just above the spectators' heads. Another gust of wind swept over the field and the movement was seen again, but this time more clearly. Coming in from the east end of the line, the tip of a red flag was bobbing up and down as it steadily came closer. Before the type of flag could be identified, another of a different color appeared a hundred yards behind the first, then another, and still another appeared, all moving westward.

Recovering from the shock of loosing the helicopter, Degan spoke into his headset. His tone was uncertain.

"What's on those flags?"

An agent a quarter-mile to the east responded nervously.

"The first one that went by was a Dixie flag, the second one was homemade. It said 'Cattlemen,' then there were farmers, hunters, miners and even an Aryan Nations flag. Now, I see...yeah, the next one is Ku Klux Klan. They keep coming, sir. They just keep coming!"

"Who's carrying those flags?" demanded Degan. "Are they armed?"

"We can't see," responded the distant agent. "There are too many people in front. Whoever they are, they're walking behind the crowd in front of us. But by the sound of the foot steps, there must hundreds of people coming your way. Maybe thousands!"

Degan looked up and saw there were now three news helicopters flying overhead. "Agent Jones, contact those news choppers. Have them tell us what they see!"

The Dixie flag passed the news trucks and continued on to the west with the other flags following at irregular intervals. Some flags were professionally sewn, but most were made from bed sheets and spray paint, yet all flew on poles of equal length.

A response came on Degan's headset.

"The news reporters say all they can see are lots of people. They are marching four abreast behind each flag. They think some of them are carrying weapons."

Anderson looked back at the van that had held the Jordans and Rico. It was empty but no one else seemed to notice. All eyes were forward.

When the Bars and Stars reached the end of the line, the flags came to a halt. Waving in the gentle breeze, flags unfurled from east to west for half a mile. With the heavy sound of marching feet now ended, another hush fell over the crowd.

For five long minutes, there was silence. The agents along the line, especially those farthest from the tents, began to sweat. Then, to the south, a muffled boom broke the stillness. Five seconds later, another was heard. A few seconds passed then an unidentifiable, low-pitched vibration rose and fell.

Degan crossed a short distance to Anderson and Anson.

"What the hell is that?"

"We'll find out soon enough," muttered Anderson. "But whatever it is, you can rest assured it's coming for us."

Again, after a few seconds another set of booms sounded, but this time they were closer. The low-pitched note followed, but now sounded more like a cacophony of human voices, male and female, melded into one bizarre cry. Like slow thunderous heartbeats, the ominous booms and cries echoed off the mountainsides. Whatever was out there was coming closer.

Degan spoke again into his headset. His agitation was growing.

"Jones, what do those choppers see. What is that sound?"

"Hold on."

Before Jones responded, the deep roar of voices was finally understandable. It was the mass articulation of a single word.

"Breeeee!"

"The people are making the sounds," said the agent. "They're hitting the sides of cars, trucks, buildings, stomping their feet…anything to make noise, and then they're yelling something. And the guy in the news chopper says there is a small army headed directly for us."

"What do you mean, 'small army'?" asked Degan, as the voices grew nearer.

"The choppers say they're in uniform…and heavily armed. And all their faces are painted green. One man, dressed in a white long sleeve shirt, seems to be in the lead."

The ground began to shake from the thundering crashes, and with everyone along the line joining in, the chant of "Breeee" was almost deafening. Degan yelled into his headset.

"Agent Jones, get the Mabry kid and bring him to me. Now!"

Anderson shook his head. He had tried to tell them, but they would not listen. It was happening just as he feared. This was it. This was the fire in the rain, and people were going to die in its flames.

As if on command, the fervid crowd once again fell silent. Directly opposite the HQ tent where the FBI cut the barbed-wire fence and set up their microphones, the line of onlookers began to separate and withdraw. A fifty-foot-wide space opened up.

Carrying a large white flag in his left hand, a lone figure walked into the center of the clearing then stopped and waited. He wore a long-sleeved white shirt. A pistol was tucked in his belt, but the grips were plain to see. He held papers in his right hand.

Degan, Francis and the others stood over a hundred yards away, but everyone recognized the man with the flag. It was Justin Mabry.

From east to west, the other flag-bearers started moving forward, making their way through the long line of people until each was fully in view of the federal agents opposite them. Next to each flag-bearer, another person appeared, but instead of a flag, each carried a large megaphone made of cardboard and duct tape.

Mabry raised, then lowered his white flag and simultaneously, the megaphones came up. Each repeated the same message to all the agents.

"You are involved in an illegal operation. Agents Francis and Degan are being served with a federal order, citizen's arrest warrant. They are involved in an illegal operation. Lay down your weapons and get down on your knees, or you will be considered hostile to the warrant. Holding a weapon will result in lethal force being used against you. This is a legal warrant. You are involved in an illegal operation. Disarm or face lethal force."

The message was repeated a second time as Agent Jones came up behind Degan. With a tight grip on Billy's shirt collar, he said, "Here's the kid."

Anson glanced down at Billy as Degan took hold of him. His face was full of fear. "Let him go, Degan," she said. "You're beaten."

"The hell I am. I have the kid. And that bunch of wannabes over there won't face down three hundred federal officers with automatic weapons. It's all bluff. And Mabry is walking into a trap. And who the *hell* does he think he is?"

Anderson took a few steps away from Degan and went to Francis.

"Tell him to let the boy go. You can see I was right all along about these people. Now they have a leader. And I can tell you, Mabry is no fool. He has our men fully intimidated. They're spread out in an indefensible position and we're trapped. This is all by design, D.J. It's his strategy and it's brilliant. He is not bluffing!"

Francis hesitated. She looked skeptically at the crowd of civilians, then at Mabry who stood alone in the clearing.

"I don't think so, John. I agree with Agent Degan. It's all bluster. It's impressive enough, but it's just bluster. We represent the federal government. They won't dare oppose us."

"D.J.," pleaded Anderson. "Look out there. It's just like the second profile said it would be. You've boxed Mabry into a corner. His child is all he has left and all he cares about. He's been beaten down to the bare metal, but now all you've done is expose a core of solid iron. He is fully capable going to war if he has to, and you're giving him no other choice. And those people over there will follow him, D.J. Justin Mabry is a natural born leader. You have to believe that!"

Anson wanted to stay near Billy, but she slowly backed away. Agent Anderson was next to Agent Francis and could handle her, but Jones and Degan would be trouble. She needed a better angle to maneuver.

Passing through the line of federal agents as if they did not exist, Mabry started forward. High overhead, news helicopters hovered in place. The wind blew gently from the north. The flags caught the breeze and waved lazily to the left and right.

As Justin came nearer, Kelly noticed something about the shirt he was wearing. She knew what he looked like without one, and he was anything but paunchy. But now he seemed ten pounds heavier. He had on a bulletproof vest!

Stopping five paces in front of his son, Mabry's penetrating eyes locked on Degan.

"You are Special Agent Degan?"

Degan snorted.

"And you must be 'Breeee,'" he said sarcastically and tightened his grip on Billy. "That was quite an entrance for an out-of-work schoolteacher."

Tossing the papers at Degan's feet, Mabry said calmly, "That is a federal order, warrant for a citizen's arrest. Named in it are Agents Phil Degan and D.J. Francis of the Federal Bureau of Investigation. Causes alleged: felonious abuse of discretion of office, and the attempted murders of Mathew Jordan and Justin Mabry. This warrant has been fully served. You are hereby subject to immediate arrest. And you can be certain the warrant is legal. I had my attorney draw it up this morning."

Degan smacked his lips and raised his eyebrows then glanced at Agent Jones.

"Do you believe this guy?"

Jones was looking at the pistol in Mabry's belt.

"Why don't I just take him out right here? He's only carrying a single action. I could have five holes in him before he drops."

Kelly Anson was now slightly forward and to the left of Degan and Jones. Her palm rested on her Berretta.

"If you try it, Jones, I'll empty my clip into both of you."

Degan wanted to look at Anson, but his instincts told him not to take his eyes off Mabry. She was just a rookie cop. Would she actually defend Mabry, and if she tried, could she shoot?

"Stay out of this," he demanded. "You'll do twenty years of hard time if you get in my way. And you won't like being a cop in federal prison."

"Neither will you, Degan," replied Anson, as her fingers slowly encircled the pistol's grip.

"Each one of those flags you see represents a platoon of armed civilians," Mabry said. "If I call them out, they will *not* go back. You and your men will be one step closer to death."

"I'm real scared," mocked Degan. "Aren't you scared, Agent Jones?"

Jones laughed and swore.

"Platoons of potbellies and beer guts. Or maybe those platoons of his are all make-believe."

Mabry's face was unreadable.

"Give me my son," he said, then raised the white flag high over his head and brought it back down.

Immediately, along the entire half-mile front, the mass of civilians began to shift. In a matter of seconds, more than two thousand heavily armed men and several women took their place. Every face had been completely covered with a disguising layer of paint or charcoal.

Directly behind Mabry, the line was replaced with over one hundred fully uniformed men, each holding an AK-47 at the ready. Waving over their heads was the red and blue flag of the Idaho Militia.

"Tell your men to give up." Again, Justin Mabry's tone was subdued. "They will die if they don't."

Instantly, the threat of death permeated the air. Both sides were armed. The slightest wrong move by anyone would trigger disaster. Time began to slow down. Hearts began to race.

"Tell your men to throw down their weapons and get down on the ground," ordered Mabry. "We are aware of your body armor. Anyone standing will be shot in the head."

"For once in your life, read what's in his eyes," begged Anderson. "Can't you see it? He's not bluffing! D.J., please, order the men to stand down!"

"No!" bellowed Degan. "That bunch of rabble is facing fully automatic weapons fire. They'll be the ones to back down. And he won't risk getting his kid shot. We still have the boy. As long as I have the boy, we're in control. He's bluffing, I tell you!"

With his eyes locked on Degan, Mabry said, "Bluffing? Where are the four snipers you sent after me, Degan? I hear they were Delta Force trained, the elite of the FBI. There names were Rogers, Bennet, Childers and Kawalski. Kawalski's wife just had a baby girl by the name of Jessica.

"At first, they thought I was bluffing, too. But then they found out I wasn't, and they told me everything I wanted to know. Everything. I know where the rest of your snipers are, Degan. They're trapped miles away behind a dynamited rockslide. But do you know where *my* snipers are?"

Mabry could see Degan and Jones were visibly shaken. Degan still had a tight grip on Billy's shirt collar, yet thankfully, had made no movement towards the pistol strapped to his belt. The FBI agent still had the upper hand, and time was on Degan's side. If the plan were to succeed, Mabry had to move quickly.

"Still not convinced?" questioned Mabry. Keeping his right hand near his Colt, he again raised the white flag with his left.

Across the field to the north, behind the tents and vehicles, the forest reverberated with another ominous boom as hundreds of sticks were slammed into tree trunks. Before the first sound faded, another one followed. The second boom was followed by the fanatic roar of "Breeee" from unseen civilians and soldiers directly to the rear.

"Better look behind you, Degan," said Anderson.

Unable to resist, Degan turned to see thirty more flags appear from the forest. When he looked back at Mabry, he was staring into the black hole of a Colt .45.

Francis was not equipped with a headset but she had seen enough.

"Order the men to stand down, Agent Degan. We will settle this in court."

Degan continued to glare at the pistol. He was calculating the odds, and Mabry could see it in his eyes.

Anderson took over and spoke into his headset.

"This is Agent John Anderson. Agent Francis orders everyone to stand down. Disarm and get down immediately."

Those farthest from FBI headquarters complied first, and like falling stacks of dominos, both ends of the line began dropping their weapons and lying down flat.

Catching the movement in his peripheral vision, Degan yelled into his own headset.

"This is Degan. Belay that order! Belay that order!"

Ten agents immediately to the east of HQ and seven to the west continued to stand and held onto their weapons.

Degan's eyes blazed.

"We checked you out, Mabry. You've never even owned a gun, much less shot a man! I still say you're all bluff!"

Mabry's peripheral vision began to disappear. Sound became muffled and everything started moving in slow motion. The man holding his son became the sole focus of his universe.

Degan shoved Billy at the same instant he dove to the ground. In a millisecond, Mabry was racing towards the agent as fast as he could move.

Seeing the movement, Agent Jones' hand went for his sidearm. Anson reacted as well, but her hand was already grasping her pistol.

Anderson wrapped his arms around Francis and threw himself downward.

Before Degan hit the ground, his pistol was in hand and Mabry was closing. He fired his first shot into Mabry the instant he landed on his side.

Anson got off two shots at Jones, who was aiming for Mabry's back as he advanced on Degan. Jones shot once by reflex. He was dead before his knees buckled.

Mabry felt the first round slam into his chest but kept closing the distance. A second round hit near the first, but now he was on top of Degan and his own gun exploded in his hand.

Guns blasted from the line of citizens, the militia and from the remaining federal agents.

Mabry's momentum caused him to trip over Degan's body. Only vaguely aware of the blazing weapons fire behind him, he rolled on his shoulder and spun around to face Jones. But the only person he saw was Anson. No one else was left standing. The shots along the line slowed and then stopped.

Slowing coming to his feet, Mabry felt Kelly's arms encircle him, and then Billy was there hugging him. Degan had blood oozing from a hole in his forehead. Jones had taken Anson's shots in the throat and face. The shooting stopped as abruptly as it had started leaving thousands of passionate citizens suspended between a cheer of victory and a gasp of horror. Except for the distant moan of a wounded man, it was deathly quiet.

Mabry took several deep breaths. His vision began to return to normal and then his hearing did the same.

"Are you alright, Billy?" he asked as he tucked the pistol back in his belt and then looked into the eyes of his son. "Are you okay?"

"Yes, Dad. But you got shot! That man shot you!"

"No, Billy," assured Mabry, as he tried to shield the eyes of his son from the bodies of Degan and Jones. "I'm fine. Kelly?"

"Me, too," she said, her voice quivering slightly. "Me, too."

"Looks like we're too late," broke in another voice.

All three looked up to see Luke Jordan and Thomas Rico. Jordan's face was flushed red but Rico's was a shade of white.

Rico stared at the bodies near him then at those lying in the field.

"My God," he whispered. "My God."

The flags and the militia had already vanished into the crowd when Mabry looked behind him. Not a single weapon could be seen in the hands of a civilian. The agents that had surrendered were walking in, but they had left their weapons on the ground and their hands were raised. It was over.

"How is Matt?" asked Mabry. "They told me he had been shot."

"He's over at the medical tent," replied Jordan, then reached down and picked up the citizen's arrest warrant. Brushing the dirt from the papers, he said, "The doctor says he won't lose his arm. He'll never play baseball again. But he'll live."

"I'm sorry, Luke. I'm terribly sorry I was the cause of this."

"You caused nothing," replied Jordan.

Pointing with his head at the bodies of Degan and Jones, he added, "It's them and their kind that are the cause of it all. Not you. Not me. And there's more of them to clean out."

Rico looked intently at Mabry, who had one arm around his son and the other around Kelly Anson.

"What will you do now, Mr. Mabry? Where will you go?"

Mabry looked around. Nineteen federal agents were down and likely dead. Some civilians must have at least been wounded.

"Canada, if they'll take me." Mabry handed the Colt to Jordan. "What will you do, Luke?"

Jordan turned towards Anderson and Francis.

"First, I'm going to court. They shot Mathew in the back when he was running for home. They're gonna pay for that. And there'll be a congressional investigation over this, an investigation that will rock this country to its core. And, hopefully, put it back on track. I want to be a part of that when it happens…and part of what happens if it doesn't. But, with you just across the border and them knowing what you could do if you came back, the politicians will stay on track. You've helped re-chart the course of this country, Justin Mabry. When this is finally over, Clark Fork will stand alongside of Lexington and Concord."

Rico surveyed the ghastly scene around him.

"And I'll keep the media honest. I'll report this as accurately as humanly possible. This is one story that won't be distorted or rewritten. I can promise you that much."

Mabry pointed at Degan's body.

"He's the one who shot Matt. I'll do what I can to testify to that."

"You won't have to," offered Anderson. "I'll testify to it."

Looking painfully at D.J. Francis, he added, "And I'll testify to a lot more."

The sound of circling news helicopters filled the air as doctors and nurses from the FBI's medical tent ran to the men lying on the ground.

One of the helicopters landed nearby but kept its blades turning. Painted on its side was a large red maple leaf.

Jumping out of the Canadian chopper and keeping his head low, a reporter ran over.

"Mr. Mabry, Idaho National Guard helicopters are on the way. The Prime Minister of Canada wishes to extend an invitation to be his guest if you wish to accept it. But we have to hurry, sir."

Aware that Kelly's arm was still around him, Mabry glanced at the helicopter. "Thank you. How many can you take?"

"Depends on the weight," said the reporter as he surveyed the size of Luke Jordan. "Two, I would say."

Jordan laughed as he shook hands with Mabry.

"Not me," he said, then pointed a thumb at Billy and Kelly. "Them, there. She'll be needing a safe place until this is settled, too."

"Oh. Then, three," replied the reporter. "We can take all three of you, but quickly please."

Mabry placed his hands on Billy's shoulders and turned to face Kelly.

"Billy liked you from the start," he said. "Want to make it the three of us?"

"From the start," said Kelly.

She smiled and took Billy's hand.

"I knew it the first day we met."

Mabry nodded a solemn goodbye to Jordan then took his son's other hand. He returned Kelly's smile as they started for the helicopter.

Billy looked curiously from Kelly to his father.

"What are we going to do up in Canada, Dad?"

Mabry looked down at his son.

"We're going to become a family, Billy. And then we're going to play baseball. Just be a family and play ball. That's all I ever wanted."

Like everyone else, Rico could not take his eyes off Mabry. Watching him walk away, he asked incredulously, "Is it that simple for him?"

"Seems so," replied Jordan.

As Mabry helped Billy and Kelly into the helicopter, a man with a black snake tattooed on his arm climbed on top of a news van. He pumped a clinched fist into the air and started the crowd around him chanting.

"Bree, Bree, Bree…"

In seconds, unseen thousands joined in.

Rico raised his voice.

"But look at these people, Jordan. Listen to them. They would follow him anywhere. He's part general, part renegade and part king. Why, he could run for president some day."

Mabry stepped into the helicopter and the engine roared. It rose quickly then hovered. When Mabry leaned out and extended a thankful wave, the masses below erupted into cheers.

Jordan waved once more at Mabry as the helicopter tilted its tail upward, then turned and headed north.

"He's too good a man to be a politician, Rico. Not him. He believes in family and freedom. Nope. But he's a patriot, my friend. And whether he knows it or not…if we need him again…he'll be back."

www.ingramcontent.com/pod-product-compliance
Lightning Source LLC
Chambersburg PA
CBHW031333170626
46807CB00002B/680